# HIDDEN
# FLOWERS

To Ruby,

Stay lovely and
true to yourself

# L A T R I C E   N   S I M P K I N S

Special thanks to my children and my little sister Ericka who challenge me to exercise my imagination daily. And thanks to my friends and colleagues whose faith in my work is invaluable and encourages me to stay the course.

**Also by Latrice Simpkins**

*Matika and the River Lion*
The escape from Uganda

*Mei Ling* (Coming June 2016)

# CHAPTER 1

"Ouch!" I yelled pulling my hand away from the smoking toaster. "How am I supposed to pull the bread and not get singed?" I had burned the toast again. I still struggled with our transition to America as far as cooking was concerned. "Using the toaster is not as easy as the commercials make it out to be for the Pop-Tarts."

"Matika, you can't put eggs on the bread before you heat them up," my older sister Suda said with heightened irritation. "If you mix it in the pot, it turns out better. You just made another mess."

"But it's French toast," I complained running my hands under the cold water. "The recipe says to add eggs, milk and sugar."

"Why does that beeping noise go off every time you cook!" she shouted above the high-pitched screech that was piercing enough to wake the spirit world.

It had been four months since my father, Suda, and I had left Kenya, and even longer since we escaped the devastation of our beloved homeland, Uganda. The nightmare we left behind was oceans away but ever-present in the darkest recesses of our minds. Because my father was a prominent military general, the rebels of the Lord's Liberation Army had come after us with a vengeance, intent on destroying us all. Of my father's thirteen wives and many, many children, only three of us made it out of Uganda. I could only hope we would be reunited with the rest of our family one day…if they survived.

I often wondered what happened to my half-brother, Lutalo, and his crazed obsession with me and vengeance in the name of our father. Did he return to northern Uganda seeking his revenge on the innocent, rejoining the River Lion, the leader of the rebels, whom he worshipped?

More than anything, I missed my beloved Chaz even more now that I was in the United States. I had met Chaz in the Kenyan refugee camp and instantly fell in love with him. He told me once that he was stationed at Camp Pendleton, not many miles from where we lived. His beautiful emerald eyes haunted my nightly dreams. I cherished our time together, how he held me, whispering loving words. I wondered if he even remembered me and the time we shared...

My father – Baba in my native tongue – worked at locating our family, and though he never discussed the progress with us, he was often frustrated with the mounds of government paperwork. The war in Uganda had torn apart our family, and we still didn't know who had survived the massacre. Baba's status as a general and his political clout enabled us to get asylum.

I dreaded the knowledge that Walyam, Suda's boyfriend, would arrive soon with his new wife, Namazzi, my older sister. It was hard to contemplate living with him when I knew what I owed him, and that he would take what was owed. I made him a deal that I would do anything for him if he saved Baba and Suda from the prison in Kenya. True to his word he saved them, and now my debt was due.

When he came to visit my sister Suda at the refugee camp in Kenya he would find every opportunity to touch me inappropriately or say things that made me very uncomfortable. I always hid it from Suda, to protect her. I still remember the day when she accused me of being jealous of Walyam's attention to her instead of me. If only she knew the truth. She was so deeply, so blindly in love with him that if she knew of his behavior toward me in that camp she would only blame me, saying that I invited or enticed him.

It would be months before Walyam or any of my other family members arrived, so for the time being I enjoyed the reprieve from him. The house Baba rented was in a predominately-African community in East San Diego, California. With four bedrooms and a detached garage, it wasn't the best house in the neighborhood, but to us it was a palace with more space than we'd ever had. The house had two bathrooms, one in the private bedroom near the kitchen, and the other in the main hallway near the other bedrooms. They each had a small cabinet with a sink, an oval mirror, and a porcelain tub. The best and most amazing thing of all was the instant water by turning a handle on the pipe. No longer did we have to go to the river or well and bring the water because it was available by turning a knob in the kitchen and bathrooms, and even in the front and backyard. The cooking room was spacious with a good-size table and white cabinets with chipped paint, broken doors, and missing knobs. Baba's favorite appliance was the cold box that we had for storing our food, which prevented the long-legged black bugs from contaminating everything. Everything lasted longer in the freeze box. Baba liked to keep his shirts in there on hot summer days since he refused to turn on the cold air, stating that it cost too much.

Suda's favorite was the flat electric cooking fire, and she learned how to use it quickly, while I, on the other hand, still couldn't figure out the correct adjustments to get the right temperature. I found a new love in the spinning plate heating box above the stove, though. I just had to be careful because whatever I put in it, such as eggs, tended to explode. I was also very good at turning any meat into rubber, rendering it inedible. I still loved to use it.

There were many things wrong with the house, like the faded plastic tile floor that pulled up around the refrigerator or the ugly tan rug with dark stains throughout the rest of the house from wall to wall. I couldn't figure out how to take it out and beat it clean because the rug fit so perfectly, and was nailed down. The faded walls were white with brown smudges, dotted with small holes and a few bent nails protruding. Baba said he would fix everything. But most importantly, it was ours, and we were happy.

We settled into a daily routine. Suda cooked and tended to the small backyard, overgrown with waist-high brown grass and weeds, but with hidden treasures throughout. I found a naked skinny doll with a crow's nest of dirty-blonde hair, along with a toy car, and a jump rope. Suda found a deflated basketball and a soiled stuffed bear. She had visions of a thriving garden complete with goats.

Baba had a job as a security manager at a company in Del Mar, so we were able to attend an elite school in the district, one of the top schools in the state, Torrey Hills High School. We had taken placement tests, and Suda and I were both accepted into the tenth grade.

With school starting on Monday, we went to shop for clothes at my favorite stores, Goodwill and Salvation Army. This was where Baba had gotten beds for three of the four rooms, dressers, and a large sectional couch. No wonder they called it Goodwill, because it was indeed very good. And the Salvation Army was the only army I wanted to be a part of.

Suda and I were so excited to go shopping because Baba rarely took us with him. I loved the store. They had so many choices with rarely more than two identical items. With such a variety of clothing, you never had to worry about having the exact same thing as the next person.

I really wanted to blend in, but Suda couldn't convince Baba to buy us pants or shorts. We had no say in our clothing. Instead, he picked out long dresses and skirts that went to our ankles, and then complained the entire time about how indecent the clothes were and how expensive everything was. We were not even allowed to try them on because he didn't want anyone to see our bodies.

"These prices are robbery," he complained to the poor store clerk as he rung up our goods. I was mortified, and Suda pretended like she wasn't with us, as Baba bargained for a better price. Baba may have learned English, but he was completely ignorant of American culture.

"I'm sorry sir, but I don't set the prices," the bored clerk responded. He was in his thirties with a medium height and large build, and a mustache that curved around his lips. He wore a blue-and-green checkered shirt and faded jeans.

"I will take these dresses for fifteen dollars," Baba said firmly.

"Sir, your total is $27.83."

"No, I will tell you what. I will take them for twenty dollars and that's my final offer. Just look at the poor quality," he said as he held up one of the dresses.

"Hey, hurry up!" a frustrated shopper yelled in the line that had accumulated behind us.

"Just pay the man," another chimed in.

"I am offering you a good deal," Baba said crossing his arms as he stood firm and ignored the growing complaints. "I bring much business to your shop, and I expect to pay fair prices."

"What's going on?" another shopper asked. "Can't you open up another register?"

The store clerk let out a weary sigh. "I'll have to call the manager." He picked up the intercom and held it too close to his mouth as he mumbled, "Manager to register two."

Baba continued to complain as the manager, a much older gentleman with white hair, approached.

"Just give it to him! I'm not trying to stay in here all day!" a petite old lady shouted from behind.

"I'll give you five bucks to get out of line," said another man.

When the clerk explained the situation to the manager, he smiled, "Sir, I'll give you a twenty-five percent discount and that will bring your total to..." he paused as he punched the numbers on the cash register, "...$20.80. Now, would you like to purchase these items?"

"Yes, I'll buy them," Baba responded happily and took out two crisp twenty dollar bills from his wallet. Everyone let out a collective sigh of relief as Baba paid for the clothes.

The Torrey Hills Goodwill was not prepared for a customer like our Baba.

"Thank you sir, we appreciate your business," the manager said.

Baba grunted as he took our bags, and we followed him with our heads hung low. Let's just say we had a new perspective on humiliation. His dignity rode high as Baba beamed with pride over the deal he'd just made. Suda and I never asked to go with him again.

When Monday finally arrived, Baba was even more excited than me and Suda combined for our first day of school. Suda was sick again that morning. She woke up early and rushed to the bathroom, her choking echoing through the room. She returned to bed and slept until Baba woke her around six. Since she slept in late, I had to make breakfast, which wasn't in anyone's best interest because I had only learned how to make eggs and toasted bread on the electric fire.

Once we sat down to eat, after I had gotten the sensitive fire alarm to stop, Suda took one bite and rushed out of the kitchen as she held her mouth.

"Matika, go check on her," Baba said with a mouthful of runny eggs, and every so often pulled shells out of his mouth. I just couldn't figure out how to get the shells out of the pan without getting burned.

I went to the bathroom. Suda was knelt down on the floor, hugging the toilet like a long lost friend. I knelt beside her, not missing the pallor of her skin. Sweat beaded around her nose as she heaved again. I wet a washcloth and put it on the back of her neck.

"Are you okay, Suda? Should I call for Baba?"

"No, no. Please. Just give me a minute," she said in her heavily accented English. She took a few deep breaths. "What did you put in those eggs?"

"You know, a little this, a pinch of that. I'm sorry you didn't like it."

"Just hold off on the garlic. I don't care if I never taste garlic again."

"You said it was tasteless the other day, so I added a whole clove of garlic." I just couldn't cook, and it was time for Suda to get well and take over again. Although Baba never complained about my cooking, she was relentless. "I'm worried because you have been sick for a long time. You really need to ask Baba to see a doctor."

She clutched my dress to stay me as I started to rise. "No, Matika! I feel fine," she said lowering her voice.

I helped her to her feet. "Are you sure?"

"Yes." She turned toward the sink, switched on the tap, and splashed water on her face. She did look a little better. "Do we have mangos? I'm really hungry for mangos. I need them right away!"

I couldn't figure out how she could be hungry for mangos after the food she spewed. I went back to the kitchen and sat back down to finish my cold breakfast smiling at Baba's clean plate that sat on the table in front of an empty chair.

When Baba took us to school, my excitement quickly wilted, then turned to fear, followed by extreme dread. I wasn't afraid of many things, but to start school here ranked just below my worst nightmare of being confined in small places. Baba didn't seem to notice or chose to ignore all the prolonged stares we got from the others. There were only a handful of black students. Suda counted a total of seven. I felt like a moss-covered tree in the middle of a flower field, unable to hide amongst the beauty.

My homely dress, which was the best one I owned, was a rag compared to the other girls' clothing. Most wore shorts or pants, and cute shirts with different cuts and designs. I was shocked that girls were allowed to wear pants to school. There were plenty of girls in dresses, but theirs were short, brightly colored summer dresses like the ones in Baba's newspaper. I had never seen so many variations of shoes from heels to flats, sandals showing polished toes, and boots to tennis shoes that matched their clothing to perfection. Our shoes were used black flats. We only had one pair to wear to school for every outfit and a pair of flip-flops for around the house.

Everyone seemed to know one another, which made me feel even more out of place. They gave butterfly kisses, embraced, and exchanged schedules, squealed with excitement, laughed, or received playful punches on the shoulder. I wondered if I would ever fit in.

At that moment, I realized that I had never had a friend. Sure, Suda was the best friend one could ever have, but still...she was my sister. I couldn't share my innermost thoughts and feelings with her, nor could I speak negatively about the family. I was there for her, and she was there for me.

"Good, you both got all the classes I chose for you," Baba said handing us each a schedule, drawing us closer to him. I had U.S. History, Culinary Fusion, P.E., Algebra II, and English. As he smiled and beamed brightly, he was surely the happiest parent there. More than a few mothers looked his way, but he didn't spare them the slightest glance. Many would say he was a handsome man in his late forties, tall, and very muscular from his long military career. These women looked at him with curiosity. Like a child as it played with a prideful lion even as it knew it was not safe, but the thrill of flirting with danger too hard to resist.

The school day moved quickly, but we went to only half our classes on an odd and even schedule. I still couldn't figure out why we didn't have all our classes every day, or why we had to changes classes in general. Baba picked us up after school. "Come. We'll go to Walmart to get school supplies."

As we pulled away from school, Suda and I were both silent in the back seat while Baba drove and whistled a tune, ignorant of our sobering experience. At Walmart, Baba let us wander around the store and told us to meet him at the checkout counter in twenty minutes. Goodwill paled in comparison to Walmart. The store had everything from food to furniture. Suda and I rushed to the clothing section.

Suda held up a short skirt with heart designs embroidered on the front and back pockets. The matching shirt was a solid pink tank that was certainly fitting.

"I bet I could make this."

"I like this one." I picked up a soft summer dress and held it to my body. I loved the blue and white colors that looked like an ocean current. The pearl buttons set it off like moons that glimmered in twilight.

"Let's go try them on."

"No, it will just make me want it more."

"Come on, it will be fun." Suda pulled me toward the dressing rooms, sweeping additional items into her arms as she weaved between clothing stands.

A line of women and children were outside the dressing room as they waited on a single weary woman who struggled with an armful of clothing while she passed out numbered cards. She clearly needed assistance, but there was no one around. The dark shadows under her eyes revealed the passing of a long shift.

"How many?" she asked while placing clothing on the rack to her left.

I began to get quite nervous as our time quickly sped by.

"We have six between the both of us," Suda responded.

When we were in the "family" dressing room, I noticed that we had nine items.

"Why did you say that we only had six?" I asked her. I hated being in small spaces but was thankful the room wasn't as confined as the others.

"Not to worry, I'll take care of that." Suda began to undress and I did the same.

I loved the dress on the hanger, but when I put it on and looked into the full size mirror, I didn't want to take it off. I wanted to cry because it looked so beautiful on me with its soft fabric that gently hugged my hips, and didn't quite reach my knees. It fit to perfection and even made my ample breasts, which I was always self-conscious of, look a bit smaller.

I peered over at Suda, as she put the old dress over the new skirt and top that she had tried on. It happened so fast that I didn't even get to see her in it.

"What are you doing?"

"Keep your voice down," she said in Swahili. "Here, let me help you." She reached for my dress and attempted to pull it over my head, but I stepped back against the dressing room wall horrified at what she suggested. "Do you want to take this home or not?"

"Yes…but this is wrong."

"Matika, look how rich this store is. This is a hundred times better than Goodwill, so they can afford to part with these clothes. They have more money than we can count."

"We're going to get in trouble. What if we get caught and Baba finds out?"

"No one will ever know. I promise you. Matika, you look very pretty in this dress…it looks like the ones the girls were wearing at school today."

I did look nice, and I really wanted to be accepted. This would be perfect for school, and by the looks of it, we needed everything we could get. "Oh...I suppose we can do it this one time..."

"Just this one time and it will be our little secret." She smiled at me as I allowed her to pull my old dress over my head. It was far longer, and it hid the dress underneath with not so much as a ripple.

# CHAPTER 2

Suda must have planned this because we walked out of the dressing room with six items; not that the overworked lady even bothered to count them. As we rushed over to meet Baba, my heart beat loudly. I was so nervous about being caught I couldn't ever hear Baba as he called to us.

"You're late!" he snapped, clipping us both over the back of the head with his free hand. It didn't hurt much, but it was enough of a warning to not let it happen again. A few shoppers glanced our way. I was humiliated. Everyone looked at me as I smoothed out my dress self-consciously, and checked for any sign of the garment underneath.

"These supplies should last you the whole year, so take good care of them," he said to us. We followed as Baba headed to the checkout counter where he unloaded the blue handheld basket. There was little fanfare as Baba received a ten percent discount for the things that were in "poor" condition. The clerk only wanted the line to stay in motion and didn't challenge him.

Once out of the store and in the car, I breathed a sigh of relief. Suda grinned as she briefly squeezed my hand in reassurance. Then the gravity of what we just did hit me like a hammer. I had done one of the most cowardly acts. I took something that didn't belong to me. No, I stole it. That was a crime in any country. That made me a thief. It was far too late to undo what I did, and telling Baba to turn back around was completely out of the question.

When we pulled up to the house, Baba gave us the plastic bags that held our supplies before he went to see the neighbor. Once inside, I went to our room and Suda followed.

"Shouldn't you be making dinner?" I asked. In our family, a man never had to ask for food, as the woman anticipated his every need. If he was hungry, then shame on her for not attending to him in a timely manner.

"I have to change. I wouldn't want to mess my new clothes."

I was more than upset at myself, but I channeled some of my anger toward Suda. After all, it was she who had pressured me into taking the dress. She left me no choice.

"You won't think about it tomorrow," she said. "You'll be happy to wear nice clothes. You are such a good pair of shoes."

"Suda, it's 'goody two-shoes' and no, I wasn't even thinking about it," I said rolling my eyes like she did when irritated.

"Yes, you were. I can read you like a book."

"No, I'm just worried about the math test next week."

After hiding the clothes, we headed to the kitchen where I watched Suda make the evening meal. I was supposed to learn from her, but I found no interest in cooking, and my mind wandered as usual.

After we ate, Baba sat in the living room on his little sofa and watched television. I went to our room, bored to tears, and observed as Suda altered her clothes. She never wanted to talk while she worked, and said that I talked too much and it distracted her.

I noticed the American food agreed with her. Suda was thinner and taller than I, but now she looked more filled out. Suda and I braided each other's hair, and took special care to make it perfect. Suda got carried away and braided my hair so tight it felt like my scalp parted instead of my hair, which caused my eyes to slant under the strain.

Baba sent us to bed early, claiming that we needed our energy for school tomorrow. As I lay my throbbing head on the pillow, I thought about what the next day would bring, which took my anxiety to new heights. Sleep was a long time coming.

The next morning, Suda was full of energy. She had fallen asleep as soon as her head hit the pillow. She woke early and had breakfast completed by the time I awoke. She made a sweet bread and bush tea. Dressed in a calf-length flower dress, with lace that bordered the neckline and hem, she looked the picture of decorum complete with her flat black shoes.

With a sleepy frown on my face, I sat down.

"Aren't we in a bad mood?" she chided, smiling as she set the table.

"No, I'm fine." I was even more irritated that she noticed I was having a bad day. The night had sucked the energy right out of me. Rubbing my eyes, I sat down for breakfast still wearing my nightgown. Uninterested, I tore into the sweet bread without tasting it. Although it was one of my favorite foods, I just wasn't in the mood.

"Matika! You dare come to my table naked? Get some clothes on!" Baba snapped sending me running to my room before he struck me.

I was dressed in no time, wearing the same dress as yesterday with my precious "secret" dress underneath it. Baba didn't allow me to return to the table, but Suda saved me three pieces of bread and wrapped it in plastic, putting it in her shoulder bag.

We arrived at school early, around six-thirty, because Baba had to be at work by seven. Being the first at school gave us the opportunity to divest of our old dresses and store them in our shoulder bags. The other kids started to arrive, and the first bell rang. Suda and I said a quick goodbye before we headed to our first classes.

I was the second student to enter the classroom and sat in the front row. The other students filed to the back. The laminated tan desks were perfectly arranged in five neat rows and could hold all of your books and supplies in a compartment underneath the seat. The class was filled with pictures of Shakespeare at various stages in life, many pictures of European kings and queens, including a large headshot of the fiery redhead Queen Elizabeth, who, in my opinion, was the most courageous of all. Queen Elizabeth stood by her vow never to marry, thus she prevented any man from controlling her life or country during her reign.

When the second bell rang, in pranced the eccentric dandy Mr. Kroger, an oddly shaped gentleman with a round stomach and thin legs that came together in a point, making an upside-down triangle from the waist down. He wore dress pants that were too short, which showed off his brown socks, plus suspenders, and a white buttoned shirt. His long graying hair was pulled back in a ponytail, matching his equally gray eyes.

"This, my dear class," he said loudly and in heavily accented theatrical English, with shoulders thrust back as his hands swept up and down his clothes, "is the only time you will see me dressed as such. So take a look now and remember it for the rest of the school year."

He walked to his desk, but he did not sit. Instead he paced back and forth, and one by one, said everyone's name and made them each say something interesting about themselves. We had a huge boy that wore a sports uniform named Brad Ashton, who inserted snide comments when some of the students spoke. He sat somewhere in the back, but I didn't look behind me. I refused to draw any attention to myself.

"Matika…" Mr. Kroger brought the paper closer to his face in concentration. "How do you pronounce your full name?"

"Matika Okello Naminiha," I responded wanting to hide under my seat. I couldn't understand what was so hard about my name when Mr. Kroger was able to say, "Rachael Esperiquerta" and "Felix Mahama."

"Wassup with *that* name?" Brad said with such disdain, as if to refer to me as an outcast.

"Do tell us where your name is from?" Mr. Kroger politely asked.

I felt all eyes of the other students boring down on me. "It is from my father."

The class erupted with Brad's laughter rising above all others. I wondered why they laughed at that. What had I said that was so amusing? Mr. Kroger promptly quieted them down with a follow-up question. "Where is your family from, Matika? What country?"

In dead silence everyone leaned forward and waited for me to answer. "We're from Uganda."

A couple of "Ohhs" and some snickers broke through the silence.

"Class, we have a student from a country in East Africa. We welcome you with open arms. Julie O'Brian…"

After Mr. Kroger went through the other names, he had us rearrange our desks in a circular formation that he said would be more engaging.

There was no way to hide. I sat directly across from Brad. I tried not to make eye contact with him while Mr. Kroger discussed the syllabus.

Brad's straight blond hair was spiked to a point above his hard face. He constantly laughed at his own jokes or others' mistakes, but the humor never reached his cold eyes. They remained insightful, and never missed a single movement. Cara, his girlfriend, championed his smart remarks and batted her long, heavily made-up eyelashes. Mr. Kroger never seemed to notice anything Brad said or did. He was in his own world when he spoke, hearing but not really listening.

Finally, the class was over, and I took my books from under the seat and headed toward the door, determined to get out of the class before anyone else.

"Matika," Mr. Kroger called, preventing my escape.

"Yes, Mr. Kroger?"

"Later, when you are settled in, I'll give you a few books by African authors you may be interested in if you like."

"Yes, sir."

"Good. I'll see you on Wednesday."

I quickly headed for the door and bumped right into Cara, knocking all the books out of her hands.

"Watch it, you clumsy black ape!"

"I'm so sorry." I was completely overwhelmed with embarrassment as everyone stopped and stared.

"No wonder she can't see – look at the size of those knockers," Brad said looking at my breasts with hateful eyes that I wanted to gouge out.

"I bet they're not even real, Brad," Cara said from down her long straight nose. She managed to look down at me even when she was at least an inch shorter. She was a petite girl and wore cut-off jeans, a pink tank top that read "Kiss Me!" on the bosom, and matching pink sandals. "She probably stuffed them with her stinky socks."

"What's going on?" asked the security guard who quickly approached. A huge crowd formed around us preventing any escape.

"Nothing sir, I was just leaving."

"She pushed me down!" Cara shouted.

"It was an accident. Really, I didn't–"

"All right," the guard said, "there's nothing to see here. Get to class everyone. Enough, both of you, get going."

He didn't have to tell me twice.

"I'll be watching you," he said only to me.

Suda and I met for lunch and sat down at the first empty table. I pulled out my sandwich, took a big bite, and nearly choked. My heart stopped as the dread sunk in. *No, this can't happen.*

"Look who thinks they can sit in our seats."

My eyes nearly fell from my head. Brad stood in front of us, like a mamba snake inciting fear and spitting cold at us. His endless group of followers cackled, lapping up my pride like laughing hyenas over a strewn carcass.

"I didn't realize this was your table," I stammered. "Let's go now," I said to Suda in Swahili and took my bag as I got up. I was more than willing to leave my lunch as I had lost my appetite.

"Who are they to talk to us like that?" Suda said rising with me, but she didn't gather her things. Instead, she put her hands on her hips obstinately. Suda wanted an answer right now. This was going to make a bad situation even worse.

"I think we need to clear the table of these niggers," Cara chimed in a singsong voice with an icy undercurrent.

Suda looked ready to jump across the table. "How dare you call us 'niggers'!"

Though Suda and I didn't know what niggers meant, we assumed it was something very bad. I grabbed her arm, dropping my books.

"*Wewemachafupanya!*" Suda cursed in Swahili.

"She can't even speak English," Brad mocked.

"Cage your monkey friend," Cara demanded, smiling broadly as she looked directly at me with her steel gray eyes and perfectly arched eyebrows.

"Who are you calling a monkey?" Suda shot back as she broke free and flew around the table. She went eye to eye with Cara.

I went over to Suda. She was quickly surrounded by Brad's groupies, which was a word I learned in a magazine for followers of rock bands. I squeezed my way in, but Brad grabbed me around the waist, under my breast. My gut nearly came out of my mouth.

"Oh, no you don't!" Brad said holding me roughly against him. "There is no interfering in a chick fight." His hand eased up my breast, and caressed me through the thin fabric of my dress.

"Not only can you not talk but you can't hear either," Cara said putting her perfectly manicured hands on her hips and took a step even closer to Suda. Only a few inches separated them.

Suda's eyes flared, and I knew what would come. With a sharp elbow to Brad's ribs, I freed myself just as she raised her hand to strike. I jumped between them and pushed them apart.

Raging and nearly foaming at the mouth, Suda cursed Cara to a fate far worse than death. The group laughed all the more.

"Suda, Baba will beat you worse if you do anything."

Finally, she calmed down, and I pushed her away as a large crowd gathered. Campus security blew whistles and demanded to know what was going on. We quickly eluded the security guards' inquiry by going to the ladies room. There I wanted to throw up the only bite of my sandwich I'd had.

Suda slammed her open palm into the white brick walls by the sinks, scaring some girls who quickly exited. I had never seen her so angry.

"I hate this place! I hate this school! I hate Baba for making us come here!"

"Suda, you don't hate Baba. He only wants what's best for us."

"The hell he does! He only wants what makes him look better. Baba has always only cared about what people think of him. He's always trying to impress people. Has to have everything, doesn't he? Cares only about himself and not about what we think..."

I listened to Suda's complaints, wishing that the things she said weren't true, as she paced back and forth like a caged jaguar. After venting, she calmed. Before I knew it, the bell rang. We were late for our next class. We had P.E. with Mr. and Ms. McKenzie, who were not married but were certainly related, since both owned a short mane of fiery red hair.

They shared more similarities than just their hair. Both were quite tall and in great shape. Mr. McKenzie's looks were common, but I was intrigued by Ms. McKenzie. Ms. M, the nickname she wanted us to use when we referred to her to avoid confusion, had a large build with defined muscles that made her almost bullish. Her breasts were large, but not overly, so that made me feel a strange connection to her. She was attractive in a unique, handsome sort of way with a strong nose that accompanied her angular face.

Mr. McKenzie, after he smiled at her, went over the rules and training schedule. Ms. M took the girls to the locker room and issued lockers, locks, and gym clothes. She was very nice.

"Ladies, I want you to know that I happen to have a large emergency stash of feminine items available in my office," she said. "So, please, don't hesitate to ask when the need arises."

After class, when the other students left the locker room, Suda and I changed into our other clothes.

"Suda, are your parents coming to pick you up?" Ms. M asked as we headed out.

"Yes, Ba – father – should be waiting for us out front," Suda responded, her brows drawing together in confusion and concern.

Suda and I exchanged looks. I was sure we thought the same thing. Ms. M saw us change our clothes.

"Is your mother at home? Perhaps I can call her."

"Our mother is not with us. We live only with our father," I said feeling a little left out.

"I'm sorry to hear that." She paused and then said, "Well, I'd like to meet your father. There are a few things I want to go over with him that could make your transition in class easier."

Ms. M followed us from the gym down the hill to the crowded parking lot that was a beehive of people as they came and went. Her whistle hung from her neck, gently bouncing off her breasts covered by her Torrey Hills T-shirt.

Most kids waited at the curb in front of school to be picked up or walked home like a herd of cattle. Baba had us meet him in the far back corner where he waited in the "Faculty Only" parking lot.

Our car looked old and beat up compared to the shiny new ones. Its rusty red paint was like a spotted dog who had rolled around in the red clay dirt. When Baba saw us approaching, he didn't look pleased. He put down his newspaper and got out of the car, slamming the door with his arms across his chest. He positioned himself in front of the car, his feet planted shoulder width apart, completely militarized. I imagined this was how he stood as he reprimanded his soldiers in Uganda, with a face and stance reserved for those who crossed him.

We walked up to Baba with Ms. M, who took the initiative to reach out her hand to Baba. Ms. M was never afraid of anything and kept her hand extended and patiently waited for Baba to shake it. The silence that stretched between them seemed endless.

"Baba, this is our gym teacher, Ms. M – McKenzie," Suda said.

"Hi," Ms. M said still extending her hand toward Baba who looked at her with stern reservation. "I just wanted to meet you and to let you know what fine young ladies you have."

# CHAPTER 3

He looked at her strangely and slowly uncrossed his arms to shake her hand. Suda's shoulders slumped as the exchange was made. I was so relieved, I let out the breath I didn't realize I held.

"Hello," he said with a granite-like expression that showed no emotion. But that was Baba.

"I don't mean to impose, but I'd like to have a quick word with you in private."

Baba fired a harsh look at us and nodded, as he shifted his eyes to the car in a silent demand for us to wait inside while he spoke to Ms. M. I got in while Suda lingered over the open car door of the backseat. When Baba looked back at her, she quickly got in and closed the door.

"What do you think she has to say to him?"

"Ssssh," Suda said as she leaned over me and slowly rolled down the window.

Even with the glass down, I couldn't make out their conversation. Ms. M did most of the talking, and Baba listened, nodding and asking a few questions. By the tone of his voice, he was in total shock. Considering that Baba knew just about everything, he seemed out of his element.

They didn't speak long, and Ms. M waved at us as Baba got back into the car. I was dying to ask what Ms. M said, but I could tell by Suda's continuous shifting in the seat that she wanted to know more than I did. Neither of us asked Baba, nor did he offer any hint, as we drove in silence. He looked to be deep in thought. When we pulled up to the Salvation Army, I knew it had something to do with the clothes we wore.

Like whipped dogs, we followed Baba into the store. He headed straight to the undergarment section and began to rummage through intimate articles. I couldn't keep a straight face and laughed quietly. Suda looked very uncomfortable. I had seen these before in magazines but never looked at them up close.

The little holsters, or bras, as they were called, only covered the breasts and came in many colors. The material ranged from thick padded cotton to sheer see-through. Arranged by size, I was shocked to see the variations.

Baba held out a white one to Suda that looked too small to me as her breasts had bloomed greatly over the last month.

"Baba what is it for?" Suda asked him as he sifted through them once again.

"It is a bra," he said not turning around. The plastic hangers made a scraping noise on the medal polls they hung by.

"*Wangie*?" I asked out of respect in lieu of a simple, "Excuse me?"

"This is to wear under your clothes," he said as he handed me one that looked as big as a dress.

"Baba, may we try them on?" I asked. Clearly he had no concept of any size and saw me as simply enormous.

"You will not undress in public. There is no need to try them on. I know I have chosen the right sizes for my daughters."

There was no argument. A woman who searched the garments on the opposite side looked at Suda and me with pity. All we could do was follow as Baba headed for the checkout counter. Most of the clerks at the Salvation Army already knew Baba.

Surprisingly enough, Baba didn't try to negotiate a better price. I think he wanted to get out of there quickly. The Salvation Army had the last laugh, however, when they had to do a price check and tag reissue because it was missing on Suda's bra. The woman held it up for the customers to see. Baba turned a deep shade of purple.

Once we were home, Suda and I went to our room to try on our new bras before she started the evening meal. As I expected, mine was much too big around the waist, so much so that it would almost wrap around my rib cage twice. The size listed on the tag was "40 DD."

Suda had the opposite problem. Although it fit around her ribs snuggly enough, the bra was so small that her breasts spilled over the top. As she stood naked before me, because we didn't wear panties since it was uncomfortable, I finally noticed how big she had gotten. Her stomach had rounded, and her breasts were almost as full as mine. She was still quite thin, but her weight gain was clearly centered on her belly and bosom.

"What are you staring at?" she demanded.

I started to shy away and think of an excuse but none came to mind. "You have gained much weight in your belly…" I let the rest go unsaid hoping she would fill in the blanks. When she didn't respond and continued to put on her dress, I asked, "Suda, are you pregnant?"

The question hung in the air between us like smoke off the African plains that wouldn't rise.

"So what if I am?" she asked with obstinacy, raising her chin before she stuffed the bra in her drawer.

That would explain a lot, such as her irritability, sickness, lack of energy, and countless trips to the toilet. We were going to be in serious trouble if Baba found out because he seemed to like group punishments. Credit that to his military experience. Our jobs were to keep each other in line, especially in matters as large as this.

"What are we going to do?" I said.

"Do you think I have not thought about it every day for the last four months?"

"We have to tell Baba. He'll know what to do."

"Are you crazy?! He would kill me – or us, for that matter. He would think it your fault for not sticking together."

"Suda, you can't hide this forever. He will soon see you popping out of your dress."

"I know, but I want to wait as long as possible, until Walyam comes. Then we can get married. I overhead Baba telling our neighbor that Walyam and Namazzi are supposed to be here in a few months."

"Suda…" I couldn't continue with my mouth suddenly dry. I had forgotten that Suda didn't know that Walyam was going to marry Namazzi in order to get him in the country as Baba's son. They had probably already completed the marriage ceremony.

"Walyam wants to marry me. He loves me with all his heart. You know that he loves me. If he didn't love me, he wouldn't have come back for me when we were captured in Kenya." She looked at me with eyes the size of saucers, as an anticipated hurt lurked in the dark shadows.

"I know he loves you. You don't need to worry about that."

"Then why do you look at me like that? What is on your mind?"

"I'm just thinking that maybe things will be different when he comes." I slipped my dress over my head.

"What do you mean?"

"Nothing, Suda, everything will be okay," I said smoothing the worry creases out of my forehead. I gave her the most genuine smile I could muster. "We just have to worry about Baba."

She smiled back at me. "I feel such a relief now that I've told you." With that, she headed to the kitchen to prepare the evening meal.

Although Suda was relieved after she told me her secret, it felt like a cramp had seized my leg while treading water upstream. Baba never kept us informed about the status of our family's immigration. I thought it unlikely that they would be here anytime soon, especially before Suda would give birth. It would be hell on earth once she found out that Namazzi would be married to the love of her life.

Namazzi was our oldest sister from Mama's womb and was now eighteen. I still didn't know what happened to Namazzi's former fiancé. When Suda and I left our family home, Namazzi had been taken by our uncle to her future husband's home. Our village was raided that terrible day, which set the course of our lives tumbling down a steep cliff.

I knew I should have told Suda by now, but I couldn't bring myself to upset her, especially now that she was carrying Walyam's child. Up until now, I had hoped she'd forget about him and move on, but that was as impossible as stopping a waterfall with your bare hands.

We had dinner alone because Baba left and told us not to wait up for him. I don't know what time he came home that night, but he looked very tired the next morning as he sat down for breakfast. Still, he seemed happy. Something was up.

# CHAPTER 4

Life for the next seven weeks was uneventful. Even Suda was in a better mood as her belly expanded. I wore my extremely itchy bra, and even though Suda had made adjustments to it, the cups still didn't fit right. Suda refused to wear hers. She would not conform to the English practice of binding a woman's breasts. And besides, her bra didn't fit her ever-expanding breasts that prepared for the upcoming birth.

With joy, I read the books that Baba borrowed from the library. Suda chased some imaginary smell with a spray bottle of green fluid, and worked in the garden. We weren't allowed to leave the property while Baba was gone. He hadn't gotten us a phone, but Baba said we would get one at the end of the month. Our sole entertainment was a small box TV with a coat hanger for an antenna; however, it was only agreeable to Baba's manipulation. Suda had a small radio that she listened to while in the garden.

I loved to get the mail. With anticipation, I eagerly waited for the mailman. It seemed like we got some sort of coupons or advertisement every day. Baba liked me to cut out the coupons for the grocery stores while I enjoyed looking at the clothes, and clipping every coupon from the nearby frozen yogurt shop. Suda loved the clothes in the magazine so much that she secretly altered some of her dresses, and made a cute top and matching skirt out of an old bed sheet.

At school, I avoided Brad like a swamp filled with mosquitos. At home, Baba missed more meals as he was out a lot. I didn't care as long as he came back in a good mood. Suda began to get more nervous, and though she tried to bind her stomach with wraps and wear looser-fitting clothes, her belly continued to grow. Baba was in his own world and didn't notice her, or anyone else for that matter.

One Friday at noon, I went to meet Suda after class and noticed she didn't feel well.

"Are you okay, Suda?"

"Yes, but I cannot sit on the ground today." We normally had lunch on the grass by the gym to avoid Brad's group.

"We can go over to the baseball field and sit there," I suggested.

"No, I need to sit right now," she said as she walked to the nearest lunch table. She barely made it to the table before she all but collapsed, and laid her head on the table.

"Suda, are you okay? There's a school nurse you can see for free," I suggested, getting nervous about the benches filling up around us as students poured out of their classrooms. To my relief, only three other girls sat at the other end of the table and were too engrossed in gossip to notice us.

"I think the baby may come early."

"How far along do you think you are?"

"Oh…my bleedings were never on schedule. I do not know for sure… but I think that I am over halfway there."

"Suda, why do we have a bleeding?"

"I do not know why, but a woman bleeds every new moon, and when it stops they say she is with child," she said switching to Swahili.

We had never spoken about such intimate and secret details of a woman's body before. Although Suda was a wealth of information and was shrewd enough to figure out many things on her own, she still didn't know everything about the mysteries of her body. In our country, a woman never spoke of such things, even to her daughters.

"How do you know this?"

"A few times I saw our mama's bloody cloth on her way to wash at the spring."

"Look who escaped from the zoo." Cara's voice was smooth and cold as a winter spring as it seeped through my skin. She wore a pink blouse – but that was no surprise because she had an endless supply of pink – and an extremely short pair of denim shorts. "Are you speaking monkey language?"

Cara and Brad stood among their followers to our left. Neither of us noticed their advance, and the girls at the other end of the table were nowhere to be seen. They must have sensed trouble and escaped.

"We're not looking for trouble," I said speaking before Suda had a chance.

"Again, you disrespect us and choose to sit at our table," Cara said.

"I'm sorry. We're leaving," I responded knowing full well that wasn't their usual table. It really didn't matter where we sat because we were not welcome at the lunch tables, or at this school.

"We're not going anywhere," Suda said slowly and we all turned toward her, the calmness in her voice feeding my dread.

"I'll give you five seconds to get up or I'll be forced to call security," Cara said in a singsong voice as she went to stand directly next to Suda. "One…two…three…"

Suda stood up ever so slowly and Cara slowed her count as she smiled confidently. "Four ..," she continued and looked back at Brad who shot her his full approval.

"Five!" Suda shouted. To our astonishment, she launched her right fist squarely into Cara's face. Cara's head flew back nearly horizontal, but somehow she managed to remain on her feet.

No one was prepared for this, and everyone stood in silence before they let out a collective "Oohhh." Suda continued her attack and forcefully pushed her to the ground, but Cara recovered quickly and deftly pulled my sister down with her. Both girls landed in an array of twisted limbs and Cara's long blonde hair.

I saw Suda fight more than a few times with our second-oldest brother, Obiajula, who was the bully of the family. She was quick, agile, and efficient, although the fights were never intended for any real harm. She fought with our brother to show her lack of fear and strength. Even if she lost, she was never subdued. Our oldest brother, Akello, would stop them before Suda was hurt.

Today her punches were quick, but the burden she carried coupled with her fatigue and sickness made her movements slow and uncoordinated. Cara maneuvered on top, straddling Suda with her long legs. The crowd roared! When did the multitude arrive? In a matter of moments, the entire school watched, rooting for Cara, or maybe they just cheered for an exciting fight.

Suda grabbed a fist full of Cara's hair in one hand and punched her with the other, while she ignored Cara's clawing fingers. Suda was still on the bottom but with a clear advantage; however, I had to stop it now because the baby was in great danger. Although Cara was slight in build, her full body weight was on Suda's stomach, and Suda couldn't get up if she wanted to.

Just as I made a move forward, I was dragged backward and slammed into a broad chest. I didn't have to look back to know that it was Brad. This time he pulled me away from the fight. He was prepared for a fight from me and anticipated every move I made. I couldn't get away.

"Let me go."

"Not a chance."

"You don't...understand," I said between fruitless struggles. "I have to help her." I felt all I needed to know that he enjoyed this way too much.

"No, you don't. Your sister is doing just fine, and Cara's getting what she deserves," he whispered in my ear. He held me so tightly to him that I could barely breathe.

I looked back at his dark, piercing, wicked eyes that shimmered with mocking amusement. The crowd didn't pay us any attention, too engrossed in the fight. "Please, let me go." I had resorted to begging him. It was all I could do to save Suda's baby.

"What will you give me if I let you go?" he asked grasping my right breast.

"What are you doing?!" Cara had stopped fighting and stared wildly at Brad. With a newfound energy she struggled out of Suda's hold and attempted to get up.

"Later, babe," he said letting me go. I ran over to Suda who remained on the ground just as a security guard rushed over. Several other teachers worked to disperse the crowd as Cara pushed passed me, Suda forgotten.

"What happened?" the security guard asked Cara before she made it to Brad.

"That jungle baboon attacked me! I was minding my own business when she attacked me...ask anyone." She motioned to her followers who nodded their heads in agreement.

"That's not true!" I cried out.

The security guard didn't even ask Suda what happened, and I was too concerned about her health to actively dispute any further.

"Suda, I'm so sorry," I said stroking her feverish brow. "Are you in a lot of pain?"

"What do you think?" She clutched her belly, revealing the obvious.

"I'm so sorry. This is all my fault. I should have done something. I should have seen them coming –"

"Matika –"

"There must have been something I could have –"

"Matika!" Suda grabbed my arm. "Will you stop that? You make a spirit grow weary the way you ramble on."

"Oh, Suda! What should I do?"

I completely forgot that she still lay on the ground in great pain. Sometimes, when I was nervous, or excited or bored, I tended to ramble on.

"Call an ambulance!" a familiar voice shouted, dropping me back to this world.

"Oh, no," I cried as I saw a dark red pool between her legs.

Ms. M was quickly by Suda's side and asked her numerous questions.

My eyes clouded with tears and I was helpless to do anything but watch until I was forcefully pulled to my feet.

"Come with me," the security guard ordered.

"No, I have to stay with my sister," I cried.

"There is nothing for you to do here. You need to call your parents."

Within five minutes, Suda had a group of medics working on her, and I was led away to the front office. By that time most of the students had been sent away or were in the process of being removed. Cara was gone.

He was right. Baba was going to find out one way or another. I'm not sure what was worse, the fight or Suda's pregnancy. I wanted to die going over the potential outcomes of this day, none of which yielded even a little hope.

When we got to the main building, I was escorted directly to the principal's office where Cara sat much too cozily in one of two chairs across from a large oak desk.

"Sit down and wait while I get Mr. Patton," the security guard said as he shut the door behind him. He seemed to direct his statement to me.

Uncomfortable was an understatement to describe how I felt in Cara's presence. As much as I wanted to stall, I went over to the other chair and sat down, my back ramrod straight. The tension in the room was palpable as we waited in the sparsely furnished but richly decorated office. On the principal's desk was a family photo of him, his wife, and two golden-haired boys on a beach as the sun faded in the background. All were shoeless, wore white, and beamed with happiness. I'd never met the principal, but hoped he was as happy and carefree as it showed in the photos.

After several long minutes, Cara slowly turned toward me with her chin pointed in the air. "If you think for one second that I'm going to get into any kind of trouble, you're as stupid as you look, little miss big tits."

"Cara, you know you provoked her," I said meeting her eye to eye. I would not let her intimidate me. Not only had I faced the Colonel and his men, who were the rebels of the River Lion, I would have to face Baba. There was nothing more that Cara could add to that growing pile. Also, my sister would be devastated if she lost her baby, which was extremely likely by the looks of it.

"I did no such thing, and you have no proof. As you saw yourself, there were plenty of people who would easily back me up."

"Say what you like, I don't care."

"Just to let you know, my father is the superintendent of this district."

That didn't mean anything to me, and she must have read it on my face. I felt like an open book, like Suda had said, unable to hide my emotions.

"We'll see how much you care when you and your sister get expelled from our school."

Things just turned from bad to worse. Baba would kill us if we got expelled from this school. He was so proud that we could attend the best public school in the county. He boasted of our success with our neighbors and others in our community.

Cara was obviously a girl of privilege and was used to getting what she wanted, which would be icing on the cake for her if we got expelled. She had no idea what it would do to our family. We were like ants beneath her feet, so insignificant.

"You don't belong here anyway – you're nothing but a *slut*," her mocking voice drawled putting emphasis on the word "slut." "I see the way Brad looks at you. Just because you're pretty and have big tits doesn't mean you will ever be good enough for him. He would use you then throw you in the trash when he's done, like all the others."

I didn't know what a "slut" was, but I knew it was something bad. I had done nothing to deserve this treatment. I was one breath away from breaking down, and the fact that Cara thought I was pretty meant nothing. I wanted to know what I had done to her that made her hate me so much. I was about to ask her when the door opened behind us and in walked Mr. Patton.

Mr. Patton looked like the man in the photo, but didn't at the same time, if that was possible. He regarded us both with a slight nod before he walked to his desk. His look was stern, almost troubled, as his brows creased together. Mr. Patton had a very distinguished look about himself, with his perfectly tailored dark-blue suit, white shirt, and red tie. His silver-laced black hair was cut short, his face clean shaven around a square jaw.

Before he even sat down, Cara gave me a look of absolute confidence that she already knew the outcome of this meeting.

"Our school is not some barbaric prison that permits behavior such as fighting," he said. "This is not San Diego Unified or Escondido School District. Torrey Hills holds a greater standard. This school has the highest academic achievement rates, the best sports programs, and the least disciplinary problems, and by gosh, I intend to keep it that way." He slammed his hand on the desk, sending his cup of pens flying off his desk and crashing to the floor. Then he took a deep breath and calmed slightly. "Cara, you mind telling me what happened out there today?"

Great. He knew her name, a very bad sign considering the number of students at this school. I bet anything with absolute certainty he didn't know all of the others' names.

Cara's story had little truth and painted Suda as a wild beast that attached without provocation. Of course, she didn't touch the fact that we had been forced to move from the lunch table.

"Me and my friends were sitting at the table before they came along demanding us to move," she said haughtily. In her eyes, there was only one side to this story.

"I've heard enough, Cara. You may wait outside until we call your family."

"Yes, Mr. Patton," Cara responded sweetly, but before she left the office added, "I really hope this doesn't jeopardize the winter homecoming game, especially being the captain of the cheerleading squad. It would be very bad if I couldn't make it."

"Thank you for the reminder, Cara."

"That's not what happened, Mr. Patton," I began. "My sister and I were sitting there first. Cara said awful things to my sister. Suda wouldn't have hit her for no reason."

"It doesn't matter what really happened or who said what first." He looked as if he almost pitied me. "Your sister started a fight and can't continue at this school. Not only that, she started a fight with the district superintendent's daughter, no less, the same man who pays my employees, our staff."

"Please, Mr. Patton, you can't do that to her. This means everything to my father and our family."

"It's not just the fighting issue. It's just been confirmed that your sister is pregnant, and we simply do not support that kind of student here. This is not your ordinary public institution. In spite of budget cuts, we have an image to uphold for our private donors who support the schools in this district."

I closed my eyes and took a deep breath. I was cursed. "Oh, please, there must be some accommodation you could make here in this case," I said. A shot in the dark. "Can she study from home?"

He made no show to even consider my question.

"We do *not* accommodate that type of student."

I felt the tears pool in my eyes. This was all hopeless. Gritting my teeth, I forced my eyes to travel over to his stern face, and made eye contact.

His eyes softened slightly as he cleared his throat. "There is a continuation option I will give your father for pregnant teens, but I will only be discussing that with him. You may go now. Your father has been informed that your sister was taken to Scripps Hospital." He got up and opened the door for me.

Where was I to go? I had no way to get a hold of Baba right then, and school would be out in ten minutes. I waited for hours in the parking lot.

# CHAPTER 5

"Get in," Baba barked before his car screeched to a halt.

I entered the car quickly, and he pulled away before the door shut. Though Baba was quiet as we barreled down the freeway at eighty-five miles per hour, I was not fooled. He was more than angry. I expected him at any moment to backhand me, but I wouldn't be so lucky to get a swift punishment. He wouldn't even look at me through the rearview mirror, his eyes only focused on the road ahead. I endured a painfully long drive home knowing that something much, much, worse was coming.

As we pulled up to our house, I found that no matter how hard I tried I couldn't get out of the car. My legs would not cooperate with my mind; they just stayed glued to the now-sticky seat, waiting for a spatula to dislodge them.

Baba threw open the door and pulled me out of the car by the collar of my flower-printed dress. "Get in the house."

I expected him to beat me where I stood. It certainly wouldn't be the first time a girl was publicly beaten in our neighborhood. Actually, Baba was lenient compared to some of the other men in our community.

"Yes, Baba," I mumbled as I scrambled into the house.

I was about to run into my room and shut the door, or hide in the bathroom, which was better because it could be locked, but I instead stopped halfway into the living room. If I ran, it would only make him angrier, like poking a hippo with a stick. I stood with my back to the door and waited.

Before the front door slammed shut, Baba was upon me with a switch off a tree that he had hastily taken from out front. It still had the leaves on it! He beat me with it, striking my bottom, legs, and back. I kept my arms across my chest and covered my face. That was the worst beating I had ever received from Baba.

My cries were overshadowed by Baba's yelling. I didn't hear anything he shouted because my ears rang from my own screams that threatened to shatter my eardrums. Baba beat me until the branch snapped, then he beat me with his heavy open palms, which sent me to the floor.

"Get up!" he shouted.

I wanted to move faster, but my aching body failed me. I was pulled up and forced to stand on my shaky legs. Baba gripped my face in the apex of his monstrous hands, so strong that he could have easily crushed me without breaking a sweat, turning my face upward so that I looked into his eyes.

"You knew she was pregnant and didn't even tell me!" he said. "You didn't even protect her! She could have died because of you!"

He didn't expect me to respond. How could I when my mouth was glued shut, while I bit my tongue, and possibly drew blood? I was so hurt for him to even think that I would stand and watch what happened to her and do nothing, especially when I knew she was pregnant.

"Suda has disgraced herself and brought shame to the family! How could she let those Americans have her? This would have never happened if your mama was here!" He let me go and turned away from me, but not before I saw the hurt in his eyes.

"Baba, she made me swear not to tell. She didn't disgrace herself with an American. It's Walyam's babe."

I wanted to come clean. He would find out soon anyway. I felt sorry for him, and for Suda. I don't know what I could have done to change the situation but it was too late now.

"I should have known. He's gone behind my back and defiled my daughter. I've already given him Namazzi. They are married and will be here soon. Now he will have Suda, too. Walyam doesn't deserve her." Baba's eyes were bloodshot and his face contorted in anger. "No one must know. I will tell them they were married before we left Kenya," he mused to himself. "She has a son on the way."

"The baby's still inside her?"

"Yes, and it's healthy, but she will need to stay in bed until it's time. The doctor said the babe will come in three months."

"Baba, I tried to help her, but they–"

"Enough. Now get out of my sight before I beat you again."

Relief comforted me now that I knew Suda hadn't lost the baby. I went straight to the bathroom, took a hot bath to soak the bruises and burning welts, thankful that it was Friday because I wouldn't be able to show my face at school.

Suda stayed the night at the hospital. I was forced to stay home when Baba went to get her in the morning. While she was gone, I kept busy cleaning up the house. I tried to make it as welcoming as possible while the distraction helped stave off my anxiety. I refolded all her clothes in the dresser. Finally, after a heated inner debate, I made up my mind to tell Suda about Walyam and Namazzi as soon as she came home.

"Bring Suda some water," Baba demanded, as he kicked open our bedroom door and stared at me. He carried the crying Suda effortlessly, and gently laid her on the bed. He must have told her about Walyam.

"Yes, Baba," I said as I scurried out of the room into the kitchen.

When I returned with the water, Baba was gone. He'd left the house again. Slowly I walked over to Suda, and placed the plastic cup on the dresser. She faced the wall, and still sobbed.

"How long have you known?" she asked, turning on her back, staring at the ceiling.

"Not long. I'm so sorry. I wanted to say something, but you loved him so much, and then you were pregnant. I don't know what Baba was thinking," I added in my defense. "I believed that it was the only way for him to come here. He's not related to us, so he can't just come to the U.S."

"Don't you think I know that?" she asked looking at me. The hurt in her large brown eyes nearly broke me. "How could you hide something like this from me? We are sisters!"

"I'm really sorry, Suda."

"You should be sorry!"

She narrowed her eyes, and though I knew she'd be upset, I didn't feel the fear that gripped me before. Instead, I was amazed at the anger I felt. "Wait a minute. You were the one keeping secrets from me," I shot back at her. "Obviously, being sisters didn't matter to you at all. You didn't even tell me you were pregnant. I figured it out and confronted you."

"Enough!" she shouted. "I want to rest."

"No! I think we need to get this all out in the open." I surprised myself at my retort. Who was this girl that confronted her older sister whom she looked up to? "I think Baba is right. Walyam doesn't deserve you."

"You think that he's better suited for Namazzi!" Suda shot up in the bed. "Baba thinks so little of her that he makes her wed Walyam?"

"You know how Namazzi is. You've said many times that she doesn't even think for herself. Wait…what were the words exactly? 'She wouldn't know an opinion if it slapped her in the face.' Those were your words, remember?"

Suda couldn't argue with that. Namazzi was the oldest of three girls from Mama's twelve children. She was as subdued as a field mouse, fitting the bill for the model African wife in that respect. She was weak in mind and body while Suda was strong and bold. Namazzi was unhealthy and always sick, confined to our hut most of her life. It was a wonder that she survived childhood, stricken with one illness or another. When we last saw Namazzi more than two years ago, she had bones protruding through her skin with a frame akin to a young boy, absent of any womanly curves.

"Go," Suda hissed, her steam left her in defeat. She laid back down and turned away from me to face the wall.

"I believe everything will work out," I said turning on my heel and left the door open in case she called for me.

———

Two months after our bitter argument, Suda was still upset, which didn't surprise me because she tended to hold on to her anger. When she spoke to me, it was about nothing deeper than day-to-day activities. Confined to her bed, she didn't follow the doctor's orders. Instead she chose to work in her garden and do light chores. When I gave her gentle reminders to stay off her feet, she would say, "What does an American doctor know of an African woman?"

School was uneventful for me. I was able to completely ignore Cara and Brad, dodging them at every turn. I continued to do well and was rewarded for my efforts with praise by my teachers. Even without Baba's "English only" rule in the house, I was very confident in my communication, though I could never hide my accent.

During Thanksgiving break, I clipped coupons and read library books. Suddenly, Baba barged through the front door with the most shocking grin on his face. He still wore his navy blue-and-white security uniform. With his hat and light jacket in one hand, lunch box and a large package in the other, he kicked the door closed with his foot.

It was after eleven in the evening, but I had stayed up to warm his food. Suda had long since retired for the night. She had very little energy, as her delivery was near. His smile broadened when he spotted me by the microwave and sat down at the table. Putting his food in front of him, I stood waiting for him to finish in case he wanted more.

"Go to bed, Matika," he said dismissing me with a negligent hand.

"Yes, Baba," I responded but my feet were rooted to the floor. I just couldn't tear myself from his smiling eyes. "Is there news?"

"Indeed," he grunted, clearing his throat, but didn't provide any further detail. "Bed. Now!"

My heart pounded in my chest. I headed to my room. Suda had just returned from one of her multiple trips to the bathroom now that the baby had squished her bladder to the size of a grape.

She looked at me perplexed. "What's with you?" she asked as she slipped between the sheets.

"Nothing. It's just that Baba came home, and he's in a very good mood," I said, as I changed into my nightgown. It was my favorite one, but the fabric had become thin from multiple washes. We got it from Goodwill, so I knew it was already used.

"Really?" she perked up. "That's not like him. Do you think Walyam is coming soon?"

"Maybe." My heart skipped a beat at the mention of his name.

I fell asleep that night wishing that Walyam was not coming. As much as I loved my family, I would rather not see them in order to avoid Walyam. There was a time when I wanted to tell Suda the truth about him, but I knew she wouldn't believe me, especially now that our relationship was strained.

When I awoke the next morning, Suda had already made the morning meal of fried bread and tea. Baba hadn't come out of his room yet, his door was still closed. I sat down at the table watching her waddle around the kitchen getting plates and cups. Her belly was enormous, and threatened to burst at any moment as she stretched to reach the top shelf.

"Wear something nice today; we are having a guest this morning," Baba said as he strode into the kitchen wearing a pair of black slacks and a white button-up shirt.

"Is Walyam coming?" Suda burst out.

"I don't expect him until next month," Baba responded with a look of disgust on his face. He hovered over the platter of fried sweet bread. "That's not enough. Suda, make some eggs."

"Yes, Baba." Suda's smile was barely contained.

Relief filled me as I headed for my room to change just as the doorbell sounded. I scurried to put on a clean school dress, not bothering to comb my hair. Returning to the kitchen, I was in awe at the beautiful woman who now sat in my place at the table.

She was Black American with skin the color of honey, with a dust of freckles – I'd never seen that on a black person – on both sides of her nose. With hair that hung straight as a bone to her shoulders, swaying ever so slightly, she turned to face me. Her eyelashes were like peacock feathers clumped together with mascara. She looked to be in her late thirties or early forties. It was hard to tell through the thick layer of makeup that was as smooth as icing on a cake.

"Why, hello, Matika," she said as her eyes traveled from my head down to my feet then settled on my breasts. "I've heard so much about you."

"Meet your new mother," Baba beamed. "Corin and I were married yesterday."

# CHAPTER 6

Suda dropped the spatula; I choked on a gasp. I should have expected this because Baba could never be alone. Even at the refugee camp in Kenya, he was married to another wife, Evelyn, when I arrived. Before we left, he'd told us all that he was going to work to get Evelyn to the United States.

"Nice to meet you," Corin said extending her hand out to me.

For a moment, I just stared at her hand like it were a foreign object. She had a tattoo on her arm that was in plain sight since she wore a sleeveless shirt. Corin also wore jeans, which made her look worldly. She was the opposite of what I believed Baba wanted in a wife. *What was he thinking?*

"Matika!" Baba's voice burned the ice that froze me, enabling me to move again.

"Nice to meet you, too," I said shaking her cold hand. "How do you get your hair like that?"

It was a rude question but slipped out before I realized it. It was too straight for a person of African descent to be natural.

"Honey, it's a perm. I'm sure your father won't approve of you getting one, but I do have a hot comb to straighten your hair. Sherri can teach you how."

We soon learned that Corin had three children. Her two sons, Thomas and Anthony, were seven and twenty respectively, and her daughter, Sherri, was seventeen, a junior in high school. With the exception of her oldest son, they moved into our house that afternoon. Words couldn't describe how Baba had changed our life so drastically with his surprise marriage to Corin. Suda suspected it was a ploy to further cement his citizenship, but I believed he was in love despite Suda's adamant dismissal of the idea.

Within days, Corin went from cool and polite to jealous and controlling, dominating every conversation. Baba was enamored with her, and every word she spoke was manna to his ears. Her kids received the best of everything, such as clothes and shoes, yet she criticized my ragged garments, as if I had a choice. Suda and I weren't allowed in the refrigerator unless we had permission. This was really hard for Suda, who needed to snack frequently. To make matters worse, we had to share a room with Thomas, her youngest son, because her daughter needed privacy. The fourth room was reserved for our family, due to arrive by Christmas.

The only positive thing about having Corin around was that Sherri showed me how to straighten my hair with a hot comb that, to my surprise, lengthened it to the middle of my shoulder blades. Still, she refused to be seen with my hair "looking like a hot mess."

Suda wouldn't engage with Corin at all. I was afraid that one day she would explode, and we would be in a world of trouble. As it was, we were never able to be alone with Baba, especially now that he worked longer hours.

In mid-December, Suda found an opportunity to confront Baba about Corin when she and her kids were out shopping one morning. We were all in the backyard, as Baba replaced a blown porch light while Suda instructed me in gardening. Her belly was too low to do it herself.

"Baba, Corin never lets me cook the food that pleases you," Suda said with her hand on her hips.

"I enjoy her cooking, but you are welcome to show her how to make African food. Remember, you are no longer the woman of the house," Baba said standing tall. "You must learn to obey her in all things."

"She's American," Suda reminded him. "Why do I fall beneath her?"

"Suda, watch your mouth and learn your place," he said before he walked off, killing any further discussion.

"He's under her spell," Suda said as soon as he was out of earshot. "She's not my mama!"

"You're right, but you are not going to get him on your side," I said. "He only sees her, now."

"He spends more time with her kids than with his own. We mean nothing to him anymore. I'll be glad when Walyam comes."

At the mention of Walyam's name, I froze. His very name sent a ripple down my spine. It was the first time she had mentioned his name in weeks. She was still hopeful that they would renew their love despite him being married to Namazzi.

"Oh, no!" she screamed like her life would end.

"What's wrong?" I asked as I stood, dropping the uprooted weeds to the ground. "Did you wet yourself?"

"My water has fallen," she whimpered looking down at the wetness oozing down her legs. "This can't be happening now."

"Come. We have to tell Baba." I led her into the house, sitting her in the kitchen before I ran to find Baba.

"Baba! Suda's water fell out," I called from outside his closed bedroom door. That was an area we were never allowed in, even if the house was burning down.

"It could be hours before the baby comes," he said. "I have to go to work soon, so Suda can wait for your mama to get home."

"Baba, she has to go to the hospital now. Can you please drop us off on your way?"

"Fine," he grunted striding out of the room dressed for work. "I'll be in the car."

Suda's pain started to get really intense on the way to the hospital and Baba was very uncomfortable as he drove at breakneck speed. I don't believe he was ever present when any of his ten wives gave birth back in our village in Uganda. A ceremony was given in which he would name the child when he returned, as Baba spent most of his days divided between his military position working in Kampala, his banks, and his wives.

"Baba, is there something we need to do?" I asked once we arrived at the emergency room. Baba usually took Suda to her appointments so I had no I idea about the process.

"I'll check her in," he said leaving us to follow slowly behind him.

Suda stopped every few steps, doubling over in pain. I did my best to soothe her, rubbing her back and reminding her to breathe. When we finally made it inside, Baba was arguing with the receptionist.

"Sir, at seventeen, she's a minor, and as her father you must be present," the receptionist said.

"She's a woman! Her mother will come–"

"She's a minor. She's only seventeen," the nurse chimed in.

"I have to go to work. I don't have time for this nonsense. Next, you'll want me to look between her legs!"

"Sir, I assure you we won't be asking that of you," the doctor said as he arrived at the counter. The doctor's voice was as smooth as silk and calming.

"Bah!" Baba threw up his hands, exasperated. He reluctantly followed the procession as Suda was wheeled through the double doors.

The hospital halls seemed full of people even though it was a Saturday. Labor and Delivery was on the fourth floor. I had never been to a hospital before. With its pristine tiles and decorative walls, it looked more like an office building than a place where people received life-saving treatment. After Suda was brought to the room, it all happened so fast. In a matter of minutes, Suda was prepped and vital signs checked. It turned out she was dilated nine centimeters out of ten.

"I know you are in a lot of pain, honey, but it's too late for an epidural."

"Pain is natural in childbirth," Baba said. All eyes, none too pleasant, turned to him.

"Ahhhh!" Suda bore down in another wave of pain, gripping the bedrail that strained under the force.

"Sir, try holding her hand to comfort her," the doctor said as he put on a set of tight rubber gloves. "It's time for her to push now."

"You'll have me do woman's work?" Baba was aghast, and looked at the doctor like a set of horns had sprouted from his head.

Reluctantly, he complied. Baba and I each held her hand as she bravely pushed and pushed. To witness the making of life was truly amazing.

Having a child come out of such a small opening was a miracle in itself. Despite his complaints, Baba, too, was fascinated with the whole process, and stole surreptitious gazes at the birth. He used the excuse that he needed to make sure the doctor was doing things properly, like he himself knew what to do since he had never watched a birth. After twenty minutes, Suda had a healthy baby boy.

"A son! You did well, Suda," Baba said smiling down at the boy swaddled in her arms.

"Thank you," she beamed, caressing her son's bald head.

Baba didn't go to work that day but instead took me with him to Walmart on the way home from the hospital to buy things for the baby. Although he didn't smile openly, he was content, and it showed in his eyes.

"Baba, can I walk to the bookstore across the street?" I asked, hopeful to capitalize on his good mood.

"All right, but don't talk to strangers. Meet me back here in forty-five minutes."

"Yes, Baba," I said, barely containing my excitement as I exited the car. I dodged a lot full of cars before I ran across the street. I'd never quite grasped the idea of a crosswalk.

Soon I was in the bookstore looking for my next great read that I hoped would soon be available at the public library. Aisle after aisle, I browsed the titles of my favorite authors, from historical romances to non-fiction novels. Afterward, I took a quick detour and headed to the small convenience store to buy an Almond Joy, my favorite candy. Turning down the row too sharply, I bumped into someone, and unceremoniously dropped my chocolate.

Then my heart dropped, my breath completely stolen. My knees weakened, and I found myself on the ground before him. It was like unseen hands tickled my belly, the familiar feeling of hunger that ate into my very soul took me back to the refugee camp in Kenya.

I was driven back to the time I'd dropped the water bucket. His eyes were even greener than I'd remembered, and shone brightly with his shocked expression as our gazes locked. He was by my side in an instant.

The energy still flowed between us and was epic, a live current that joined our bodies. His boyish face was gone and was replaced with masculine features, a more square jaw making him look harder than before. His body, too, had changed and had filled out significantly with arms nearly the size of my waist.

"Matika?" he asked bewildered, his brows knitted together gently. "My God! Have I died and gone to heaven?"

"Chaz," I said, my voice hoarse with emotion.

# CHAPTER 7

This was more than I could bear and yet…how quickly my emotions flowed from the shock waves that coursed through me, to the deep pain of regret and betrayal, followed by a deep-seated anger that bloomed forth, washing over all other emotions in a matter of moments. How could I be so angry when I wished for so many nights and dared to dream of being with him again?

"I thought I'd never see you again." he said reaching for me. "Oh, how I've missed you."

"It was you who left me!" Pulling away from him, I burst into tears, as I scurried out of the store.

I needed to be alone, so I scampered to the side between the two buildings. This couldn't be happening just when I finally settled into a comfortable routine.

"Matika, I never wanted to leave you," Chaz's voice awakened my soul. His presence filled the space to capacity. "You have to know it was the last thing I wanted to do. My unit had to evacuate the camp. You know I had no choice. Is that why you never met me that day? You could have a least told me yourself that you didn't want to see me again instead of sending your brother."

"What are you talking about? Walyam told me you never came," I looked up at him. He was so close to me, our bodies only inches apart. "I wasn't allowed back outside."

I thought back to the horrific day when chaos ruled the camp. The aid organizations had run out of supplies, so the people rioted, killing and wounding many. During the confusion, Chaz had told me to meet him at the water pump. It was where we'd first met. He was going to give me his information so I could keep in touch with him, but Baba wouldn't allow any of us out of the tent because of the violence. I'd begged Walyam to meet Chaz for me, but he told me that Chaz never came. For many nights, I'd cried myself to sleep regretting that awful day.

"I never would have done that – I loved you," he said moving closer, the passion in his eyes undeniable. "There hasn't been a day that's gone by without you on my mind, in my heart. I had so much time to think about our relationship and I realized that you're my soul mate. No other woman can compare to you. Matika, I love you."

He lifted my chin up so that I looked at his beautiful face before he kissed me gently. My response to him was immediate. I threw my whole body at him, making him catch me as I desperately clung to him, wrapping my legs around his waist, and yielded my body and mind. There wasn't a care or a thought in the world. Lacing my fingers in his neatly cropped hair, I consumed everything he offered. I gave and took all while his hands roamed my body with a desperation that matched my own.

The sensation he'd given me so long ago flared to life with such authority that my womanhood wept with need as it was pressed against him. His lips slanted over mine as he thrust his tongue in and out of my mouth in a rhythm that matched his hips; quick, hungry and fierce.

"Get a room!" someone shouted.

Slowly he let my feet touch the ground. Panting like we'd run many miles through the desert with no water in sight, we each struggled to find our breath. Chaz didn't let me go but instead leaned against the wall taking me with him, looking down at me with his precious green eyes. I was at full liberty to breathe in his essence that fed my soul.

"Where can I find you?" he asked breathless. "I'm not going to lose you again."

"I go to school at Torrey Hills."

"I know that area. How old are you again?" he asked with concern in his eyes.

Chaz was always uncomfortable with my age. We had this discussion before at the Kenyan camp. When we met, I had stretched the truth, and told him I was fourteen. That was more than two years ago. I was sixteen now, but there was no need tell him. The truth was, in my country I would be married and pregnant with my second child by now. Chaz was about twenty. The four-year difference was minuscule compared with the old man I would have ended up with in my country had Baba arranged my marriage.

"Old enough," I challenged.

"OK, we won't go there. Can I pick you up next Monday? I really want to see you before the holidays are over. We can go on a real date."

"Chaz, I would love that!" I exclaimed, though I didn't understand what a date was. I heard about it a lot in TV shows but never really understood its purpose.

I told him a little about how things were going in our new home and that Baba had married the Wicked Witch of the West, who happened to be named Corin. He laughed. He said he wanted to introduce me to his father one day and had told him all about me.

"You'll just say you're eighteen, and no one will question anything. You are close to it, anyway. I'm still in the Marine Special Forces, but no longer detailed to the U.N. I still get really great assignments and get to meet very high-ranking individuals. As a matter of fact, we have a special party for diplomats and ambassadors. I can bring a date, too. I know people who can get you on the cleared list easily. I have friends in high places," he said sporting that brilliant smile of his with a perfect set of white teeth. "It pays to be in the intelligence field."

To hear Chaz talk about the future, folding me into his life, was elating. I wanted him in my life always. At that moment, I knew that I would do everything in my power to never lose him again. He was my Chaz, and I would fight for him. His upbeat and excited tone was strange on a man of his stature and military background. He was completely different from the military men I'd met in my country. And, most definitely, he was the extreme opposite of Baba.

My life had shown me that military men used women for sex even if they were married. Women were no better than cattle to be eaten when men were hungry. I think Baba knew this and therefore never allowed any of my brothers to join the service, nor arranged any of his daughters' marriages to servicemen. I think that was one reason why he never approved of Walyam, who was a former child soldier for the rebels.

I could listen to Chaz speak for hours. He would have been the only man that talked more than I did. Imagine that… "Oh! I have to go," I said giving him a quick kiss before pulling away. I was so excited to see Chaz again that I'd forgotten about the time. "I have to meet Baba…um… my father across the street."

"So, I'll see you in a week? I'll be waiting at the grocery store parking lot down the road from the school, next Monday morning."

"Yes, see you soon!" I said before I ran across the street, barely missing a fatal swipe from a fast car.

I was on cloud nine, even after Baba yelled at me for being late. To think, if I hadn't taken the chance of asking Baba about the bookstore, I would have missed Chaz, possibly forever. The thought scared me, and brought me back to reality. Sometimes it was easier to stumble through life and miss out on our fate that's waiting for us to take a chance.

Determined to see Chaz as much as possible, I concocted ways to secretly meet with him, and devised the most plausible excuses. Bottom line, I had to learn how to lie. Well, at least be better at it, because I was as readable as the Sunday paper. On a positive note, Suda would be too busy with her new baby to pay much attention to me.

"Matika, move Suda's things into the spare bedroom," Corin said as soon as we entered the house. "I can't have the baby waking up Thomas at all hours of the night."

"Yes, madam," I said before heading to the room. That was the nicest thing she'd done for Suda, who would need her space with the new baby. I took my time getting the room ready for Suda, who was supposed to be released from the hospital Sunday. Her birth was considered routine, and she and her son were healthy.

When she arrived home, she was exhausted. It was more than that, she was depressed. The dress she wore hung off her body, her stomach now deflated. I imagined that she hadn't eaten since the birth.

"Suda, what's wrong?" I asked after I'd settled the babe, Walyam – I refused to utter that name to him – in the bed next to her.

"I just wish he was here for the birth of his son."

"I know, but Baba said that they will be coming in less than two weeks. It will give you time to recover and fit into your new skirt," I said handing her a bag. They were supposed to come before Christmas or soon after, but a delay in paperwork had prevented them from leaving on time.

The skirt wasn't even wrapped yet because I'd planned to give it to her on her birthday in January, a few weeks away, but she needed it now more than ever. If she was miserable and wasn't eating, like I suspected, her milk wouldn't come the way it should. I had made money "helping" others with their math homework. It had become pretty lucrative for me, and I received a dollar for every assignment.

"It's beautiful!" She held up the floral print skirt that was stylishly fitting, yet long enough that Baba couldn't complain.

"There's a top, too," I added, laughing at her excitement.

"Oh, this is perfect!" she exclaimed hugging the solid blue, button-up blouse. "Thank you so much. I'm going to look great when he sees me. I may steal some lipstick from Sherri. She leaves her makeup all around the bathroom, anyway."

"Yes, she does," I said absently as my mind churned at the prospects.

I couldn't walk out of the house with makeup on, but if I took some with me I could put it on before I met Chaz. Sherri wouldn't even notice it was gone, and I would return it when I came home. I was sure it wasn't that hard to figure it out how to apply it. There were so many girls at school who wore it, and it looked simple enough. Although some of them looked like the clowns in the cartoons on TV.

Monday morning didn't come soon enough after I'd spent the longest, sleepless evening of my life. Usually Baba would rush me around the house to get moving, but this morning I was already dressed with my hair straightened by the time he came out of his room to bang on my door.

I stole into the bathroom and locked the door behind me before Sherri, who could monopolize it and leave it steamy from too long a shower that would instantly frizz my now-straightened hair, could get there. We all had to share that one bathroom, yet another drawback of Baba's marriage to the witch. Sherri attended a nearby school, so she didn't even have to get up that early, yet she normally made sure she took over the bathroom before me.

I looked around the cluttered counters, counting the eyeliners, mascaras, concealers, and shadows. I picked up one of eight brushes, running its smooth edge against my check. I didn't know why Sherri could wear makeup and nice clothes, yet Suda and I couldn't dream of asking Baba about it. At eighteen, she was the oldest but she was still not much older than Suda.

"Get out of the bathroom!" Sherri's shrill voice startled me, sending the makeup brush to the floor with a click. "What was that? You'd better not be using my hairbrush."

"I'm not. I'm almost done," I responded and took a deep breath. I hid mascara and a lipstick in my blouse. She was already onto me, so I didn't want to take too much and risk her noticing anything missing.

I didn't have an appetite, even for Corin's pancakes, which were my new favorite – I loved anything sweet – and scrambled eggs.

"You're already dressed?" Baba asked eying me suspiciously as he helped himself to the syrup and drenched his pancakes.

"I have to study for a test this morning," I responded with lie number one. I poured myself a tall glass of milk. Having cold milk each morning was a luxury I'd become accustomed to. It still surprised me Corin and Sherri couldn't tolerate dairy products. I'd never heard of a "lactose intolerance" illness. It would send them to the bathroom nearly instantly with diarrhea after consumption. One day I'd decided to be nice and made a big pot of grits to please Corin. I'd seen her make it numerous times, so I thought it would be easy. Adding milk instead of water was my mistake, unbeknownst to Corin and Sherri who'd eaten two helpings. Let's just say I was officially banned from cooking after that.

"Eat," Baba grunted through a mouth full of food.

"My stomach is too upset, but I'll take a snack with me."

"Your grades are good, so if you're not feeling well, you can stay home," Corin chimed in, flipping over a pancake.

Even if I wasn't going to meet Chaz that day, I wouldn't stay home. She would have me do chores all day and wait on her hand and foot. The only thing Corin did was cook the meals, and although she was good at it, she couldn't make African food. Unfortunately, Baba didn't seem to miss it. I did.

"No, thank you. I don't feel that bad."

With Baba's approval, I hurried out of the house to wait for him in the car, and pretended to go over my math notes. Inside, the car was cold, the windows fogged. I was so thankful for the sweater I had on top of the two layers of clothing I wore. It was my only sweater.

Soon, I would see Chaz. I still couldn't believe that he'd recognized me. I had changed so much since we'd been together last. I was certainly taller, five feet seven inches to be exact, although still above average. I grew into my breasts, and my hair was longer and straightened. In fact, one would argue that I was not the same girl inside and out.

I was buckled into the backseat of the car when Baba opened the door, and let the cold breeze seep inside. I pretended to study the whole way to school to avoid any conversation. Baba was never one for talking, but felt he needed to ask a question or two.

"Did you study enough for your test?" he asked glancing at me in the rearview mirror.

"Yes, Baba."

"How are you doing in your other classes?"

"Very well, Baba."

"Do well on your test," he called as I exited the car in front of the school.

"I will, Baba," I called over my shoulder.

# CHAPTER 7

Immediately I went to the school bathroom, took off my cover-up dress, and put on the makeup I took from Sherri. After applying the mascara, I realized that my eyelashes were extremely long, and touched my cheek with every blink of my large eyes. The lipstick was a little too dark, so I blotted it with tissue paper to lighten it up. I looked in the mirror at the final product, and was pleased. My cheekbones were high, my lips full, and my smile showed brilliant, straight white teeth. I didn't need any foundation because my creamy coffee skin was as smooth as satin. I looked beautiful.

Stuffing everything in my shoulder bag, I briskly walked to the grocery store parking lot to wait for Chaz. He was already there and pulled up to me in a red Toyota pickup as soon as I arrived. With shaky hands, I opened the door on the passenger side and slid in next to him. The stick shift was between us which prevented me from sitting too close.

"Good morning," he said, his smile was radiant and infectious.

"Good morning," I repeated as we pulled out of the lot. "How long were you waiting for me?"

"Oh, just an hour or so," he said making a left turn on Del Mar Heights road. "I couldn't sleep last night. Since I was tossing and turning anyway, I decided that I may as well wait for you here. I thought for sure, you'd be at least another hour. I'm really glad you came early."

"My father drops me off at seven before he goes to work."

"Thank goodness for that. I think I would have lost my mind by then."

We made our way up Interstate 5 engaging in light conversation about our lives. I told him about my sister having a baby with Walyam and he, in turn, told me about his mother's most recent cosmetic surgery. Why anyone would have someone insert plastic breasts in her body was unimaginable.

"She doesn't seem to have anything else to do with her time and money," he said as he exited off Mission Avenue in Oceanside. "I'll introduce you to my parents in a couple of weeks, maybe. My father will love you."

Chaz pulled up to his apartment. "My roommate is from my unit, but don't worry, he's not here today," he said as we walked toward his door. "I figure we can hang out for a while and then have lunch by the beach."

"The beach? That sounds so fun. Believe it or not I've never been to the beach. Baba…Father said we couldn't go because people are dressed inappropriately there."

"As cold as it is, there won't be anyone in their bathing suits," he smiled at me.

Chaz lived on the second floor. It was hard to believe that people lived literally on top of each other. As we ascended the steps, it felt more like we were headed into a cave with the door carved into the gray rock walls. I was surprised at how sturdy the steps were even though I could see the gap between each step.

"Welcome to my humble abode," he said stepping onto the welcome mat as he fished around for his keys in his pocket. He found them quickly, freed the deadbolt and pushed open the door.

I didn't know what to expect as I followed him into the apartment. Since I'd moved to America, I'd never been in another person's house. I always wondered how other houses were decorated and what their kitchens and bedrooms were like, or what they kept in their refrigerators.

The living room was to the right; the dining room was on the left, like an "L" shape next to the long narrow kitchen. There was a hall straight ahead that I presumed led to the bedrooms. It was not very big but wow! I would never have guessed that two single men lived in the apartment. It was richly decorated with paintings and art pieces on the walls, shelves, and end table. Beautiful masks made of fine porcelain, glass, exquisite fabric with plush multicolor feathers captivated my attention.

"My mom collects those from Rio, and she insists that I display them," Chaz said as he followed my stare. "I believe she wants them to be a deterrent to women somehow. See these here?" He pointed to some blown glass pieces housed with dishes in a china cabinet. "These are also from Rio, made by my mother's favorite artist."

"I've never seen anything like it. They are so beautiful."

"Not as beautiful as you," he said looking into my eyes. "Matika, I can't keep my eyes off you. I still can't believe you're here with me."

The butterflies in my stomach returned anew. As though tied to an invisible string we were drawn to each other, the tension that had built up for so long threatened to explode. Slowly we came closer together, but Chaz stopped only centimeters from me.

"Matika, if you don't want me to touch you, I need you so say so now. I've waited so long for this moment and I won't be able to stop once I start. I need you, all of you, so badly."

"Chaz, I've never been with anyone before…I'm really nervous."

"Oh babe, I won't hurt you. I'll never hurt you," he vowed.

"I trust you." Those were words I'd never uttered to a man.

"You are so beautiful to me. You know…I could look at you all day."

"Well, please remember that I don't have all day so try not to stare too long." I smiled up at him and was soon drawn to his lips. They were sensuous and ready to be kissed. Still, he denied me and hadn't given me what I craved so badly. "Chaz?"

Just when I thought he looked to turn away, he captured my lips with his, devoured my mouth, and stole the very air from my lungs. With one hand at the back of my neck, the other around my waist, he held onto me tightly. I gave in to him, and it was as natural as a beating heart. With reckless abandon I held onto him, lacing my hands through his finely cropped hair.

I didn't want to close my eyes and miss anything, but they closed of their own volition, blissfully soaking in the passion of our kiss. Even as he lifted me gently and carried me to his room, my eyes refused to open and our lips were fused together. It wasn't until my feet touched the ground that he broke the kiss long enough for him to pull the sweater over my head. At that moment, I felt as though I wore too much clothing, every ounce of it a barrier between us.

"Let me," he said and stopped me when I began to unbutton my dress. "I've dreamed of doing this for so long."

He worked painstakingly slow, and though I wanted to protest, the expression in his eyes was mesmerizing. As his finger grazed my skin, a shiver flowed through my body, like I'd been exposed to frigid air. He finally let my dress fall to the floor, and I sucked in a sharp intake of breath. Embarrassed that I hadn't worn a bra that day, I looked down at my feet and bit my lip.

"You are stunning, even more so than I'd ever known. Look at me."

With a finger under my chin, he gently forced it upward until I looked at him once again. Feeling my confidence restored, I smiled as he looked at me like I was a precious five-carat stone. When he pulled down my panties, I let them fall to the floor and kicked them to the corner.

"I'm at a disadvantage standing here bare while you are fully clothed – it's really not fair," I pouted, my hands on my hips.

"Ok…so what do you want to do about it?"

"I'll have to think about that," I said pulling on my bottom lip in mock contemplation. With shaky hands, I pulled his T-shirt over his head, nearly melting at his masculine smell of soap, aftershave and…Chaz. There were no words to describe his heady scent that was deliciously intoxicating and purely primal. I paused for a moment and inhaled all of him greedily. I got close enough to feel his warmth but didn't touch him.

"Oh, I almost forgot your pants," I said a moment before dropping to my knees to unbuckle them.

"Whoa, whoa…be careful down there. I don't want this to be over before we even get started."

Soon I had him out of his pants, then boxers, and finally pulled off his socks. "Much better," I said breathlessly. He was breathtaking, with a body sculpted like an African warrior.

For long moments we looked into each other's eyes, as if afraid to lose the moment. I could barely breathe when his hands slowly spanned my hips and pulled me to him. I could feel his erection against my belly. A breathless moan escaped my mouth as his lips came down on mine. I wanted him so badly. Tentatively placing my hand on his muscular chest, I was surprised at its firmness as it flexed with each caress to my backside.

My hands roamed freely now, around his biceps, up his neck, before they settled in his neatly cropped hair that was soft as a newborn chick. He groaned as I deepened the kiss, sucking on his tongue, threatening to swallow him. I whimpered when he pulled away, robbing me of his warmth. But he scooped me up and gathered me closely in his arms before he all but threw me on a bed that was soft and inviting.

Chaz stood before me, his manhood standing tall and proud, looking longingly at my body. I never felt so cherished and loved, and my eyes began to water.

"Are you okay?" he asked as he instantly lay at my side and touched my face with a deep concern his green eyes.

"Yes. I'm just so happy to share this with you."

"And I you…"

"Chaz…I've never done this before."

# CHAPTER 8

"You are a virgin?" he looked awed and skeptical at the same time. "I've never been with a virgin before. Are you sure you want to do this?"

"More than anything." I kissed him gently. "I want you."

"Matika, you never cease to amaze me. You are so special. I will be gentle with you. I truly don't want to hurt you. If at any time you want me to stop, please let me know. I love you so much and I want you to enjoy this, babe."

I nodded, unable to speak as my throat had gone dry with anticipation. He kissed me deeply, and then trailed his tongue down my throat before lapping its hollow. "Ah," I groaned when he made his way to my breasts and gave them the attention they begged for.

My nipples pearled as they stretched forth to meet his mouth, sending waves in the pit of my stomach. He blew gently on one as his hands moved to my other breast, and his thumb slowly rubbed my nipple. Steadily, Chaz made his way even lower, his rough hands on my hips; his tongue around my belly button before it slid across my hipbone.

Everything seemed so perfect. I had found the love of my life, and I was completely alone with him for the first time. Yet my heart constricted with a sudden cold fear that seeped through my veins, creating tremors within me.

"Are you okay?" Chaz asked looking up at me.

"I-I can't," I said turning away from him, ashamed at my reaction to intimacy. This was supposed to be the perfect day and I ruined it.

"Matika, look at me," he said and pulled me in his arms, "It's okay. We don't have to do anything."

"Chaz, I'm so sorry. I don't know what's wrong with me. Do you still love me?"

"Of course I do. You need never question my love for you." Chaz kissed the top of my head and held me tighter. "I don't know about you but I'm starving. You just wait right here."

Chaz quickly left the room. While he was gone, I got dressed and fixed my hair. He returned ten minutes later with a tray of food. He wore a pair of board shorts while sporting the most handsome grin.

"Just so you know, I can only cook breakfast food, so I'm apologizing upfront if the omelet isn't very good."

"I'm sure it's fine, although I've never tried an omelet before," I said looking down at the cheese-covered egg with curiosity.

"You should meet my mom. She makes a mean omelet that even our cook cannot compete with." When I sat up, he placed the tray between us. "It's nine o'clock, so this will have to serve as our picnic, minus the beach of course. But not to worry, we will still go to beach today."

"Can we just stay here today? I'm actually kind of tired."

"Sure. That's sounds like a good plan."

"Chaz, this is perfect. Thank you."

Like a meal from a coupon book or magazine, the tray contained two omelets, toast, assorted fresh-cut fruit, and apple juice. It warmed my heart to see the effort Chaz had gone through to make this for me. As a matter of fact, I'd never heard of a man who cooked before, especially for a woman. Baba never stepped foot in the kitchen unless the food was ready, especially with Corin's rule about food only in the refrigerator. Baba could no longer store his shirts there. He didn't even get his own drink because there were plenty of us to wait on him.

"Tell me about your mom. She has a cook?" I asked when he joined me on the bed, the food between us.

"Yeah...." He was obviously uncomfortable about the subject. "You wouldn't want to meet her. We don't get along too well lately. My mom is not the nicest person. She and my father are in Rio for the winter. Anyway, how do you like it?"

"It's really good," I said after swallowing a mouthful. Because I'd skipped breakfast I was really hungry. "What's your father like?"

"My dad is great, although he's forever under mother's dictatorship. I'd like you to meet him one day soon. He knows all about you, as I said before. I'll make sure to invite him to have lunch with us when they get back."

"That'll be great. I look forward to meeting him."

We chatted idly as we ate our extremely late breakfast, and talked about our families and dreams.

"I love you," I said when we arrived at the shopping center parking lot by the school.

"I love you too, babe." He reached over and kissed me gently. "See you soon? You have my number, so let me know when I can get you again."

That day, I made a crucial decision. Since Chaz was in my life, I took every opportunity I could to see him. I didn't miss any more school, but I convinced Baba to let me join the "Science Olympiad" team that required me to take additional study courses three days a week until seven at night. It was a real program, and I had obtained the permission slip from my science teacher and told Baba that the fifteen dollar application fee was waived because of my outstanding grades.

It wasn't all a lie, well, except for the fact I never turned in the application Baba had spent at least an hour filling out. I even told him there was another girl living in our neighborhood whose mother volunteered to take me home. When he offered to meet her, I told Baba that her husband would not let her speak to other men, which was something that Baba agreed with. Luckily, Corin, who was on one of her many Christmas shopping trips, wasn't around when we got home, or she would have known that was a far stretch for an American wife.

I was normally a horrible liar, but at that moment the lies flowed from my mouth like running water. As I set this plan up I felt invincible, and realized how easy it had become to fool Baba. Now I was able to spend three afternoons a week with Chaz and every Saturday. During our time together we had protein shakes – which was truly a vile substance, but I didn't let him know that – Chaz taught me to drive, or we just had wonderful picnics on the beach. Our Saturdays were spent lazily at his apartment watching old movies, listening to music, and eating omelets.

Sometimes Chaz left for a few days to unknown locations for training or operations. Although I missed him so much when he was gone, I knew that he would come back and I'd see him again. He'd given me so much to look forward to…

"He's here!" Suda screamed at the top of her lungs. "Walyam is here!"

# CHAPTER 9

She had been looking out the window all afternoon, in fact, within an hour after Baba had left and gone to the airport to pick them up. It wasn't like he could even drive from San Diego to LAX in that amount of time. I was on pins and needles, and there was no amount of household chores to keep me busy enough to not think about Walyam. It was Saturday, and I wouldn't normally be here had Chaz not gone to another training exercise. His squad was getting ready for a six-month deployment that was scheduled for May.

When I considered the argument Suda and I had a few months ago about the marriage between Walyam and our sister Namazzi, I was surprised she was so excited. She probably just wanted to use the opportunity to flaunt Walyam's new son in front of Namazzi. Oh, I dreaded what was to come because I was sure the newlywed couple was unaware of the babe. That's just how Baba was, forever withholding the details many of us needed to make informed decisions in our life.

"Go on without me, Suda," I said as I continued to fold laundry.

"That can wait," she said as she pulled me to my feet, knocking over the basket of warm, dry clothes, leaving me no choice but to be dragged outside.

"Matika, you're so clumsy!" Corin shouted as we headed out the door.

Baba got out of the car followed by Walyam, who sat in the passenger's seat. He was so tall and had filled out even more, but other than that he looked the same. Handsome in a rough sort of way with piercing eyes that lanced into your soul. As always, he made me feel naked as he sneered in my direction before he caught Suda, who had launched herself into his arms.

"Namazzi, wake up," Baba said tapping a knuckle on the back window. He quickly went into the house without another word.

She was asleep in the backseat, and I felt for her. It was an exhausting journey that was very taxing on her health, which had always been fragile. She got out of the car slowly, clearly exhausted. The dark circles under her eyes made her look older than her eighteen years.

"Hi, Namazzi," I said in English, but immediately saw that she didn't understand me. "How was your journey?" I asked switching to Swahili.

"It was very long," she said giving me a hug.

Namazzi was still very thin but not nearly as skinny as before. It had been almost three years since I'd seen her last. She was dressed very nicely in a stylishly long dress that was tight around her waist, hugging her small breasts.

"Come inside and see our home," I said tearing her gaze that was focused on Suda, who was behaving inappropriately with her husband. There was much to be said as so much had transpired while they were apart.

Namazzi chose to say nothing and followed me into the house instead. She probably would never bring up the issue, as it was her way to not question her husband, or any man for that matter. Suda, on the other hand, would bring up the painful subject, which was the most likely scenario.

I gave Namazzi the grand tour, then introduced her to Corin and her children, and finally told her the rules of the house, which basically consisted of do as you're told and stay out of Baba's room, which was easy enough. She would have no problem with that as she was as submissive as they came. Namazzi and Walyam were to share the room with Suda and the baby. Their room consisted of two twin beds and the baby crib – a tight squeeze to sleep in, but a luxury nonetheless.

"Namazzi, why don't you take a shower and rest for a while?" I was concerned because she looked dead on her feet.

"How do you work this?" she asked confused when I showed her to the bathroom.

"Let me show you," I said turning on the water, waiting for it to heat up. "So tell me, how have you been?"

"Good," she responded with a forced smile as she sat on the closed toilet.

"You know you can always talk to me. Our other mamas are not here, and we only have each other." I was concerned when she didn't respond right away, noting the tears brimming at the corners of her eyes.

"Matika, you must not say a word." Her hand shook on her chest as she drew in a few solid breaths.

"Never. You can always trust me." I turned the shower off, deciding to run a bath instead. Namazzi wasn't in a right emotional state to be alone right now and a bath was much more comforting.

"I'm not a good wife to Walyam," she cried, the tears flowing freely.

"Of course you are. You are the perfect wife and always will be."

"No, you don't understand. I cannot please him in the way that he needs. He comes to me every night for me to perform my wifely duties, but I find that I cannot please him; so he comes to me again and again in the same night. Sometimes I'm so tired by morning that I cannot get out of bed to make the morning meal. What am I doing wrong?"

I was furious with Walyam. He was completely insatiable. He was not the husband that Namazzi needed. She needed someone who was kind and gentle to her. Someone to take care of her needs in her fragile state. Walyam on the other hand, would kill her. For the first time I was glad at the thought that Suda would provide some relief. But I knew Namazzi, and she would feel like a failure at her inability to please her insatiable husband.

I worked hard to swallow my anger before I answered. "There is nothing wrong with you Namazzi. Walyam–"

"He is a good husband. Matika…I have yet to conceive." She immediately began to cry in full throttle.

"It's OK," I said, but quickly turned to stop the water that threatened to overflow. "Take a bath and you will feel much better. We can talk about it later."

Always obedient, Namazzi didn't utter another word. I got her undressed and helped her bathe. Afterward, I led her back to her room and tucked her into bed. She was so tired and fell asleep within minutes. I was headed straight for my room when Suda burst through the door, Walyam at her heels.

"Isn't he precious!" she beamed, picked up her son, and handed him to his father for the first time.

"Suda…" Walyam stammered in shock, holding his son awkwardly. "He's so small."

"No, he's big, actually. Tell him, Matika."

She caught me as I was headed out the door. Walyam turned slowly to face me, as he saw me in the room for the first time. His demeanor changed as he looked me up and down, his eyes taking in my body. I glanced down quickly to make sure I wore clothes as the blood traveled to my face.

"He's healthy and very large for his age," I said, then changed the subject. "I really should go now because Namazzi needs her rest," I couldn't get out of that room fast enough, even though in her exhaustion she hadn't even stirred. And, as much time as she had spent in our hut in Uganda while she was stricken with one ailment after another, she had to be used to the noise.

"He's waking," Walyam said handing the whimpering baby back to his mother. "Matika, why don't you show me this garden that Suda's been talking about?"

"Oh, no. That's her pride and joy. I wouldn't want to take that from her."

"Don't be silly, Matika," Suda chided as she pulled out a breast to feed her now-wailing child. He was frustrated as he rooted around and tried to find her nipple.

"Come on, I want to see it," Walyam said enthusiastically, like a child himself as Suda's grin reached from ear to ear. He pulled me out of the room before I could respond.

In the family room, Baba, Corin, and my step-siblings sat watching the television that, thanks to Corin, was four times the size of our old one and ten times as heavy, according to Baba. When we passed, Anthony waved, Baba nodded, Sherri stared, and Corin didn't even acknowledge us, which was fine with me. There was a time when I sought out Corin's approval but found that was as impossible as catching rain with a strainer.

"There really isn't much to see," I said opening the sliding-glass door and waiting for him to walk through.

"Ladies first," he said and took the handle, then gestured for me to go outside.

*Great!* I really planned on showing him where it was and, as Chaz would say, "ditch him stat," but he put a stop to that. I walked out to the garden and didn't bother to look back when I heard the sliding-glass door shut behind me. Winter had just begun, so there wasn't really much to see.

"Matika, Matika…" Walyam came up from behind me, placed his chin on my head, and encircled me with his arms. His manhood rested firmly against the small of my back. "I've waited a long, long time to take what is owed to me."

"What do I owe you?" I asked innocently, pulling out of his grasp and turning to face him. I knew what he wanted but needed to hear him say it out loud. I made a promise to him that if he saved my family, I would do anything. Those were bold words, and I meant it when I said it, knowing what it would take to get him to help them.

"I want you in my bed. I've been dreaming about you every night." He started to touch his erection through his pants.

# CHAPTER 10

"Really, Walyam?" I grimaced in disbelief. "You thought about me when you were married to my sister?" I forced my voice not to escalate, but it was a challenge as I thought of Walyam dreaming of me, then waking up Namazzi to satisfy him. "Meanwhile, Suda is head over heels in love with you and has given birth to your son."

"I never wanted to marry her," Walyam hissed through gritted teeth and then grabbed me roughly by the shoulders. "She is like a mouse, and you know I like my women feisty and full of life. Your father practically forced her down my throat. Do you not think I hadn't tried to marry Suda?"

"Why didn't you tell her this?"

"I was too ashamed at Baba's rejection after everything I'd done for your family. I had asked Baba many times, and he just ignored me like I wasn't good enough for her. I even asked for you, and he just laughed in my face!" His anger was palatable, his eyes intense as he remembered the encounter. "He may have not thought I was worthy enough to have Suda, but now I have won because it is my child she bore. He may have mocked and humiliated me with that insult when I wanted you, but again I will win because I'll take you any way I want."

"What if I refuse?"

"You won't, I'll make sure of it." His confidence scared me. "I can think of many things to say to Baba and the family to make them all hate you."

He was right. There was so much he could do or say that would ensure that outcome. He resented Baba for not allowing him to marry Suda. Baba just didn't know Walyam couldn't be trusted; I was the only one who knew this, but I couldn't do anything about it. Fine! If he wanted a feisty woman then that's what he'd get. But at that moment, I needed to talk to Chaz because there was no way I could live under the same roof as Walyam. He would always use that against me any chance he'd get.

"I never go back on my word." I said. Turning on my heel I headed back into the house.

The week passed by along with Christmas. I was actually shocked at the amount of gifts Corin bought us all. Baba, too, was astonished, but she said she did it because it was our first one. In reality, she was a shopaholic, as Chaz would call it, and spent every dime she got her hands on. Although my four gifts paled in comparison to the legion given to her kids, I was very thankful because I really needed the underwear and hygiene items.

"Baba..." I said when he came into the house after a long shift of standing guard. Everyone else had gone to bed, but I stayed up because I needed to speak to him about the event that Chaz invited me to.

"Matika," Baba said wearily. He'd been working many hours to help support the family. Luckily, Walyam would start work next week with Baba and would help support the family too. Corin, although she now worked part time, didn't contribute to the household expenses. "Why are you still awake?"

"I wanted to make sure you had your meal," I said putting his covered plate in the microwave.

"What do you need?" he asked bluntly. Leave it to Baba to get to the point.

"Well, after studying Saturday the team is going to have dinner and watch an educational movie afterward. Would it be all right if I go, too? I will have a ride home."

"We have plenty of movies that come on the television here at home. Why do you need to go out and do that?"

"Yes, Baba, but it will give me a chance to do something social with the team besides studying...I've missed many outings already. Please, Baba..."

Right on cue the beef fat popped in the microwave.

"Are you trying to kill my food?"

"Oh, sorry!" I rushed over the microwave, took out the hot plate, and sat it in front of Baba. The beef sizzled, and the dark fat curled up around the edges.

"Matika, you should be staying home and learning to cook, but I fear you would give your mama a heart attack." Then after he took a resigned breath, "Fine, but be home by midnight."

"Thank you, thank you!"

"Be off so I can eat this rubber steak," he said waving me away.

When Saturday arrived, I was beyond excited. I picked out the best dress I had, which was truly a rag compared to what I knew the other women would have. Still, being with Chaz was more than I could ask for, and I'd gladly suffer the ridicule and stares to be with him. I walked down to the street corner five minutes before 10 a.m. I couldn't wait to see him.

As I got into Chaz's truck, I saw Walyam who looked angry, though he apparently didn't see me. Hopefully he was just out for a walk and had not followed me. Maybe he had hoped to get me alone, but that proved impossible with the dynamics of our household. With Corin constantly riding me to be at her beck and call, I was always in public areas of the house doing chores. Not to mention little Anthony followed me around the house to irritate me out of boredom.

"Chaz, we need to talk," I said as we drove out of my neighborhood.

"When a woman says she needs to talk, that's never good. Is this going to put me in a bad mood because if it is, I'd like us to wait until after the party."

"It's not good or bad, but we can talk about it later. Baba let me stay out until midnight!" This was the longest time he and I would have together in a single day. "I hope you don't mind, but this is all I had to wear."

"I picked you up this early so we can go shopping." He grinned over at me before he held my hand. His truck was a standard, but he had mastered steering the wheel with his knee to shift gears.

Chaz took me to the mall in Oceanside to a department store called Macy's. My world just kept getting better. The store was covered with clothes and shoes, all neat and organized, from wall to wall. This was such a welcome convenience that Goodwill or Salvation Army couldn't compete with.

"I want you to pick out a dress, shoes, and anything else you'll need for the party tonight. It's a formal occasion, so we can start in this formal section," Chaz said leading me to the dress section of the store.

"Are you sure?" I asked in apprehension though I was secretly beyond thrilled.

"Of course. I want my babe to look and feel her best. I have a confession and have to be honest with you. I have no sense of fashion, so don't look to me for help. As a matter of fact, I'm not a shopping type of man, so I'll be looking at sunglasses on the first floor. Just come and get me when you're done." He handed me a card.

"What's this?" I asked perplexed.

"It's a MasterCard. You can buy whatever you want with this." He gave me a quick kiss. "See you soon. Enjoy!"

With my head in the clouds, I explored the endless options with no clue where to start. The dresses came in many different colors and lengths. Some were sleeveless while others were more modest, yet sparkled with sequins and rhinestones. Stroking them at random, I was losing time and nowhere close to picking one.

"May I help you?"

I was startled by a sales attendant who leapt out of nowhere. She was tall and thin, and wore a tan suit and matching flats. If not for her kind, soft brown eyes that matched her hair, I would have refused.

"Yes, please," I began in earnest. "I have a really important event to attend tonight. A formal one, and I haven't a clue where to start."

"My name is Delia, and I'll be happy to help. So, will you need a dress and shoes?" the attendant asked with a Spanish accent I hadn't noticed at first.

"To put it bluntly, I have nothing, and I need everything."

"A total makeover! This will be fun. Do you have a price range that you're looking at?"

"No, no price range."

"Great! Let's start with your dress. Do you know your size?"

"No, I don't know my size."

Delia whipped out her measuring tape that she had slung over her shoulder, and measured my waist and bust. She also had my foot measured. She was more than eager to assist with everything I needed.

"Your waist is so tiny. You're a size two dress, a 34 C-D cup size, and a size eight shoe." With that she buzzed through the store and picked out several dresses for me to try on, all of which Baba would never approve of but Chaz would adore. I would definitely need a jacket for every one of them, and Delia was one step ahead handing me various sequin wraps that were exquisite.

I fell in love with a deep-purple dress that was both daringly bare, sleeveless in fact, and sensuously low cut, and hugged my body to perfection as it complemented my skin tone and shape flawlessly. Delia picked out a pair of black suede high heels that would require a cane to help me walk in. The accessories were rhinestone earrings and a matching bracelet with purple stones that accented the dress. The wrap was black lace, light, and airy, and matched the small, shiny beaded purse. Delia picked out pantyhose, panties that were strangely missing the butt part, and a strapless bra that actually held up my breasts in place magically.

I felt wonderful picking out anything I wanted and being able to buy them with a swipe of a card, yet I found myself feeling a little guilty for taking advantage of Chaz's generosity.

"You should stop by Penny's to get your hair done," Delia said once the transaction was completed. "They have a really great stylist named LaShean who specializes in ethnic hair."

"I think I might just do that," I said with stars in my eyes. I didn't bother to tell Chaz, just quickly headed in the direction she'd instructed, and didn't stop until I found Penny's. I felt no guilt and even felt justified in getting my hair done. After all, Chaz did say he wanted me to look my best.

As my hair was shampooed, conditioned, and straightened, my nails were manicured and finished with a delicate French tip. As I went to pay the cashier, Chaz busted through the front door.

"My God, Matika! There you are," he said as he gave me a hug.

"What's wrong?" I asked.

"Babe, I couldn't find you anywhere and searched all over the mall for you."

"I'm so sorry. I got a little carried away."

"It's okay. Wow! You look beautiful. Your hair is so pretty, and longer than I thought."

The stylist had put in loose curls that flowed to my shoulders. I smiled and had to agree as I was very pleased when I looked in the mirror. I loved it. I just hoped it would last through the night. At least until I left the party.

By the time we got back to Chaz's apartment after we fought the Saturday night traffic, there wasn't much time to get ready. In fact, we only had two hours left before we needed to leave.

"Do you mind if I take a quick shower?" I asked back at his apartment.

"Of course not. Take your time. I'll make us a sandwich."

I took a bath to avoid getting my hair wet. I also made sure the water was cold to avoid any potential steam. When I was done, I realized that there wasn't a towel on the towel rack – Chaz must have been doing laundry. Freezing, I crept into the room in search of a towel.

"I'm making sandwiches. Do you want mayonnaise?" Chaz asked startling me.

"You scared me," I gasped, my hands trying to still my heart that ricocheted in my chest. I found it hard to catch my breath as a strange sensation passed over me.

"Are you all right? I didn't mean to scare you," he said as he came closer and licked his fingers.

"I need a towel, please."

Chaz quickly went to a basket in the corner of his room and took out a towel.

"Here let me help you," he said coming over to me cautiously.

Chaz proceeded to dry me, and though I was cold only moments before, I now felt extremely hot. Then he wrapped the towel around me and quickly headed for the door.

"Wait," I said not sure what I wanted to say to him. I just didn't want him to leave and the thought of him going to next room was unbearable. "I need you."

"Matika, I am a man. I can only hold back for so long. And right now, you standing naked in front of me is driving me crazy."

"I want you," I amended, letting the towel drop to the floor. I loved Chaz, and I felt loved by him. He had shown me his love many times, and at that moment I knew that I wanted him to have all of me. I didn't want anything to stand between us again.

"Are you sure?" he asked coming closer to me. But he didn't wait for an answer. He devoured my lips as if on the verge of starvation.

Chaz lifted me onto bed and quickly divested himself of his clothes. The reality of what was about to happen finally sunk in. After everything that happened to me in Uganda and everything that I'd seen, I made the decision right then that my past would no longer dictate my future. I finally took a stand – from that moment on, I would forever be in control of my future.

# CHAPTER 11

Chaz joined me on the bed with his signature smile. "I want you so badly that I'm afraid I'm going to make a fool of myself if I don't take my time."

I smiled back at him. "Lucky for you that I will only have you to judge by."

Chaz took his time, though it pained him, and kissed me thoroughly until I was breathless with need. Trailing his tongue down my neck, he continued on until he paid a good amount of attention to my breasts before making his way down toward my hips.

I couldn't hold back the small cry that broke free. Another moan escaped me, and I panted with need. When his mouth caressed my womanhood, I nearly wept. It was so unexpected. His mouth was so hot, soft, and utterly moist. My hands that were fisted at my sides released and stroked his head. This was too much, my body on sensory overload.

I looked down at him, caressing his short hair, as each lap of his tongue sent spots dancing across my eyes as my hips moved involuntarily to meet him. I was nearly undone when he slipped a finger in me.

"Mmm, you are so ready. Your smell and taste is unbelievable."

Even his feather-light breath heightened my arousal. I knew what would come, and I squirmed with need. I'd felt it before with him a few years ago, when he'd sent me over the edge with his fingers.

"Chaz," I begged, so close. I panted, wanted, and begged for release. Then it happened so suddenly that I convulsed, my body thrown over the edge, and I screamed with an intense force.

I looked in his eyes and was momentarily frightened by the raw need within them. Chaz came up over me, jerked my legs open with his knees, his deft fingers still going in and out of me before he gripped his manhood and poised for entrance.

"I'm going to do it fast. Matika, are you ready?" His voice was deep and raspy.

I nodded once again, breathless, unable to speak. Then without preamble, he slammed into me.

"Ahhh!" I cried, feeling a tear deep from within as he broke through my innocence. I closed my eyes briefly as they teared up at the foreign fullness.

"Are you OK?" he asked, pausing, his eyes bright with both pleasure and concern. "I'm sorry, but you are so tight."

"Yes." I rasped, my eyes wide as I grabbed his arms, holding him tightly to me. I needed to feel all of him and know that everything was okay. Slowly, I wiggled my hips as I thought to seek a more comfortable position, but instead found the movement was an exquisite feeling deep within. "Oh."

"Babe, babe…hold on a moment," he panted. "I'm trying not to lose it here."

After a minute, he began his gentle thrust, and I joined him right away, my body stretched to its limits, accepting all of him. He eased in and out of me slowly, creating a steady rhythm that was so natural to follow. Grasping my head between his hands, he pulled me close for a gentle kiss. But I was anxious again with need as my teeth pulled his lips. He was so warm. A sheen of sweat covered us, making our bodies erotically smooth as silk.

I could feel my body building like before as he picked up the pace. My womanhood quivered with every thrust, with a mind of its own, as it opened up further for him. Then I exploded around him like a flower in full bloom. I screamed before I bit his chest, powering through my orgasm.

He moved into me harder, faster. It was a mixture of pleasure laced with pain, and just as the latter began to take over, he yelled my name and he released his seed into me. Our hearts vied for dominance as he laid his full weight on me. In that moment, I didn't care that I couldn't breathe; I wouldn't have cared if I had died in his embrace.

He rolled off of me and cradled me in his arms, my cheek on his chest. "I hope I didn't hurt you. Next time it won't be so bad, I promise."

"Chaz, I'm fine. It was wonderful, and I would gladly do it again." My limbs felt like jelly, though my hips were sore from being spread for far too long, not to mention that I wouldn't be able to sit properly for a while. Despite all that, I was elated.

When I saw the bruise on his chest, I nearly died from embarrassment as images of our lovemaking surfaced. I was also much too bashful to ask if I hurt him. That was a topic I wouldn't breach.

I got out of bed and felt every ache and stiff muscle. I gasped, horrified. Blood and semen were on the sheets and flowed down my leg.

"Makita, it's okay. That's supposed to happen the first time. It's completely normal," he assured putting an arm around me.

"But there is so much blood," I said biting my lip. "Are you sure that you didn't poke a hole up there?"

"I'm sure," he stifled a laugh before he kissed me. "Let's take a long shower. Umm…I think you should take one alone because you might come out in worse shape if I join you."

As suggested, I took a nice long shower, careful not to wet my hair, and washed away any remnants of our lovemaking. Though the shower relaxed me and felt good on my sore muscles, I regretted the loss of Chaz's wonderful scent that was all over me.

Chaz brought a girl to his apartment, but she was now a woman. I felt so strange now that I understood what Suda felt with Walyam. To share your body with the one you loved was beautiful, fulfilling, and utterly breathtaking. The coming together of two souls, when they joined to become one body, was truly a blessing. I wanted to spend the rest of my life making love to this man and wake up to him every day….

After showering, I applied a little makeup and salvaged some of the curls the hairdresser put in before I headed into the bedroom where I found Chaz laying out his dress blue uniform. I only had a towel wrapped around me, as I knew his roommate wasn't around.

"Maybe we could skip tonight and have a party of our own," he suggested then nipped me on the neck before tugging the towel free.

"Not a chance after I spent all afternoon getting beautiful for you."

"The best beauty is this," he said rubbing his hands down my waist.

"Hurry and shower, otherwise we'll never get out of here. Besides, this is work for you."

"Yes, the dullest work in the world, so I'll just have to grin and bear it." He smacked my bottom playfully before heading into the bathroom.

I was dressed and ready to go by the time Chaz came out of the bathroom. With the strapless bra on, my breasts spilled deliciously out of the top of the fitted purple dress. With my black suede high heels, beautiful rhinestone earrings, and matching bracelet, I didn't look like myself. I clutched the black lace wrap and the matching small shiny beaded purse, and smiled to myself. Baba would be horrified and I adored the thought definitely.

"You look amazing."

"Thank you," I said, truly believing his words. I felt so good about myself. I didn't want to be full of myself, but there was no denying how pretty I looked and felt. Maybe Chaz would change his opinion once he saw his credit card bill, but at that moment, nothing mattered.

"You got dressed so quickly," he said. "I should have been the one to take a shower first."

Within twenty-five minutes, we reached the Thames clubhouse on a cliff that overlooked a stunning view of the ocean. The driveway was in a semicircle around a three-tiered fountain with what looked like bathtubs of descending size. The country club was bigger than the public library and was two stories high. It was majestic as the floor light amplified its brilliance. A few palm trees and miniature gardens completed the landscape, which was also lit with floor lights.

It was only eight, but Chaz needed to arrive early for the security detail. I waited for him in the beautiful reception area near the bar, sipping on a club soda, shaking. It wasn't cold even though my wrap was collected at the door; I was just so nervous now that I was alone, and felt completely out of my element. Watching the men have early cocktails and the ladies collect in small groups sipping wine, I felt even more excluded.

I was the youngest person there for sure, with the closest person to my age at least twenty years my senior, aside from Chaz, and a few other men in his unit; none of whom brought dates. Most of the gentlemen were older, and some were very old with women in their early forties that hung on their arms.

"My, you look stunning," an elder gentleman said as he approached the side of the bar. He stared down at me with piercing eyes.

# CHAPTER 12

"Thank you," I smiled back at him, flattered by his compliment that seemed genuine.

"And such a beautiful smile you have. Why is such a lovely young lady alone tonight?"

"I'm not alone…Well I am for now, but I'm waiting for someone."

"Would you like some company?"

"Sure, thank you. That would be a lot better than being alone right now." I was relieved to have someone to talk to, and it would certainly make the time pass by more quickly.

"You know, the people at these parties can be so uptight and stuffy. It's really a breath of fresh air to speak to a normal person. Here let me get you a drink." He motioned for a bartender and ordered a wine and a martini.

"I've never been to one, so I'll have to take your word for it, sir."

"Please, call me John. There is no need for formalities," John said handing me a glass of white wine.

I was so thankful the wine was clear instead of red. Red just wasn't a color I would ever choose for a drink. In fact, I wouldn't even eat anything red and politely steered clear of Corin's red beans. It reminded me too much of blood, of the colonel's blood as it flowed from his neck…

"My name is Matika," I said taking a much too large gulp instead of a sip. I'd never tried wine before and was surprised that it didn't taste anything like it looked. At least it was cold.

"That's a lovely name. Where are you from?"

"I came from Africa," I responded, feeling the same discomfort I normally felt whenever I discussed my origin. "Do you live nearby?" A change of topic was normally my best bet.

"Very good," he remarked. "Actually, I live in D.C. and I'm just here for work. What languages do you speak? I bet you speak quite a few."

"Not really. So what's it like in D.C.? I've never been anywhere but California," I said eagerly.

"D.C. is an interesting place if you love the politics and the Bible." He took a large swallow of his clear drink. "What do you do?"

"Nothing special, I'm a student actually. What about you?"

"I do all sorts of interesting things that one can only dream about. I get to travel all over the world and meet a lot of interesting people. Did you come with family or did you immigrate alone on a student visa?"

"That's still to be debated." I began to feel uncomfortable with the whole line of questions that were innocent enough at face value, but led me down a road that I didn't wish to travel.

"You have managed to deflect every question I asked you, smoothly and effectively providing general answers."

"As did you," I said smiling at him. He truly seemed like a nice man but I could feel the secrets he had hidden in the depths of his soul.

"You're very smart, you know. You are also very beautiful. If you find yourself bored with your life," he said as he produced a card, "contact me."

"Thank you," I said putting the card in my purse that housed only a lipstick. "Are you trying to offer me a job? I ask because the last person who offered me one was quite shady, to put it mildly."

"I'm not offering you a job. On the contrary, I'm offering you an exciting lifestyle that only the elite can obtain and only a select few are qualified for. This is a unique new program that has the highest level of security imaginable."

"That's sounds like a great offer, I'll think about it." NOT. "Thank you."

"You're quite welcome. Now if you'll excuse me, I must go and mingle with the dinosaurs." He kissed my hand gently before he departed.

That was a strange conversation. To humor myself – my cheeks were growing numb from the wine – and out of morbid curiosity, I reached into my purse and looked at the card. *John Lee*. I flipped the card over but it showed only a phone number. That's it? There was no indication of who he was or where he worked. He must be joking! Looking around for a trash can, I saw it was on the other side of the room, which would require me to walk through the crowd, so I dropped it back into my purse.

"Are you enjoying yourself?" Chaz approached, with the most brilliant smile reserved only for me.

He looked so handsome in uniform and happy to see me. He reached out and placed my hand on his forearm, then led me into the ballroom. I felt like a princess and somehow managed an elegant walk to our table, thankful that my feet didn't hurt just yet. I'd heard many horror stories that ladies would get huge blisters from high heels, but, as they say, there was always a price for beauty.

That was the happiest night of my life. The company was superb, the food beyond terrific – take that, Corin – and the atmosphere was elegant. There couldn't have been a better venue and I felt privileged to be among the few to attend with diplomats and high-ranking officials, both military and civilian, in attendance. Unfortunately, as was my weakness, I couldn't remember anyone's name but John, who I truly admired, yet who also turned out to be the head of a top secret international program, whatever that meant.

Most of all, I was thrilled to be here, to share this wonderful moment with the love of my life, Chaz. His job, as well as a few others from his command, was to serve as an inconspicuous security liaison for John, posing as guests. There were obvious ones posted in the corners throughout the room as security, but they were not privy to the dialogue as a guest would be. To make it look more covert, members were encouraged to bring dates, and here I was, enjoying every moment of it.

Chaz had an important job, and I was proud to be by his side. I marveled at his world, his job, and appreciated the complexity and nuances of security. I made a candid observation that when each of the five courses was served, Chaz or another from his unit discreetly switched plates and glasses with John. It was like a great game of chess, a beautifully coordinated work of art.

I felt warm, after enjoying another two glasses of wine, I received the eye of all at our table. I realized two things that night: first, I was truly beautiful, and secondly, I loved the attention of being looked at.

When we left that evening, my head was light with happiness, and giddy with expensive wine. We were among the last to leave. Chaz made sure all guests had departed and nothing was left behind before we found our way to his truck. It was a chilly night, the stiff breeze was brisk, but I was warm from the inside out.

"I really don't want to go back home, Chaz," I said once we were in and he started the engine to get the heat going.

"Oh, Matika, I would love for you to stay the night with me, but your father would kill you. Then he would never trust you to go out again." He turned down the radio that we had rocked on the way here.

"I know, but Chaz, I need you. I mean, I really need you…"

"It's the wine talking, and you shouldn't have been drinking." He smiled at me but then grew serious. "We are talking about your dad here. Any other time you would be paranoid. I'll do the responsible thing and take you back to your house on time. Sober up and look lively. And look, we even have a little over an hour to spare with no fear of breaking your midnight curfew."

"I can think of a lot of things we can do in an hour…" I began to stroke the back of his ear, unable to help myself. He just looked so good, and I wanted him so badly it hurt.

"We don't have the time to go back to my apartment and make it all the way back to your house in an hour. Not to mention you still need to get dressed and sober up."

He had a convincing argument but made no move to stop me as I started to nibble on his ear. He smelled wonderful, like brisk aftershave, a little sweat, and Chaz. I just couldn't take my hands off him. This was the boldest I'd been with him or with anyone. He shivered as I trailed kisses down his neck and leaned up against him.

"Who says we have to go back to your apartment? Besides, I can't make it another moment without you inside of me."

"Babe, what am I going to do with you?"

"Anything you want within an hour…"

"You're not making this easy for me…"

Without invitation, I straddled his hips while he sat in the driver's seat, and my dress rode up my thighs to accommodate the position. Stealing his mouth for a passion-filled kiss I thrust in my tongue to taste his sweet mouth, moaning at the ambrosia within.

Chaz lost the little resolve he had, grabbed my hips, and pushed his erection against my core. There was still too much clothing between us, but I could feel my wetness saturate my thong, and make its way down my inner thigh. I felt incredibly sexy, indestructible, and Baba be damned, I wouldn't be home on time.

With deft hands, he pulled my underwear aside before his finger plunged deep inside me. I moaned with delight as he was finally gave me what my body had craved so badly. In and out he stroked, sending me dangerously close to the edge.

With his teeth, he bit at my nipple through my dress, making it wet and so very warm. Then he placed his face in my cleavage, lowered my dress with his chin, and exposed two nipples to the frigid air that waited for soft lips to suckle. Coming down on them hard, he devoured them like his last meal as I arched my back to feed him more.

I was about to explode but didn't want to do it without him. I reached my hand into his pants and I worked at his buckle before freeing his member that boldly sprang forth. "I need you now," I moaned, adjusting his sex to my womanhood. I sat down on him, enfolding his *makende* with all my warmth and love.

Together our scent was heady, feral, and in the confines of the car, we fogged up the windows. Chaz held onto my hips as he pumped into me wildly. I met him stroke for stroke, hanging on to him for dear life as his service medals dug into my skin. We performed a natural dance that was as ancient as the beginning of time and clung to one another.

My peak was explosive. I screamed his name as my sheath quivered around him. He soon followed, moaning, deep in the throes of his own release. With my hands laced through his short hair, I milked every last drop he offered.

I fell forward in the afterglow of passion, resting with my head on his shoulder, unable and unwilling to lift a finger. Chaz and I had only made love twice, but I could see that each time it would get better and better. My stomach quickened as I imagined what it would be like if we spent the rest of our lives together.

"We really must be going," he said bringing me back to reality.

Reluctantly, I crawled over to the passenger seat, and adjusted my dress. Before we drove away I changed back into my old dress and shoes and took off the accessories. *Goodbye beautiful clothes.* Placing the precious garments into the shopping bag, I put it lovingly on the seat beside me. I decided to keep the purse and put it inside my shoulder bag.

The drive home was peaceful as we rode in silence. Though I wished so badly that I could stay with Chaz, I was thankful to have had such a great night of dinner and dancing with him. I vowed to do my best to spend more time with him.

"I really don't like leaving you like this."

I looked over at the clock and saw that it was almost one-thirty in the morning. I was an hour-and-a-half late, but found myself sad to leave Chaz instead of afraid of Baba. My love for him was now on a whole new level.

"Chaz, tonight was the best night of my life. I would do it all over again in a heartbeat. So please…don't worry about me."

"I had a great time, too. Please call me if something bad happens. I'll come and get you. I love you, Matika."

"I love you too, Chaz."

He kissed and hugged me goodbye before I headed out of the vehicle. The night was cold so I walked quickly down the street to my house.

With no lights on, I was confident that everyone was asleep, and Baba tended to be an early sleeper and riser. When I reached the door, I retrieved the spare key from the plant. It was late, and I certainly didn't want to wake anyone. I crept through the door and tried to shut it silently as possible, but the door had squeaky hinges that Baba refused to oil. He stated that it provided a natural alarm.

True to his assertion, he heard me and bounded into the room, meeting me before I made it halfway through the living room. Corin was at his heels. "Where were you?" Baba voice boomed a deep baritone that was chilling yet painfully calm.

# CHAPTER 13

There were three obvious clues that foretold the deep sewage I'd stepped in. First was the tone of Baba's voice that showed he was on the verge of dishing out a painful punishment. He always did his due diligence and thought things through before he laid into the unsuspecting victim. The second was his question. He clearly knew where I was supposed to be, yet he asked the question anyway to bait me, and put me in a position to lie; hearing a lie told firsthand was a great motivator for him. And thirdly, Corin was by his side, never one to miss out on Baba's precious children if they got into trouble, which bolstered his ego and fed his anger.

"Baba, I'm sorry…" I began, surprised that I wasn't as frightened as I should be. It must have been the alcohol that still pumped through me. My time with Chaz was so worth the beating that I was sure to get. "I'll never do it again. I just wanted to have some fun like the other kids at my school."

"You call this fun! You want to be a slut and get pregnant," Corin threw out.

*Like your sister*, is what she didn't say in front of Baba. She always looked down upon Suda. She labeled her the black sheep, and used her as an example to her own daughter, Sherri.

"What are you talking about?" I challenged, fed up with her intrusion. I felt emboldened to stand up to her tonight.

"Walyam said he saw you get into a truck with a white man." Baba said "white man" with a menace that nearly choked me.

I had completely forgotten that I'd seen Walyam when we drove away and assumed that he hadn't seen me. Apparently, I was wrong. He'd met Chaz before and would have probably recognized him. This situation had just gotten a whole lot worse.

"And I checked to see if you were even going to meet with the Science Olympiad," Corin said. "It turns out that you're not on the team, and never were." Her smile was sinister at best as she relished the moment.

"Do you deny it?" Baba asked. His expression remained unchanged, but the hurt in his eyes was evident.

"No, I'm sorry." Just as I put my head down in shame, Corin smacked me across the face.

"How dare you put your father through this! He was worried sick about you." She stepped back quickly as Baba followed suit, hitting me so hard that I nearly fell to the floor.

Corin handed Baba a paddle she had so graciously brought into our home. It was the size of an open hand, and shaped like an oval. It was used to play ping pong, so I was told, but it was not used due to the number of small holes she'd put in it to increase the speed, which yielded a harder blow. Just as I put down my shoulder bag, it began. For ten minutes I was beaten on my butt, legs, and back. I tried not to cry and wondered if that night was worth it. With each blow dealt, it was a resounding *yes*. When I couldn't take the pain any longer and started to sob, Baba stopped, and threw the paddle to the floor. I had awoken the entire house with my cries and saw heads peer out the dark hallway.

"You have brought shame to this house. You will never see this man, or any other, again," Baba said. "You will go straight to the office every day after school and wait for me to pick you up. No phone, no TV, and you will do what anyone needs you to do in this house until I say otherwise. It sickens me to look at your face."

Those were Baba's final words to me before he left the room. It hurt so badly. How would I ever see Chaz? I couldn't believe how this night had ended so badly. Just an hour before, I was in Chaz's loving embrace only to be beaten and bring shame to my family. There was no way I could ever recover from the stunt I'd pulled, no matter how obedient I was in the future. Baba would never let me forget this day.

I sat on the floor and cried about how my life was going to be. The only thing I had to look forward to now was to finish school and move out. If I was lucky, I could start a new life with Chaz. We could get married and have our own family.

Footsteps alerted me that I had company. Walyam, Suda, and Namazzi came into the living room. My sisters were covered with their robes, and he wore a pair of sweatpants, completely shirtless. Walyam parked himself in Baba's chair while Suda and Namazzi hovered over me, their expressions completely opposite of each other.

"Are you all right?" Namazzi asked in Swahili. She hadn't learned English, so I imagined that she was oblivious to what just happened because I knew Suda wouldn't take the time to translate.

"Shame on you," Suda said. She, too, spoke in Swahili for Namazzi's benefit. "Please tell me you didn't do anything with a white man. That is unspeakable!"

"I love him," I declared looking straight at Walyam, who lost his smugness. He looked angry as he narrowed his eyes at me. My sisters both gasped in unison, their expressions priceless. "He was the one I spoke about in Kenya. It was always him." Despite Suda's insistence, I'd never told her who I had seen at the camp because I knew that she'd be angry, like now.

"That is a disgrace! You must never tell that to Baba." Suda was furious as she stared down at me.

"Suda, she doesn't mean that. She doesn't understand love," Namazzi said in my defense, as she knelt beside me.

"Don't try and defend her. You are too stupid yourself to understand love. It's all your fault, Namazzi. You are so, so...argh!" Her deep-seated anger at Namazzi breached its ugly head. "Walyam...honey, I'm going to bed so I'll see you soon," she said as she sashayed out of the room.

That was the ultimate disrespect. Namazzi was hurt. Her large eyes shone with unshed tears, but she said nothing. Instead, she stayed by my side and rubbed my back like a mother would soothe her weeping child. I really felt sorry for her. Her whole life was destined to be ruled by others. She didn't even have the strength to stand up to her younger sister.

"Namazzi, go to bed," Walyam snapped at her.

"Yes, sir." She nodded and left immediately.

That was my cue to go to my room. As I got to my feet, Walyam was two steps ahead of me, blocking my way. He looked angry and aroused at the same time, like a tropical storm, both surreal and deadly.

"Get out of my way. I can't deal with you tonight," I grumbled as I attempted to push past him. Inside, my heart thumped loudly in my chest.

"You're not going anywhere until I say so. You will do as you're told." He pushed me back to the floor.

"What do you want?" I couldn't believe this was happening. Walyam was despicable. It had to be after two in the morning. I was dead on my feet. And the knowledge that Corin would have me up early only made my head throb worse.

"Get me some water." I stood to my feet and padded toward the kitchen stubbornly. He followed me. The glasses were beside the cold box, or refrigerator, that faced the backyard. After I poured water from the tap into a clean glass, I placed the cup on the table with a solid clink.

"I want cold water," he ordered coarsely.

We never drank our water cold, which had to do with the fact that none of us grew up with refrigerators, but Corin and her children drank it chilled, and sometimes added ice cubes to it to make it even colder. Walyam was just being difficult to show that he now had some control over me. I might have had to do what he told me, within reason, but at least everything about Chaz was out in the open, and he couldn't use it against me. It was a relief, though a small one. But Walyam was creative enough to invent more dirt on me.

When I went over to the sink to pour out the water, his muscled chest was right behind me, flush against my body. I dropped the glass in the sink and turned around to face him.

"What are you doing?" I attempted to push him away, but he lifted me on the counter. He had me sit on top of it, merged between the stove and the toaster. I whimpered involuntarily because my backside was so sore, which made it impossible to sit on the hard surface without pain. To make matters worse, Baba's bedroom was on the other side of the wall, and he would be able to hear if we spoke too loudly. I swallowed as Walyam's hands roamed over my breasts.

"You better be quiet or Baba will come out of his room. You and I have a score to settle. I will take it now."

"I owe you nothing. It was you who got me in trouble in the first place."

"That wouldn't have happened if you had given me what I wanted to begin with." He pulled up my dress to my waist and ripped off my panties.

"Stop it now or I'll scream."

With one hand he restrained both of my hands behind my back, the other headed to the apex of my legs. Just as I opened my mouth to scream, he covered it with his, and plunged his tongue down my throat, nearly choking me. My cries were muffled as I struggled to no avail. He was too strong. I was torn between angering Baba further, or trying to fight him on my own.

When he found my core he shoved in at least three fingers, and began to thrust them in and out rapidly. He was hurting me and had no remorse. I bit his lip hard, but he didn't pull away and instead head-butted me in the face. Stunned and dazed, the back of my head hit the cabinet. Tears ran down my face; my nose stung in protest. Walyam was about to use my body in my family's home while they were asleep in their beds. They would never believe me. I'd lost all credibility and was now labeled a liar and a whore.

"I love my women feisty and full of life. I know that you changed. Oh my…you are so wet for me," he said in surprise. Walyam was defiling the afterglow of Chaz's and my earlier coupling. It had nothing to do with his assault. "I see it in your eyes every day. You've always wanted this. I'm going to make you feel real good. I can be as rough with you as I want because I know you like it that way." He pulled down his sweatpants, freeing his manhood.

In my efforts to get away, I sent the toaster crashing to the floor. Walyam gripped my hips, pulling them towards him, where he nestled further between my legs ready to penetrate. His mouth came down on mine again to stifle my cries, daring me to bite him again. He was effective because I had learned my lesson.

"What's going on?" It was Suda's voice. She carried the baby who whimpered in her arms. "No...no!" Her horrified expression was of a woman on the verge on insanity.

"I can explain," Walyam said pulling away quickly, leaving my dress up which exposed my bare bottom. "Matika was seducing—"

"No!" She practically dropped the babe on the table and ran over to me. "How could you do this? You always take everything from me." She slapped me across the face. "I hate you!"

Just then Baba, Corin, and Namazzi ran into the kitchen. Anthony slept like the dead and Sherri was over at a friend's. Her absence was not missed because, knowing her, she would have eaten popcorn and watched the fireworks.

"Suda, listen to me—"

I was cut off as she launched a full-on attack. In a split second, I was off the counter and on the floor wrestling with her. She pulled at my hair that had to have stuck straight up at that point as I worked to pin her to the ground. I refused to get beaten up again. Suda had no right to attack me when it was Walyam who was the culprit.

It was tough to fight against her, but lucky for me, she was not as strong and was still recovering from childbirth. While she had dropped most of her baby fat, she was still vulnerable and weak from the pregnancy.

"Stop it, this instant!" Baba shouted. He tried to lift me from her, but Suda clutched my hair, refusing to let it go. Baba backhanded Suda, who fell away from me. "What's going on?"

"I caught her seducing Walyam," she wailed with a crazed look in her eyes. "I can't live here anymore. I hate her!" She went over and picked up the crying babe off the table, and handed him to Namazzi. "This is what you want from Walyam, a child. Take him. You can have it all because I don't want it."

`

# CHAPTER 14

She ran out the front door barefoot before anyone could stop her. Everyone was in total shock and slowly turned to stare at me, including Walyam who had the audacity. I could have died from the look in Baba's eyes. If he'd had a machete, he would have cut me down.

"I didn't do it…" I began, but I was too late. Baba turned his back to me and walked calmly out of the kitchen. Walyam filed out behind him and Namazzi, holding the wailing babe, did the same. That single moment was worse than any actions that preceded it. I had lost my family.

"Corin, please speak to Baba," I begged now on my hands and knees in front of her. "I didn't do it. Walyam tried to force himself on me." I rubbed at my eyes and swiped the smeared makeup mixed with blood from my nose on my hands. I was a mess or, as Corin would say, "a hot mess."

"Listen to me and listen well," Corin said looking down at me with her hands on her hips. "You have caused enough trouble in this house with your lies and deceit. You are a bigger whore than Suda, who had the audacity to sleep with her own sister's husband. Now here you are, doing the same thing. I see the way Walyam looks at you as you flaunt your big breasts in front of him, encouraging him no less. You have brought this on yourself.

"You have destroyed your father's hope for and image of you. To think that he believed you would one day go to college and make something of yourself. You're no better than a common slut." She paused briefly to let her words sink in. "You are dead to all of us now. Get out of this house and never come back. If your sister knows better, she would stay away too. I don't need your filth around my children. Get out of my house!"

There was nothing to say. It was clear Corin and Suda hated me, so it didn't matter if I begged and pleaded my case. The outcome would be the same. So I said nothing but got off my knees and headed toward the door, grabbing my shoulder bag off the living room floor on the way out.

Once outside, I hurried down the street toward the strip mall to find a phone so I could call Chaz. It was freezing – well, close enough to it anyway, considering I came from a much warmer location in Uganda. Outside, the thick layer of fog made the air moist and dreary. No lights came from the other houses on the block and I imagined everyone nestled in their beds, peacefully asleep.

I envied the neighbors and what seemed to me like their less complicated lives. It's funny how it seems that everyone else always has it better. Our lives were supposed to be so much easier in the States. Sure we were well fed, housed, and safe from the government, but we'd brought many problems with us from Africa. Why did Baba marry Corin? Why did he bring Walyam into our home? Those two, Corin and Walyam, were the real cause of why our family was falling apart.

Like a blow to the gut, I realized that the issues maybe didn't stem from Corin and Walyam, but from me. It was I who should have told Suda about Walyam years ago, and left it up to her whether she believed me. Instead, I hid his behavior and protected him, and in the end it was no good for any of us.

Then, on that day at the camp when Suda had asked me to speak to Baba about her love for Walyam, I should have told her that Baba planned to arrange a marriage between Walyam and Namazzi. Instead, she was caught completely off guard while pregnant with his son. As a matter of fact, she and I could have spoken to Baba together about the pregnancy long before Walyam came to the States. Maybe things would have been different for all of us, and lessened the tension in the house between my sisters.

Then there was Corin. There was nothing I could've done to make her like me. But as long as Baba loved and cherished me, there was nothing she could have done to break that bond. Now I had broken his trust, his love, and respect for me, and Corin had her ticket to kick me out of our home.

Maybe I didn't belong there if I corrupted her children, but I wasn't the only one who was in the wrong. Once again, I blamed Suda for some of this. She tended to put me in situations that never ended well. Plus, Suda disrespected Namazzi, her own sister, choosing a man who was not her husband over her family.

A car sped by and caught my attention. Few were on the road at this time of night so the light turned quickly at the intersection. I crossed the street and headed to the 7-Eleven to use the pay phone. Suda was in the dimly lit parking lot, bent low to the passenger's side and while she spoke to some men in a dark Chevy Impala.

When I tried to flag her down, she ignored me. I ran over to her and pulled her arm, forcing her to face me. I refused to let us part like this.

"Suda, I need to speak with you right now," I insisted.

"Go away. I'm busy," Suda said turning back to the car. "So what do you have in mind?" she asked sweetly to the passenger. The man had neatly slicked-back hair glued together with pomade, which made it far too shiny to be natural.

"Babe, we can go anywhere you want," he purred, his lips spreading into a wide grin. The passenger was of Hispanic descent, as was the driver, whose buzz cut revealed a circular scar on the right side of his skull.

How could Suda speak to these two strangers, let alone consider going anywhere with them? They looked dangerous with visible tattoos on their arms, and teardrops etched on their cheeks. They were clearly out of place in our predominantly African neighborhood. To make matters worse, the driver looked around a lot, as if searching for someone because he knew that they didn't belong here.

"No, I won't leave it like this between us," I said more sternly, getting between her and the open window.

"Sweetie, this will only take a minute." Suda turned around and pulled me to the side. "Matika, I have nothing else to say to you."

"Suda, you know that I would never try to hurt you on purpose. It was Walyam–"

"Stop there," she commanded holding up her hand. "You don't need to say any more about him. As long as I live, I don't care if I ever hear that man's name again."

"I'm so sorry about everything. I failed you as a sister and a friend. Please accept my apology."

"No, Matika. It is I who should be truly sorry. I have condemned you when I am far worse than anyone of us."

"What do you mean?"

"I always knew that Walyam had a thing for you, but I didn't realize that he would try something so disgraceful. After everything you and I have been through, I'm sick to my stomach. I chose to ignore his behavior because, for the first time, I felt like I had something that you didn't. I closed my eyes to everything. To be with him I put you in a situation that…that…" She sniffled as she swiped away a falling tear.

"Please, Suda, don't blame yourself for his actions. You had his son to think about. Remember, he is the father of your son and will always be. Walyam is your family now. You need to go home to him. He loves you and you know it."

"You don't understand." Suda's voice became hollow like a shell. It was a tone that I never heard, as if she was a mere vessel and her soul had left her body. "It was what I always wanted from him. To have a family with him and be his wife was all I ever wanted. But no…" She shook her head violently. "…the more I tried, the more it backfired. The baby is not Walyam's son."

# CHAPTER 15

"What are you talking about? He has to be!" My mouth had gone instantly dry. A swarm of bees could have stung me and I wouldn't have been more surprised.

"It happened in the prison in Kenya."

Because of our half-brother Lutalo's obsession for revenge, he revealed our whereabouts to our father's enemy. We were taken one night to an underground prison on a military base where my father was beaten and tortured within an inch of his life. If it wasn't for Walyam and the hidden diamonds, Baba would have been killed. Who knew what would have happened to the rest of us.

"I was ruined by more men than I could count. So, the truth is I don't know who the father of my bastard son is. I don't think Walyam can have children because God knows we tried. I wanted to get pregnant so Baba would let us marry."

"You don't have to tell anyone, Suda. Just go home and he will take care of you." I tried to hug her, but she tore out of my grip and pushed me away.

"Don't you get it!? We are not in the 'bush' anymore. He'll know sooner or later. Maybe not today or tomorrow, but he will find out. That is for certain."

"What about your son? He needs his mother. Who will care for him?"

"Namazzi can have him. She always wanted him, anyway. She's envied me the moment she laid eyes on our son, wanting him for herself."

Just then a quick beep of the horn sounded from the Impala. The men urged Suda to hurry.

"Suda, please don't go with them. You don't know anything about these men."

"Hah! The one thing I do know is men. I'm leaving and never coming back. I suggest you do the same. One thing is for sure. I'm going to do everything in my power to kill Lutalo. And when I do, I'm going to kill him with my bare hands."

With that, she held back bitter tears in her eyes and got into the back of the car. She rolled up her window quickly to stave off the chilly air, and didn't look back as the car pulled out of the parking lot.

Suda needed her space, but she didn't know those men. Again, she proved how reckless she could be. I had to trust that she'd take care of herself and stay safe because there was nothing I could do. Walking over to the far side of the store, I stepped into the phone booth, and deposited thirty-five cents. After I dialed Chaz's number from memory, I waited for him to pick up.

"Hello," Chaz said when he picked up after the fourth ring. His voice was groggy but was still wonderful to my ears.

"It's me," I said twirling the metal cord holding the shredded phone book.

"My God, are you okay? Are you hurt?"

My heart warmed at his caring words. He really did love me; I could truly count on him to care for me. Truly, I was a lucky girl, much more so than Suda, who left our home only to get in a car with strangers. "I was in a big fight with my family. Can you pick me up at the 7-Eleven?"

"Of course. I'll be there in half an hour. See you soon."

After the phone died on his end, I sat down in the phone booth and waited. There was no reason for me to leave the little warmth it provided. The sweater I wore was as thin as a silk slip. I felt cold, and the moist air stole my warmth. Of all things that could have happened that night, leaving Suda was the worst.

I had failed to see her pain. I should have asked her what happened back in Kenya. When she left the camp, she was beaten and bloodied, her clothes nearly torn from her body. At first glance, her spirit didn't look broken, but something in her had changed that night. Deep down inside, I knew. I tried to hide it, and simply ignored it altogether. The signs were plain before my eyes. She had torn off her dress to take a shower at our cousin's house, who had sheltered us after we escaped the prison. She had scrubbed her skin so hard, like she wanted to scour residue from her body. I was young then, so the signs were lost on me.

Then there was Namazzi's confession about her inability to conceive. It was Walyam who couldn't have children, not her. It was too much of a coincidence that Suda had gotten pregnant right before we left Kenya when she and Walyam had been lovers for over two years. Why didn't I make the connection?

Baba was with her in the prison. We all knew something was wrong, yet we all kept it a secret because surely Baba had to know. Because of that, she blamed herself for the web of lies that we all helped build. Then the fact that she kept the pregnancy a dark secret for so long was tragic. To think, she had to carry the burden alone that the child had been created from an act of violence. Unimaginable.

Baba, Walyam, and I were all to blame, not Suda. As a father, a lover, and a sister…we each should have recognized it within our own unique relationship to her. She needed us, and we failed her in the worst way. Now she was lost to us all, perhaps forever.

While I waited for my beloved Chaz, I thought about our relationship and where it was headed. I loved him so much and I wanted it all; marriage, children, and a home together. What did he expect from me? As lucky as I was to have him in my life, I had to know his intentions.

I had risked and ultimately given up so much for him. I'd lied to Baba and Suda about him the whole time. If I'd been upfront and spoken to Baba in the first place, he may have understood. Well…maybe I gave Baba too much credit. But if you loved someone, there shouldn't be secrets. You should be able to shout to the world your love for each other instead of sneaking around like thieves in the night.

When Chaz pulled into the parking lot, I exited the booth with my shoulders back and head up. I would demand to be introduced to his parents because if he loved me he wouldn't be ashamed. As soon as the time was right, I would bring it up and leave him no room to disagree.

"Matika, I'm so sorry…" he said as I opened the door and crawled into the seat next to him.

"It's not your fault," I said rubbing my hands together in front of the heater. I never understood why my hands were always cold, even on the hottest of days. "It was a long time coming."

"You can stay at my house as long as you need."

"Thanks." I moved closer to him and rested my head on his shoulder. The feeling of safety and warmth was such a comfort when I was in his presence. The clock read 3 a.m. I was exhausted and found I dozed off and vaguely remembered Chaz carrying me up the stairs. I awoke later in the morning with my head in the crook of his arm, nestled in his soft bed under the covers.

"Are you all right? You were crying in your sleep."

"I'm fine. I need to take a shower," I replied as I got out of bed and headed promptly to the bathroom. My entire body was sore, and I was tender in an area that made me queasy to think of Walyam having touched me. I wanted to wash off his filth immediately.

I started the shower, swiftly took off my dress, and got under the spray before the water even warmed up. Taking a wash cloth from the rack, I scoured my body. I was on the verge of losing my top layer of skin when the water began to run scalding hot.

The door swung open letting in the chilled morning air. "Can I join you?" Chaz asked with a devious smile on his face. He stepped out of his loose shorts and entered the shower before I could respond.

Truthfully, I needed to be alone to gather my thoughts this morning, but it was too late as he shared the water with me.

"My God!" he gasped. "Who did this to you?"

"It's nothing. I'm fine," I said firmly placing my hands across my breasts.

He stepped out of the shower and pulled me with him. Our soaked bodies dripped on the floor. With the shower steaming up the bathroom, Chaz used his free hand to wipe a clear spot on the mirror. Then he pulled me forward roughly.

"Look at yourself. How can you tell me it's nothing?"

Reluctantly I gazed into the mirror and saw the legion of bruises on my face and body. I had a large hand print on my left breast, and I couldn't recall how it got there. I was an awful mess to see, but I would recover. Being estranged from my family was another tragic matter entirely.

I wanted to be honest with Chaz about everything because I wanted him to be a part of my life. He needed to know who I was, and that meant all of me. It was time to tell him. Right then, I told Chaz what had happened, even about Walyam, right down to the very last detail of when Suda left with the men. I didn't mention anything about Suda's revelations because that was her own painful story to tell.

Chaz's body tensed. "If I ever see that jerk–"

"There is no need for that. Just let it go because I have," I said trying to calm him. A lot worse things could have happened, and for that I was thankful.

"So she threw you out, just like that?"

"Yes. I can't go back there." I waited for him to respond as my last words hung in the air like mist in a valley.

"Babe, you never have to go back there. You can stay here with me." He pulled me close to him. "I know I'm leaving in a few months, but I'm sure we can make something work. I may not be here, but I'll take care of you. You won't have anything to worry about."

"There is something I want before I agree to stay with you," I said looking up at him. The issue burned at my soul and I could no longer deny it. "I want you to introduce me to your parents."

"Why do you want to meet them? Believe me when I say my mother isn't the most pleasant person to meet." Chaz shifted and wouldn't look me in the eyes.

"I don't want us to be a secret anymore, especially not with your family. I just want things to be right. Besides, I've had my share of unpleasant people, as you know. I hardly think your mother can be worse than mine."

"Matika, you don't understand my mom. She always finds a way to ruin my life. She's an elite socialite used to getting her way. She's the reason I joined the service...and if I don't agree?"

"Then I will go somewhere else, wherever that might be." And I vowed to myself that I would do as I threatened.

"All right, I'll take you to meet them when I get back from assignment."

"Why do we have to wait that long? That's months away."

"For one, I have to make an appointment. God forbid I show up unannounced. Two, I need to tell my father, so he'll have time to prepare her."

"What? Am I that bad that she has to be prepared for me?"

"No it's not that–"

Just then, the phone rang. Chaz used that as an excuse to bolt out of the bathroom as if running from a fire. Any other time when we were together at his house he wouldn't have considered answering the phone.

Irritated, I dried off and wrapped the towel around me. Picking up my clothes, I walked to his bedroom. With nothing to wear, because I refused put on the same clothes I came in, I sat on the bed with my arms crossed in frustration. I couldn't help but feel that Chaz was ashamed of me by the fact that he wouldn't introduce me to his parents. He was a fully grown man and no longer under their roof, so I couldn't fathom the reason. I just hoped I wasn't overreacting.

"Is everything all right?"

"Oh, it was just a telemarketer," he said but he began to put on clothes. "You need something to wear. I figure we can get something to eat and take you shopping."

"OK," I said coyly. The prospect of shopping improved my mood significantly.

Chaz gave me a pair of his sweats and a T-shirt for me to wear that was much too big. It was comfortable but awkward because I'd never worn pants other than the time I'd dressed up like a boy soldier. I did it then to escape my crazy half-brother, Lutalo, who was determined to marry me and take me back to Uganda. During that time, I was desperate and had done many outrageously risky maneuvers to gain freedom for me and my family.

Since Chaz despised shopping, he didn't go into any of the stores with me, but we decided to meet back at his truck in two hours. I was amazed how hard it was to keep track of time when you're enjoying yourself with someone else's credit card. There were several "oh, no" moments when I'd forgotten about the time only to check and find out there was still some left. This trip I only picked out the basics. I chose to purchase jeans, which were not as comfortable as they looked, and plain T-shirts. I bought a jacket, which I considered a necessity, and a pair of lace-up shoes. I didn't want to over indulge, so I picked out three pairs of underwear and one bra.

Chaz was pleased when I finished with ten minutes to spare, and took the bags from me before he opened the door. On our way home, we stopped at the grocery store to stock up on food. Chaz must have assumed I knew how to cook, because he allowed me to pick out all the food. I decided to buy a cookbook and learn some recipes. I would have plenty of time to practice while he went to work each day.

Chaz's roommate, though rarely present, was nice enough. He wasn't as kind as Chaz was about my cooking, but he admired my drive to keep trying. After three weeks, when Chaz left for several days on assignment, we had settled into a comfortable routine. I enrolled in home study, or alternative education, which was at my own pace but so easy that I was on track to graduate one year early. I did most of the cooking and cleaning and made sure he had a meal waiting for him when he came home from work each day. We would watch movies and talk until we were tired, and then we would make love before falling asleep. On weekends, we spent quality time together and always found a fun activity to do such as bowling. Chaz was also an avid shooter and loved going to the range, where he spent hours teaching me to shoot a pistol.

"I'm so happy that you're here. Everything is so much better with you, Matika," Chaz said one night as we lay sated, entwined in each other's arms.

"This is the happiest time of my life. I don't think it can get much better."

"It can and it will get better. You'll see. Once I get back from deployment, our lives will move in a new course together."

I stayed quiet, though my heart pounded. Did this mean that he was going to propose marriage? I could only hope because I wanted to spend the rest of my life with him. Nestling closer to him, I kissed his shoulder with a mouth that had gone dry with anticipation. Finally, my life had turned around for the better and not once had I cried for my family, though I missed them very much.

The phone rang, jolting me back to the present.

"Oh, no. Who would be calling this time of night?" Chaz asked looking at the bedside alarm that showed midnight.

"You might want to get that. It could be important."

"I really hope they are not calling me in," he said getting up from the bed.

I regretted telling him to answer when my body instantly grew cold without his warmth. It was raining, and the air was chilly. Whereas I enjoyed warm weather and an equally toasty house, Chaz liked the cold and was completely at odds with me when it came to that. His theory was you could always put on more clothes to stay warm, but you can only take off so much to get cool. He had a valid point, but I hated wearing layers of bulky and uncomfortable clothes.

Just then Chaz burst through the door. "My father had a medical emergency. He's been medevaced here and is undergoing surgery. I have to go to the hospital."

# CHAPTER 16

"I'm so sorry. What's wrong with him?"

"I don't know yet. I can't get anything out of my mother. She's hysterical. Probably because their trip was cut short. I've got to leave now."

"Of course." I got up and began to look for something quick yet decent to wear. After all, I was going to see his mother for the first time so I should at least be presentable.

"Matika, there is no need for you to get out of bed at this hour," he said in a strange tone that I'd never heard from him before. "I won't be too long. I'll call you from the hospital to let you know how things are going."

There was no denying that he didn't want me to accompany him. At a time like this, petty things like his mother's dislike of me shouldn't matter. I could have let it go, let Chaz be with his family during this difficult time, but I found I was unable to concede.

"I'm going, too. I refuse to stay here instead of supporting you. I promise I won't be any trouble."

"Now is not the time for me to introduce you to my mother."

"It's the best time. We are living together, after all. She should know about me." Now standing with my hands on my hips gearing up for a fight, fire in my eyes, I dared him to argue with me.

"Fine. But for the record, I think this is a horrible idea and not the best time."

Within minutes, we were dressed and headed to the hospital. Still struggling with the cold weather, I wore a pair of blue jeans, a fitted pink sweater under my warm denim jacket, and a colorful scarf around my neck. After we arrived, Chaz headed straight for the nurses' station on the fourth floor.

"I'm here to see William Landry," Chaz said, calling a nurse's attention.

The nurse directed us down the hall to his father's ICU room.

"It's about time, Charles," his mother said with a perfectly manicured hand on her hip. She stood outside his father's room apparently waiting for his arrival. Dressed in a blue high-waist pantsuit and honey-blonde hair pulled back into a tight bun, she looked more appropriate for a corporate office than a hospital. "You've got to be kidding…" her voice trailed off.

"Mother, I'd like you to meet Matika. Please be nice to her. She's a good friend."

I nearly choked. Did he just refer to me as a friend? I'd read in a fashion magazine once that being called a friend was not a good sign. As a matter of fact, it meant that the person didn't value your relationship enough to introduce you as anything but. When had our relationship been reduced to a friendship? We would have to talk about that later.

Chaz gave me an apologetic look that I chose to ignore. His eyes pled with me and silently urged me to respond. I had a mind not to, but the silence was beyond uncomfortable as his mother stood in open-mouthed shock.

"Nice to meet you, ma'am," I said politely extending my arm as was customary for a handshake.

She looked at my hand as it if it were diseased.

"Mom," Chaz said breaking the silence, giving her a look that I didn't understand.

"A pleasure," she said placing a cold hand briefly in mine. Her grasp was loose, her skin thin and full of veins, with narrow fingers sporting multiple rings that glittered under the fluorescent light. "I'm too young to be called ma'am, so we can get rid of the formalities. You are Chaz's friend, after all. Please call me Mrs. Landry."

That wasn't what I expected, but if she preferred Mrs. Landry then so be it. Her response wasn't too bad considering that she had just met me for the first time.

"How is dad doing?" Chaz asked concerned.

"He was stable after the surgery but now they are having a hard time keeping his blood pressure down."

"What happened?"

"He was playing golf and apparently on his upswing he just doubled over in pain and passed out. They thought he had ruptured something, so we were left baffled when he didn't come to right away. Long story short, your father had to have quadruple bypass surgery. There was no way I'd have them operate on him in Mexico when we have the best doctors here. But I must say, it cost a small fortune to have him medevaced.

"It turns out that he also had bleeding ulcers, so it's a good thing he had the heart attack, otherwise we would have never known. I always tell him to stay away from that artery-clogging pork or that spicy stuff the cook makes for him sometimes." She finished with a wave of her hand.

"Can we see him?"

"Yes, but you'll have to go in alone because they only allow one visitor at a time at this ungodly hour."

"OK. Makita, please wait here."

I was an afterthought, but I didn't mind. Chaz's father was sick and far more important than me being stuck with his mother. "Yes, of course," I responded as I watched him go into the room.

"Matika, is it?" his mother asked with hard eyes.

"Yes, ma– oh, Mrs. Landry." I had to concede inwardly that Chaz was right, but there was no way that I'd let him know it. His mother was colder than the other side of a pillow.

"Well, then, let's go down to the cafeteria and get some coffee. There is no sense waiting around here for Charles. We can chat and get to know each other." Before I responded, she had turned on her heels and was headed for the elevator. As expected, I followed.

She was a very shapely woman who looked to be in her early forties, but I knew she was in her mid-fifties. The only thing that gave her true age away were the gentle lines and age spots on her hands and neck. Her bun was severely tight and pulled at the corners of her blue eyes, which made her look closer to Asian than Caucasian. Chaz must have gotten his green eyes – and other traits I was thankful for – from his father.

She glided down the hall, as regal as a queen in a castle. With shoulders back and head held high, she received many looks from nurses and guests. We rode the elevator, along with a medical assistant, down to the second floor in uncomfortable silence. The assistant's eyes were fixated on the patterned design on the ceiling as if counting every ridge proved more important than saving a life.

As soon as the elevator stopped, Mrs. Landry walked out and the assistant breathed a sigh of relief. I followed her down the white corridor that smelled of fried foods that grew stronger with every step. The cafeteria was noisy with the medical staff talking and rushing around like it was the middle of the day instead of the wee hours of the morning. It seemed so unnatural for anyone to be this active and chipper at this hour.

"Do you have any hazelnut creamer?" Mrs. Landry asked the tired cook by the coffee pot. If he'd had any more bags under his eyes he would have had trouble holding up his face under the weight of them.

"Whatcha see is whatcha get." His tone left no room for argument because he simply didn't care and was not intimidated by anyone. He'd seen it all.

"What are you waiting for, get a cup," she said directing her irritability at the cook toward me.

I'd never had coffee before but didn't have a choice. It was a dark brew with a sign that said Maxwell House. Deciding not to put in any cream or sugar – I didn't take any extras in my tea, anyway – I headed to the cash register where I was told by the cashier that Mrs. Landry had already paid for mine.

I joined her at the booth closest to the darkened window, sitting opposite her as she sipped her coffee. She sat and watched me expectantly with a critical eye. Deciding to take a draw of the coffee, I was both shocked and appalled that anyone could drink such a bitter brew akin to muddy water. I set it down quickly, failing to stifle a little gag.

"Let's cut to the chase. What is your relationship with my son?" Her eyes were so sharp they threatened to cut me in two.

How was I supposed to answer such a direct question? Chaz should have a least warned me about this or told me what to say in this situation. He did introduce me as a friend so perhaps I should just go with that for now.

"We are friends, very good friends," I answered placing my hands in my lap. I sat up straight and got ready for the intense interrogation that was sure to come.

"Really? That's odd, because Charles never mentioned you before. Good friends? Such a good friend you are to show up at the hospital in the middle of the night."

I didn't like where this was going. Her tone was nothing short of disrespectful. What was her issue? Chaz was a grown man and didn't need his mother's permission for anything.

"Maybe we should go back upstairs. Chaz will be wondering where we went."

"Do not call my son that childish name. His name is William Charles Landry III."

I took a deep breath to calm my nerves that threatened to erupt, and closed my eyes briefly before I responded. "I'm sorry. I'm really not feeling well, so if you'll excuse me, I'm going to see how Charles is doing, Mrs. Landry."

"We are not done yet. I don't want you to ever see my son again. How dare you have the audacity to show your face here tonight. This is a private family matter that has nothing to do with you."

"Why is it your concern? You don't even know me or my relationship with your son. I will not stop seeing him. We are in love, and there is nothing you can do about it." I got up.

"Sit down. We are not finished." She calmly took a long draw of her coffee that must have grown cold under her glacial hands.

"You can't talk to me like that." It was my turn to be upset. For some reason, despite my desire to flee, I sat back down and looked her straight in the eye. Perhaps it was time I had it out with someone, and she happened to be the perfect candidate at the moment. "You're going to have to learn to accept me. I'm in a serious relationship with your Charles, and in fact, we live together."

"What?" She sat in open-mouthed shock, but it only lasted for a few moments before she gained her composure. Still, the look on her face, even briefly, was a great victory.

"It's true. He loves me, you know." Although I was never one to brag, I couldn't help but rub it in some more.

"You are living together in sin. He will never be with you in the end."

"That's not true. We'll get married one day soon. And when we have children, I won't let you be around them if you don't learn to accept me."

"Married?" She shook her head as if talking to a misbehaving child. "You silly, silly, girl. My Charles will never marry you. He is already married. His wife is William's business partner's daughter. So you see, you are nothing but a temporary distraction for him. You should be ashamed of yourself playing house with a married man. I'm sure your parents are very proud of you."

Her words hit me like a punch in the stomach that stole my breath. How could she say such a thing that was simply not true? She was cruel in the worst way imaginable.

"He may not see her as often as he should," she continued, "but Charles will never divorce her and jeopardize his father's business relationship. Nor will he disappoint his father, to whom he is very close."

"Stop it," I said breathlessly. "Why are you saying this?" My legs, though unsteady, finally allowed me to get up from the seat and walk toward the elevator. Mrs. Landry followed me and continued to talk but I'd tuned her out, unable to hear anything past my rapid breaths that threatened to overtake my lungs.

"Matika, are you OK?" Chaz was quickly beside me, his strong arm wrapped around me, supporting my body that was too heavy for my legs. "Mother, what happened?"

"She doesn't react well to the truth. It seems you never told her about Aria."

"Mother how could you? It was not your place."

I couldn't believe my ears. Chaz had lied to me all this time, and he was married. Not able to be around him another moment I began to run toward the elevator.

"Matika, wait!" Chaz followed.

"Let her go, Charles."

"Listen to me for a minute, please," he said holding onto my arm.

"Is it true?" I asked with a small ray of hope that maybe Mrs. Landry had told lies. She could have been just trying to get under my skin to break us apart.

"Let me explain–"

"You lied to me and…" I couldn't finish. What he had done was unspeakable. A simple slap in the face – although my palms itched for it – was not enough. He couldn't have married me because he already had a wife.

"Leave me alone," I said tearing my arm out of his grip.

Not wanting him to see how bad he had hurt me, I sprinted to the elevator, thankful that the door opened right away. It was the longest ride to the first floor. Storming out of the hospital was ironic. I had entered with a heart full of hope, the love of my life at my side, but now leaving, my heart was cleaved in two, all hope dashed against the sharp rocks at the bottom of a deep cliff. Every part of my soul was exposed and vulnerable for Chaz alone, and at that moment, I made up my mind that I would never allow another to hurt me again. Shame on him for doing this to me, but next time I would have only myself to blame.

No one noticed the tears that ran down my eyes. The staff and other visitors had their own world to tend to. Endless work and patients waited for their care. They were used to the distraught or grieving visitors.

Once again I was greeted by the cold night air, but this time with truly nowhere to go. I found myself walking to a nearby pay phone down the street, deposited a few coins from my purse, and waited with my ear to the cold receiver. The phone rang only two times and it surprised me.

"Hello," a heavily accented voice spoke in English.

"Namazzi? Is that you?" I spoke in Swahili. It was hard to be certain for sure because I'd never heard her voice over the phone.

"Yes, it's me. Who is this?" she asked.

"It's Matika. Um…how are things?" I didn't know what to say. I hadn't planned for anyone to answer and if someone did, I would have hung up.

"Not well. Suda never came back," she began quietly as the babe cooed softly in the background. She must have been making him a bottle when the phone rang. "Baba is very angry still and is not talking much. Mama… she hasn't been very kind."

"I'm really sorry," I said imagining how Corin would take everything out on Namazzi. She was the lowest in the family in terms of rank so she would certainly have to bear it all. I should have been there to help her.

"Walyam forbids me to speak to you, so I have to go, else I will be in trouble with him.

Goodbye, sister."

She hung up the phone before I had time to respond.

Who was I kidding? I could never go back there. If I called back I would only get Namazzi in trouble with the whole family. As it was, she had to deal with Walyam, and that was a huge undertaking in itself. I don't know how she'd managed to survive with him all this time. There was truly nothing left for me. I had nowhere to go.

Rummaging through my purse, I found my wallet and counted the money; $23.63 wasn't going to last long. As I replaced the wallet in my purse, a fingertip touched a card. I pulled it out and read it again as if I'd never seen it. The card read *John Lee* on one side, his phone number on the other. Maybe he could give me a job and a place to stay.

Dialing his number, I felt I had nothing to lose. The worst he could say was "no," and it wasn't like I hadn't heard that before. When we met at the party, he seemed pretty interested in helping out. He offered me "an exciting life style that only the elite can obtain."

When the phone stopped ringing, I knew that someone had picked up it up but had remained silent. "I'm looking for John Lee," I said timidly.

"Who's this?" a deep voice sounded on the other line.

# CHAPTER 17

"My name is Matika. I met John at a party a few weeks back. Could I speak to him?"

"Speak." The deep voice sounded interested now. It was John, who was apparently using his "telephone" voice.

"Is your offer still open? I'm in a bind and need a job and place to stay. I'm stuck at Mercy Hospital off of Fifth. I'm alone and have nowhere to go and no one to turn to. If you could help me out now, I would be forever in your debt."

"I could certainly arrange something. You have to know that if you are serious about this, there is no going back to your past."

"I'm more than ready. As far as I'm concerned, I'd be glad to leave it all behind."

"Matika, I like you, so I'm going to give you some time to think about this because it isn't the sort of decision to be made in the heat of the moment at…2 a.m. I've just traced your call so listen to me carefully. There is a motel called Comfort Nights about three blocks to the right of your current location. Check in using the name Jasmine Yancy for one night. I will be in contact with you tomorrow, so tear up my card now."

I was desperate to humor him to see what else he would say. How would he know where I was? Not to mention the fact that I didn't even have an ID to check in under that bogus name he gave me.

"I don't–"

The phone was disconnected.

I was hung up on twice in one evening. What nerve. I tore up the card and let it drop in a nearby trash can, then headed in the direction John had instructed. If this proved to be a lie then there was no need to ever call him again anyway.

This "three blocks" took much longer than expected because the blocks were very long in this questionable neighborhood. I was glad I'd dressed warmly, the scarf a godsend that I wrapped around my head and neck to defrost my ears. As I made my way to the final block some twenty minutes later, I was on a street with several motels and inns, none of which looked inviting.

I almost missed the Comfort Nights Motel because most of the letter lights were out, spelling "…M…ORT…N…HTS" instead. I was afraid there was no occupancy because there were a few men and many scantily clad women that stood around outside, but then I saw the "vacancy" sign lit under the motel name.

I walked quickly into the small office, took my hands out of my jacket pocket, and clutched my purse that held the only money I had. It was not a clean lobby. The green carpeted floor was stained and hadn't been vacuumed in a very long time. The paneled wall space was completely bare. A wooden chair sat against the far wall and faced a protective glass window that housed the attendant, an older gentleman in his late fifties. Since I'd been in the United States I'd become accustomed to higher standards, and by the looks of it, this was on the lower end of the spectrum.

"I'd like to get a room," I said through the small holes in the glass no bigger than a fingertip. Smoke came through from an ashtray that held a dying cigarette butt, which was a fire just waiting to consume the endless stacks of clutter.

"For how many hours?" the man asked, loath to tear his eyes from a small TV in the corner of the booth. He continuously turned back to the set, swiveling his head multiple times. Though he'd turn to me, he wasn't really paying attention.

What a strange question. I suppose if I wanted a place to sleep for a few hours, this would be the place to go to save money on a full night.

"I need a room for twenty-four hours," I said not sure how long it would take for John to contact me. "How much will it cost?"

"Sixteen ninety-five." He turned his head again to the TV where a soccer game was in full swing, the score tied at one.

"I'll take it." That would leave me only six dollars and sixty-eight cents to spare for food. John had better come through for me.

After I filled out a small form with the fake name John gave me, and added two years to my age, the attendant gave me the yellow carbon copy, along with room key twenty-one without much fanfare. He was eager to get back to his show.

"Unbelievable!" he shouted at the TV, throwing up his hands. "Can you believe this guy?"

As I walked to my room near the end of the building I ignored the catcalls from both the men and the women. I opened the door and my nose was immediately assaulted by a repugnant odor. With only two dim lights the room seemed shabby, and although it was very neat, it was far from clean. It's strange how quickly I'd acclimated to the standard of cleanliness in this country, which came as naturally as breathing for me.

The walls and ceiling were stained from cigarette smoke, other un-identifiable substances, and what I hoped were water spots. The carpet was in desperate need of a good twice-over from a steam cleaner and was littered with several needles that the previous occupant, who must have been diabetic, had failed to throw away.

The bathroom wasn't much better. Again, it was neat but with no trash can, and the heart-shaped tub sported an unsightly ring around it with hair at its base that clogged the drain. Shower shoes would certainly be desirable in this case. Although the toilet wasn't bad, I'd still hover over it, just in case.

I turned off all the lights, and pulled back the fitted bed cover, laid down on the sheets fully clothed, and waited for this night to be over. I just wanted to sleep and not think about anything…but…it made me so angry to think about Chaz and how he'd hurt me. If I hadn't snuck around in the first place, I wouldn't have gotten in trouble with Baba. And if I hadn't been in trouble with Baba, Walyam wouldn't have been so bold with me. Well, at least my family would have believed me. Instead, I'd lost all credibility.

I really didn't need go down this spiral of blame. It was just too easy and only left me feeling betrayed. One day I was going to wake up and realize that I was in charge of my own destiny and I shouldn't depend on anyone else for my own happiness and well-being. For me, the decision was a simple one. Or was it?

My Chaz. Who was I kidding? I still loved him with every fiber of my being. He was my first love and nothing or no one could take that away. I had given him everything I had, my heart, my body, and my mind. My heart pounded in my chest at the thought of his lips on mine. The nights he had spent holding me when I couldn't sleep or was plagued with nightmares came to the surface as hot tears ran down my cheeks.

I couldn't leave him even though I knew that I could never be his wife. I loved him so much. Still, I wondered what his intentions were with me. Could I live with myself being his mistress? Too many thoughts raced through my head that swayed me to and from Chaz, back and forth. When I had finally stopped crying my head hurt. I had to speak to Chaz tomorrow. Sometime between the constant moans and yells from the rooms on both sides of mine, I fell asleep.

——

I awoke, startled by the phone as it rang beside my bed. The small clock beside the phone read 7:30, but the heavy drapes on the window didn't allow for any sunlight to come through. I reached over and picked up the phone.

"Hello?" My voice came out lower than I'd intended.

"Have you made your decision?" John asked. As promised he had found me, and yet I wasn't surprised. He was certainly a man who valued his words.

For a moment Chaz flashed through my head, leaving my chest burning in pain at what he'd done to me. I was hurt and angry all over again. The idea of speaking to Chaz faded with the night. "My decision is the same. There is nothing left here for me."

"Good. There is a white sedan parked at the end of the lot, two doors down from your room. You have three minutes. He will take you to the airport and give you instructions along the way. Good luck, Matika. I'll be in touch."

Again he disconnected the phone. In a matter of a twenty second, one-way phone conversation, my life had changed with no time for a second thought...not that I had any. I made my way to the restroom, hovered over the toilet, and splashed some freezing water over my face. Then I left the key on the bedside table and headed out the door. The air was brisk and cold, the sky clear, but aside from that all I noticed was the white sedan looming before me.

Bravely, I pulled the metal handle and opened the door to my destiny.

"You ready?" the driver asked, but it wasn't question. He wore a golf shirt, slacks, and a baseball cap that covered his salt and pepper hair like he was headed to a tee-time instead of the airport.

I nodded and sat in the front seat. The car was nice and warm. I wasn't sure how long he'd waited for me but it was clear he was ready to go. As soon as I'd closed the door he backed out of the parking space and exited the hotel.

"So, I was told you have instructions for me," I began once we were on the freeway heading north. The driver was quiet and the suspense killed me. Still, I felt very safe and comfortable with the decision I'd made to leave everything behind.

"I'm taking you to Los Angeles International Airport where you have a ticket waiting for you at the American Airlines counter under the name of Jasmine Yancy," he began as he reached for the pink shoulder bag beside my leg, letting it drop on my lap. "In there is your birth certificate, passport, and Nevada ID. You are from North Las Vegas and came out to San Diego to visit a friend. Now you are headed to college in D.C.,

Georgetown University to be precise. Although I don't anticipate any problems, that's your story in the event you get questioned."

"How did you get my picture?"

"Surveillance videos at the cocktail banquet. We were able to extrapolate some pictures and change your clothes and background using computer imagery."

I was impressed. Although they were mostly facial shots, I wore a different outfit in all of them. Somehow they'd also managed to change my hair slightly, which made each photo a unique snapshot in time.

"What am I studying?" Inside was a large yellow envelope that had everything I needed, including a college acceptance letter and the dorm address. The information was so complete it was strange, as if this person really existed.

"Liberal studies for now. Freshmen don't seem to know what they want to do at this point. You need to study the paperwork and know it inside and out. You can't hesitate if someone asks your date of birth, for instance."

"Yes, of course."

It was easy for me to remember Jasmine's life. She was not a typical teenager. Shuffled from foster homes to group homes throughout her life, Jasmine ended up in Las Vegas her senior year and graduated from high school soon after.

After six months of being off the grid, she applied to Georgetown University and was accepted with a full scholarship based on her diverse background and hardship. So it seems not everyone in this country had it so easy. She would turn twenty on July third.

I looked up from the files out the window as we passed the power plant. When I first arrived in this country, I remembered thinking the twin round structures looked like a woman's breasts complete with a square structure that resembled her nipples. There was nothing else around it but vast land. Even when our host called it a power plant, I still didn't understand what he'd meant. I thought I'd never see it again, but there it was.

"So what about this six-month gap? She had no address and no contact with anyone."

"Who knows? You could have lived with an abusive boyfriend or someone else you don't want to talk about. A six-month gap is nothing for a teen that has no one and nowhere to go. You did get a post office box before you applied to college."

"Is this going to be my identity from now on?" I asked, looking down at the documents before me. The fact that he referred to Jasmine as "you" wasn't lost on me.

"No," he chuckled deep in his gut. His eyes looked rather nice when he cracked a smile. "Once you get trained up, they will give you an assignment and that will determine the name you will use."

"I see. Do you know what I'll be doing? Will I be working for the FBI?" I was very interested and excited because I'd watched a show about some of their secret missions. "Because that would be amazing!"

Then it hit me. Working for the FBI would be scary, dangerous, and secretive. All were things that I feared and despised. Secret agents in the shows killed people, and sometimes they died. My mind raced. Agents were also able to jump off buildings and land on moving cars. Some could even fly with the help of a balloon.

"No, not the FBI."

"The CIA?"

"Sort of, but not directly. You will be working as a subcontractor for a private company that provides intelligence to government organizations. However, I'm not at liberty to identify them. The work the company does is so top secret and unorthodox that the government cannot even get directly involved. The company is called MEI. Not very many people are familiar with it, but it checks out as a top-secret psychological research institute. So you won't be a direct hire to MEI but will fall under a subcontract because of your status. I don't even know everything about the research they do, but they will fill you in when you arrive."

"What's the difference between the FBI and CIA?"

"They both collect and act upon information that is related to criminal activity or national security. However, the FBI focuses on domestic security and crime investigation, while the CIA focuses mostly on international intelligence."

"All right..." It was all I could say at this point. This was not what I'd expected, but hoped things would be made much clearer to me. Maybe I would work at a desk for all I knew and handle paperwork. I wouldn't mind that at all – a steady job, income, and more importantly, a life of my own. Except when I looked for our father after being separated from Suda, I had never in my life been on my own. Still, I was nervous, apprehensive, and excited all at the same time.

The driver smiled again as he looked at me briefly before turning back to the road. Then he lifted up the console to retrieve a pair of sunglasses. We rode the rest of the way in silence.

"Remember, you cannot have any contact with anyone until further notice, so don't make any calls at the airport," the driver reminded me as we pulled up to the curb.

"You don't have to worry about that," I said unbuckling the seat belt.

"That's what they all say," he said as he reached for my purse. "You don't need this anymore. You have your bag now. Also, someone will find you at baggage claim when you land."

I got out of the car and he followed me. "What are you doing?"

"Helping you with your luggage. You can't very well travel across country without any bags now, can you? You are going to college after all."

He had an excellent point. MEI was good at what they did and had clearly thought of everything, even on such short notice. The driver pulled his cap, bidding me farewell, and there was a slight pang in my heart as he pulled away, leaving me with two overstuffed black suitcases. I couldn't turn back. At least for now.

# CHAPTER 18

Although I was nervous, checking in was easier than I thought. As promised, there was a one-way ticket to Reagan airport in D.C. for me at the customer service counter. I didn't get a single question when I passed through security after checking my bags and no matter how curious I was, I didn't look inside them.

I'd traveled on a plane ten months ago. The first time was the long trip from Kenya to the United States. After two days of travel, the only thing I'd remembered was how exhausted and overwhelmed I'd felt. Today, alert and observant as I waited to board, I watched passengers from all over the world move through the airport. Despite my earlier experience, I was nervous to fly. The thought of being as high as the clouds unnerved me, and I still didn't understand how an airplane stayed in the air. Sure, it was physics, but it was magic to me.

On each of the two legs of this trip, I was crunched into the back near the latrine with little leg room. Fortunately, the food and drinks were free because I didn't have a penny to my name. Much of this trip was like before, nothing to my name, traveling to the unknown. One thing was different for sure, although I would never call Baba, knowing where he was gave me hope. He wouldn't move anytime soon. And having Chaz as well gave me courage, though I'd hate to admit it because I was still angry with him at the moment.

After I stepped off the plane I headed straight to the baggage area to retrieve my luggage. I was greeted by a fair-haired lady who identified me right away.

"Hi, Jasmine. You were the last to arrive. Come this way," she said as she led me out of the airport and took both my bags in her strong arms. Her hair was cut short, the loose curls bouncing with every clicking step she took in her low patent leather heels. She wore a black pantsuit, a light-blue collared shirt, and a heavy wool jacket.

At 7 p.m. Eastern Time the sun had set hours ago. The air was beyond chilly, my scarf and jacket, which now felt as thin as lace, did nothing to protect me from the cold. The wet, slushy ground seeped through my canvas shoes and numbed my feet. Quickly, I followed the lady to what looked like a utility van with tinted windows. It was what some of the kids at my high school would call a "kidnapper" van. The irony was not lost on me considering that I didn't know where I was going.

"Hop in," the lady said as she slid the door open. "These are some of your teammates."

"Thank you," I said climbing into the van, which was deceiving because there was a section between the driver's seat that prevented the passengers from seeing the driver. In fact, we couldn't even see out the shadowed windows. Four other girls sat stiffly in two of the van's rows. The woman, who wore the same black suit as the driver, sat in the last row alone. I chose the first open seat closest to the door. Then the van pulled off and we were on our way.

"OK, I'm going to give you a quick brief. For security purposes, your training location will be unknown to you," the woman in the suit began as we turned our heads to listen. "There will be no contact with anyone, as I'm sure you were made aware of this prior to selection. As of right now, you will no longer use your birth name or whatever name you've been using. During this training you will be referred to as your team color, which will be assigned after in-processing. In short, we don't know nor do we care who you were before you showed up here."

"How long is the training?" the girl beside me asked. She was pretty with dark-brown hair pulled into a loose ponytail and light eyes, a striking contrast that favored her. She looked as nervous as the rest of us.

"Ladies, there aren't many questions that I can answer for you right now, again for security reasons. I assure you that all will be revealed in due time. But I will say that it's not very long. The training, that is. So please, I urge you to hold your questions and get some rest. You have a long night ahead of you and longer days to come."

Although I knew the value of sleep, I was too excited and nervous to heed her advice. I wasn't the only one who stayed awake. One of the girls, a curly haired brunette, wrung her hands as if getting water out of the cloth before hanging it to dry. Her expression was of one waiting for execution, looking as if she'd burst into tears at any moment. But the person that stood out to me the most was the tall blonde girl who just looked mad. She looked angry at the world and ready for revenge. Life had given her the rotten meat and she had been forced to eat it or go hungry. I knew that look. It was like my Suda's before she left Baba's house that cold night.

After we drove for three suspenseful hours, we finally arrived. The doors were thrown open, we filed out of the van sleepily, leaving everything behind as instructed, and took in our first look at…the compound. Although I was exhausted from hours of travel I perked up quickly.

The air felt like below zero. The compound, for lack of a better word, was an interesting place – quiet, like a morgue, with lights so dim around the building it was difficult to make out its size, or to know if there were more than one. It was a small single-story building surrounded by trees and darkness, like a horror film waiting to happen. Once the van pulled away, there were no other vehicles present – again, very strange. I felt like there was no way out.

Our feet crunched on the recently fallen snow as we were led to the building in silence where the woman used her fingerprint and a code to unlock the door. Inside, the light shined brightly. It was both warm and inviting, night and day, compared to outside. A series of closed doors, equally spaced, filled a long corridor. We followed the lady through a door on the right, and were taken to a room with an elevator hidden behind a wood-paneled wall.

The woman used her fingerprint and code to activate the power, and we descended several floors underground. Once below, the small building was more like a small city, with several high-ceiling passageways, more doors, and foyers. I would certainly get lost if I had to navigate my way down here. After we took a left, then right, right, left tunnel – or was it right, then left, left, right – she opened a door to a large rectangular room. The room had at least thirty beds, some occupied, with half on each side of the room, and a metal locker to the left of each bed.

"You sleep here tonight so choose a rack. The bathroom is on the left if you need to use it. Breakfast is at 0530. You'll be meeting T. Brown soon. Good luck, ladies," the woman said before the door locked behind her as she left.

I looked around and noticed two girls that stood watch who looked as tired as we all were from traveling. They didn't speak to any of us as they stood, one by each door. As my travel partners headed to the restroom I chose a bed, took off my wet shoes and socks, and slid into the tightly made bed. It felt so good to stretch out my legs that had been confined the entire trip between the plane and the van ride. I put away my excitement, replaced it with my fatigue, and quickly fell asleep after my head hit the pillow.

———

"Get up! Get up, ladies!" a lady's voice shouted dragging me out of a deep sleep. "For those of you who don't know me, you may call me T. Brown."

So that gravel-filled voice I'd heard– compliments of years of yelling – was T. Brown's. She was very pretty with an angular, hard face. With piercing blue eyes and perfect pink lips she looked ready for a photo shoot, especially with her regal height, impeccable black pantsuit, and light-blue collared shirt. That seemed to be the uniform of the employees here. Her hair was pulled perfectly in a French twist and not a single hairpin showed.

Looking around, I was loath to see the other girls standing at the foot of their beds ready to go. Reluctantly, I crawled out of bed and stood in front of mine as well. It was unnatural for anyone to get up at this ungodly hour; even the goats would complain at a milking during this time of morning. And, the three-hour time loss made it much crueler for me.

"For all you newbies, your uniforms will be provided this morning. In the meantime, put on the sweats located in your locker."

I donned the gray sweats, which were identical to everyone else's, and my shoes and socks that were not quite dry. I followed the other girls to the door that could only be unlocked with T. Brown's fingerprints and code. It appeared that you needed a fingerprint and code to get in and out of any of the rooms throughout this place. In the next section over, which was connected with an enclosed circular walkway, we ate a quick breakfast in a cafeteria-style setting where I choked down as much food as my stomach allowed. Everything was pristine white, perfect, and sterile.

Shortly after we returned back to the sleeping dorm, for lack of a better word, we were taken to get our uniforms, which consisted of various yoga pants, sports bras, a jacket, gloves, a beanie, and two pairs of running shoes.

Over the next six weeks, we only saw T. Brown – I discovered that "T" stood for trainer – in the morning and at night. There were thirty-five of us total. We ranged from the late teens to mid-twenties, but it was hard to say for sure because we weren't allowed to disclose anything about ourselves. She said our names didn't matter until after we graduated from the program. This reminder was drilled into us daily. I didn't feel out of place, as I realized we were all from different countries, with various unique accents. None of us was U.S.-born, which I thought was strange.

Through vigorous medical and dental exams, each one more intrusive than the one before, we were checked, inside and out. They discovered I had a cavity. I had to get painful shots in my gums that made me talk like I had a speech impediment for two hours, and endure the torturous drilling, which I refused to even think about ever again. I never had to keep my mouth open for so long. Then they cleaned my teeth, which was another first for me. Some of the girls had to endure extensive dental work to correct crooked and missing teeth, so I couldn't complain too loudly.

Then the nurses took ten vials of blood, saliva swabs, urine samples, and hair samples. The doctor examined my vagina and butt, for what was still a mystery. We were given various immunization shots and a birth control device was implanted into our arms, which they said would stop our woman's cycle. Many of the girls had to get breast implants and other cosmetic surgery. I was given hair treatments, facials, and body scrubs that left my skin as smooth as butter. At all times we had individual counseling and coaching.

After more weeks of healing for those who'd undergone surgeries, we began with some light physical fitness tests. I had a four-mile run on a treadmill hooked up to heart monitors, push-ups, sit-ups, and a swim test in a heated indoor pool. I was not the fastest runner, but I was the fastest and strongest swimmer, which surprised everyone, the trainers included, who looked at me as if I had walked on water. Swimming was one skill that saved my life in Uganda, and I felt great pride in being the best at it.

Finally, we each had to undergo an intense four days of psychological grilling with little sleep while we were hooked up to machines. Since they asked the same questions over and over, I had my answers memorized. Many of the girls were either removed or perhaps sent to another facility. By the end of the three-month processing period, fewer than two dozen of us remained. Some of the girls weren't found fit for the program.

After I was hooked up to a machine that I was told would detect all lies, I was forced to recount my entire life. By the time it was all over, the organization knew everything about me –my journey from Uganda to Kenya; who my father was, his ties, and finally my role in the killing of the colonel. Though it was painful, no matter how hard I tried to detach my emotions, I was forced to tell them about Chaz as well.

I kept my mind focused on completing the training, and wouldn't let them break down my resolve. Soon, I would be someone important, doing work that I could be proud of to help my new country, and no longer be the "shame" of my family. Government work was the type of career path Baba would be most proud of.

Finally, T. Brown gave us the formal introduction in a brightly lit room with no furniture or windows – most of the rooms didn't have windows – and a large flat-screen TV bolted on the wall. Twenty-three of us stood, waiting for the next order. The other twelve were sent home. We were young, most would say beautiful, and eager for the next stage in our lives.

"Before I get into the details of why you have all been called here," T. Brown began, "I'm going to assign each of you a team. Each member has been screened and picked to promote the best possible combination of multiple attributes, personality, and mix based on primary assessments. There is no 'I' in team. This will be your group throughout training and when you are in the field, so you better make it work. If one person on the team fails, you all fail. Always remember that you are only as strong as your weakest link."

T. Brown proceeded to call out team names and instructed us to sit with our group. There were seven total – Pink, Brown, Yellow, Green, Orange, Purple and Blue. Each had three members with the exception of the Green and Orange teams, which had four. I was on the Pink team with the tall blonde and a shorter Asian with kind eyes. The blonde girl was the one who was in the van that day when we came from the airport. She still looked angry and mad at the world, though not as outward as before. She had also undergone breast augmentation when we first arrived.

"From now on you will eat, sleep, and shit with your team. Never will you be separated," T. Brown said looking around the room waiting from someone to protest. "Training here is going to be aggressive physically but downright savage mentally. It is arranged in three phases with the sole purpose of weeding out the weak. Each phase will be more difficult than the one before. Now, I'll give you more information about the training in a minute, but first I'm going to go over our mission. Turn your attention to the video on the screen."

As if on cue, the video began. It started out mildly enough, and told of three girls who lived in poverty in three separate developing countries. Then, it changed. The first girl was sold into slavery by her father in order to take care of the family. He could no longer feed and care for his large family, and therefore, felt his only option was to sell his eldest daughter to a brothel. The girl was repeatedly beaten and raped into submission. After only a few years, she died from a solid blow to the head by the madam of the house.

The second story was of a girl who was recruited to work abroad to better her life and support her impoverished family. After she spent all the money her family had borrowed to support this effort, she arrived in the foreign country only to find out that the job promised to her did not exist. Her passports and documents were taken from her by her recruiter. She was forced to sell her body to up to ten men daily, only to give all her earnings to the recruiter, who beat and starved her regularly.

The third story chilled me the most because I'd had to leave my home and live with Chaz. Set in the United States, the video was about a young girl who ran away from home to be with a boyfriend she trusted. First, he made her dependent on drugs and alcohol, then he coaxed her to have intercourse with his friends for money. He would pressure her until she complied. Then he took her across the Mexican border and sold her into sex slavery. She was chained in a basement for many years, where she was repeatedly raped and assaulted by the men who owned her.

When the video was over many of the girls were in tears, while others were visibly angry or disturbed. Although it was very sad, it didn't affect me that way. I couldn't let it. For some reason it was as if I was unnaturally detached, numb. I felt nothing. It could have been because of the horrific things I had witnessed in Africa that made me this way, but I still felt guilty that I hadn't reacted. Besides, these were clearly actors, and I'd never cried over a movie in my life.

"Ladies, there are millions of women and children who are forced into sex slavery all around the world. There are some girls who have been kidnapped and are the daughters of U.S. government officials and parties of interest that fall within our mission, and are a threat to our national security."

"What do these girls have to do with national security?" I asked, puzzled.

"Good question but don't speak unless you are told to do so," T. Brown said pointedly to me. "These individuals do important work for our government and have knowledge of top secret information. So, if their children are taken, then they pose a risk to our government because they can be manipulated and used as a weapon to extort information. These government officials or persons of interest cannot be suddenly removed from their post because the classified information they have that requires their top secret clearance must be safeguarded."

Her arms crossed her chest as she surveyed the room. "The first phase of training will be physical endurance and the arts. The second phase is the mental challenge. The final phase will be the practical application. If you make it through training, it will be your job to help find the children of these individuals and return them home by whatever means necessary. You, ladies, will act submissive in the field with an operative that will help rescue these girls. Those of you who are strong enough in mind and body will make it, because only fifteen of you will be given assignments. The rest of you will not."

She grabbed a very thin hose from the corner of the room. "You all have many things in common. Some of you have worked the streets, danced in the local clubs, or sold drugs. All this we are well aware of. There is nothing you can hide from us. You are also all U.S. citizens and were brought to this country on questionable terms, perhaps, but are perfect for this international program.

"Look around this room," she instructed with a wave her hand, and we each turned our heads to look at one another. "We are well aware of the secrets you carry that could easily land you in prison or worse. You have all killed someone in your past for survival. Therefore, you are capable of doing whatever it takes to save your life as well as those you care for. You have what it takes to care for your team and the agent who will be your handler."

There was a collective gasp among us because up until now, none of us knew what our jobs would be or why we were chosen. It all made sense now.

"You will play the role of the girls who have been trafficked. This training will teach you to be just like them, and is a specially designed curriculum that will push you to your limits. Like the victims, you must learn submission, obeying every order and questioning none. You cannot convince anyone if you cannot convince yourself."

"You'll be called many things but you can't react." T. Brown towered over us, suddenly spraying water in the faces of those who flinched when she approached. "The water represents the strikes you will receive for disobedience. It will be water for now, but that will change later in the training. And, never, ever, look anyone in the eyes."

Then T. Brown reached up to touch my face. I stepped back and was immediately greeted by a blast of cold water that chilled and stung my face.

"You can't react to anything unless you're told to do so. The enemy will have no mercy on you and will strike you down without warning. You must trust your handler in all things. He won't let anyone harm you. Understood?"

"Yes, madam!" we bellowed in unison.

"You are the submissive. You cannot save those girls if you cannot *be* those girls. You must learn to think, eat, and sleep like them. Only then will you be equipped to relate and communicate with them on their level. As of now, your former life is gone. You will not discuss the past because from this point forward you are dead. Obey your handler in all things, no matter what. Understood?"

"Yes, madam!"

"Will you question your handler?"

"No, madam!"

"Excuse me," I began in earnest, unable to help myself. "What if I have a really important question, or I don't understand what the handler is asking me to do–"

"If you keep your mouth shut, Pink Team," she said referring to my team name, "you will be able to listen to what's he's telling you. You will not eat, sleep, or shit unless he alone tells you to do so. If you fail to obey, you will not only jeopardize the mission, but you will risk your team's and your handler's lives. Ladies, you are the key to making these operations work. The roles you play are critical. You'll be the eyes and ears for your handler. It's you who will learn the layout and analyze the threats of each assignment. Now it's time for your first lesson."

# CHAPTER 19

The training was an intense drilling of obedience and submission. I was soaked from head to toe when it was over. Although being respectful – or "submissive," as they termed it – was second nature to me, it was really hard to understand T. Brown's orders because she would give them so quickly, one after another. Get up, sit down, eyes on the ground…. It was like playing a game of "Simon Says" like I'd seen the kids play on TV.

There was only one girl, "Pilly," who didn't get wet the whole time. Since she was a tough one, I was glad she was on my team. I secretly named her Pilly because she always wore an expression like she had swallowed the most disgusting pill imaginable. I didn't know anyone's name and no one offered. They were so secretive and untrusting, which made me feel the same way. Instead, we were forever referred to as our team color. In those groups we ate slept, studied, and strategized.

I instantly fell in love with my other teammate. She was Asian for sure but her country of origin was a mystery to me.

"I'm glad we are on the same team," I remarked to her one early morning while we sat on the floor waiting for T. Brown to emerge from her room.

"I am, too. I just know that you and I are going to get along great. I wonder how long this training is going to be. Not that I have anywhere to go." She drew her perfect brows together in puzzlement.

"Me, too. I wish they'd told us. It's like they always keep us guessing what we are going to do next. Everything is so unpredictable."

"Quiet, you two," Pilly snapped but didn't turn toward us. She sat on the other side of the Asian girl.

"And that is why I call her 'Pilly,'" I whispered in my teammate's ear.

"I don't get it," she said turning toward me.

"Doesn't she always look like she's chewed on the nastiest pill ever?"

When she burst out in giggles it was hard not to laugh along with her. From that moment on, I deemed her "Giggles," which fit more than "Asian girl."

T. Brown was in front of us in an instant. "So you like fooling around? I'll show you what we do to those who think that this is a game. Push!"

My arms ached so badly from the countless push-ups T. Brown made us do for "fooling around." All this was even before the morning meal, for which Giggles and I were late.

After breakfast, we stood by our foot lockers in our "B" uniforms that were nothing more than a pair of black tights and a matching sports bra, which I considered undergarments. I really hoped the training wasn't out-side this morning because of the cold, and I certainly wasn't used to being in the snow in May. In fact, this was the first time I'd seen snow.

T. Brown led the group up the second floor of our building to a room covered in mirrors. The room was almost empty, devoid of furniture ex-cept for narrow poles that went from the wood floors to concrete ceil-ing. Speakers were mounted in each of the four corners; a tower podium housed a wireless radio, where a tall instructor stood with her hands on her hips. There seemed to be no shortage of trainers over five feet ten-inches. She was dressed as we were except her underwear was gray, which matched nicely with her steel-gray eyes. Her face was beautiful – again, no shortage there – yet she bore a large, angry scar that went from the side of her cheek down to her neck and finally hid under her bra.

"Each of you, stand by a pole," she said pleasantly, in contrast to yell-ing at us as we were accustomed to. "I'm T. Rayes, and I'm going to teach you the art of exotic dancing. But first we are going to stretch. Reach down and touch your toes." As we followed her instructions, she walked us through a series of stretches that even my high school gym teacher wouldn't understand. Some were odd, pulling muscles I didn't know I had; others were downright embarrassing, making me thankful that we all had to do it in unison and no one was looking at my big butt in the air.

"Can anyone tell me what exotic dancing is?" T. Rayes asked after the stretching was completed. "You may answer."

"It's stripping," a girl said with a heavy accent. "I used to dance to make extra money sometimes."

"Yeah! You can make good tips," another added.

"While that may be true, exotic dancing is a way to control and entice. There will be times in the field where you will be asked to dance to entertain men while business is discussed. This is a safer alternative to other riskier jobs you may be forced to perform. While you're dancing, you can control your body, your movements, all of which controls your audience to follow you with their eyes. When you dance, you'll have the control, and they will not be able to touch you. It will be the only platform that you will be able to express yourself while in the field. It will be your refuge. While your hips sway..." T. Rayes undulated her hips, her hand following the gentle motion. "...your audience will be drawn to you, and so will your enemy. It is a distraction that can provide valuable time in the field. Now let us begin."

While a collage of international music floated from the sound system, we attempted to follow the dance instructions. But even those who had done it before had trouble keeping up. All benefited from T. Rayes' excellent tutelage. Thankfully, I wasn't the only one who fell, but I won the record for four, of which she kindly reminded me. She had us work out on the pole, which was a lot harder than it looked, and had me saturated in sweat before our first break. It was not just a dance training but strength training, and built up muscles needed for "the field." After three hours of an intense workout, T. Brown collected us and returned us to our floor to shower and get ready for our next training session.

"Follow me," T. Brown said to me only as she turned on her heel.

"Yes, madam," I murmured following her out into the foyer. She took me to a section of the facility that I'd never seen and used her code to open another door. When T. Brown stepped aside, I walked into the room full of computers, and hesitated when I saw who waited for me inside.

Standing in front of a massive screen on the far wall was John Lee. Dressed in a navy-blue suit and black shoes, he stood taller than I'd remembered. His jacket opened, showcasing his pressed shirt; one hand was in his pocket while the other was behind his back. Baba always said to never trust a man who hid his hands from you. Immediately, I stood on alert.

"Well, hello there, Matika," John Lee said as the door was shut behind me.

I glanced around the room to confirm that we were alone. Save for the huge screen that was filled with red and purple dots on a world map backdrop, it was only the two of us. The only sound was its low beeping.

"Hi, John," I said closing the distance between us.

"It seems as though you are doing quite well with your training. That doesn't surprise me. All the recruits that I select fare very well in the field."

"Excuse me. I'm not trying to sound ungrateful, but why did you choose me?" I just had to know. Of all the girls he could have come across, why did he choose me?

"For one, you are street smart and intelligent–"

"A dime a dozen, John. Now, I'd appreciate you being honest with me." I fought the urge to cross my arms. I didn't want to be rude when I was the one requesting information.

"See what I mean?" He let out a solid laugh and removed his hand from his pocket. The other remained behind his back. "You, my dear, are fluent in several African languages, including some difficult tribal ones. And recently, over the last year, there has been surge of missing girls taken from the African communities in the States. San Diego seems to be an easy target due to its proximity to the border. They make their way to Europe, which is another story in itself. Many of these missing girls go unreported."

John was right about that. Many African immigrants didn't report crimes, let alone missing girls. They never wanted to bring negative attention to the family, not to mention get American officials involved. They would even go so far as to lie to avoid that situation.

"Well, it's not like I know all the Africans. Maybe just the ones in my neighborhood."

"True, but perhaps you know some of these women." The hand behind his back held a white folder that he offered to me. "We need to find common connections to identify the trafficker. Take a look."

I opened the folder and headed to the nearest desk. There were dozens of pictures of women of all ages, taken at various locations. Most seemed to be taken in the field while others seemed to be pictures from their families. My heart went out to each and every one of them, and I was nearly in tears by the time my eyes scanned a familiar face.

"I know this one. Her name is Ashaya. She lived a few blocks away from me." I pulled out a picture that was coded with a letter and number combination, and handed it to him.

"I figured you would," he said, not looking at Ashaya's picture but at me instead.

I continued to look very carefully and was able to identify two others. Then my heart jolted in my chest. It couldn't be. Right before my eyes was a picture of Suda. It was clearly taken in the field as she was dressed in the skimpy clothes like the American girls that she despised so much.

"My God! Suda," I gasped, dropping her photo to the floor. I stood up quickly as if the chair had burst into flames. "Where is she?!" I pointed an accusing finger at John throwing all training to the wind.

"I take it that you know her," he said coolly, studying my reaction.

"Like you don't know? What games do you guys play here? I'm leaving. I quit! I'd rather live in the streets than stay here another day." I ran over to the door and naturally found it locked, which made me even angrier.

"Matika, you know that we had nothing to do with her being missing. Yes, I admit that I knew she was your sister. I know everything about you and your family because it's my job to know."

"Why didn't you tell me?" It was only pride that held back the tears that threatened to breach the surface.

"According to our sources, she went missing the day that we met."

He was right. I hated him for it. I remembered that dreadful day and I knew that I needed to tell him what I knew.

"Yes," I confirmed with a slight nod of my head. I told him everything about the two men I'd seen in the car that day. It wasn't much, but John seemed to appreciate the information.

"I want you to know that my team will do everything in its power to find her."

"No, not your team. I need to be the one to find my sister and I will accept nothing less." I crossed my arms and waited for him to deny me.

"You must understand that she's been missing for several months now. This is what we call a cold case. It could take months or even years to locate her. Besides, I cannot authorize you to be on the team until you've completed your training."

"John, if I'm not on this case then I quit. There is no way that I can continue this knowing that she's out there."

He seemed to contemplate my decision and then he finally nodded. "You complete training, and I'll make it happen. I will see what we can do to expedite things."

As soon as he spoke those words, T. Brown came and got me. Her timing was impeccable.

# CHAPTER 21

Training became more extreme and focused on softening techniques, which temporarily disables an individual, and killing techniques. I couldn't believe the number of ways you could kill someone with just your bare hands and body weight. I wish I would have known this when I was being chased by the colonel. I worked as hard as I could every day knowing that Suda counted on me.

We trained in dance, language studies, hand-to hand-combat, short and long range shooting, surveillance, physical fitness, psychological corrosion and manipulation, and submission. The training was drilled into every aspect of our very existence.

The weeks flew by, followed by months. T. Brown would wake us randomly during the night for what Giggles would call "mind-training." She said, "You must always be vigilant, even while you sleep." Pilly was a light sleeper and would wake us before T. Brown. The idea was to have your team alert, dressed, and ready to go before the others. The Orange team, which never slept, was always first and our Pink team was a lucky second. It didn't matter as long as we weren't last, like the Blue team that had to do push-ups in the middle of the night.

"Everyone up," T. Brown said prying us from much-needed sleep for the third time that night.

We scurried out of bed and stood by our bunks. The dorm was cold, and the lack of windows made it impossible to determine the time of day. But I felt as if we'd just gone to sleep from the second rude awakening.

Goose bumps covered my skin as I waited for our next order, hoping it would be quick before the warmth left my bed.

"Take off your clothes," T. Brown ordered.

I exchanged a brief glance with Giggles, who was as uncomfortable as I was. We had been ordered to do many things, but never this. Not sure what test this was going to be, I followed the others and pulled off my T-shirt, followed by the tights. Some of the girls slept in their bras, which I could never do because to me bras were confining. So there I stood in my underwear and no bra, while my nipples made a stunning appearance to greet the cold air.

"All of them!"

Again we complied. Her tone allowed no room for argument.

"You must be comfortable in your body, because many, many will see it," T. Brown said just as several men entered the sleeping quarters.

Some of the girls gasped in shock and proceeded to cover themselves with their hands as others looked down at their feet. I followed Pilly's lead from the corner of my eye, knowing that she always did what pleased the T's, and stood my ground, looked straight ahead, and observed the new entrants.

"Don't move," T. Brown said spraying cold water with a water gun in the faces of the girls who foolishly covered their breasts and private areas. "You must get used to being looked at by the opposite sex. Failure is not an option."

The men came forward, spreading out to cover the first girls in the row. Each wore a pair of latex rubber gloves. When one came up to me, he first touched my head, and moved it from side to side. He lifted my arms before he let them fall to the sides. Placing his hands underneath my breasts, he tested their weight. Since everyone had been touched in this manner, systematically, as if scripted, I knew it was only another test so it didn't bother me like it did some of the others.

The men didn't stay long, leaving as quickly as they had entered, after which we were permitted to get dressed and go back to our beds.

Thankfully, our team did well. And with that thought, I fell back to sleep.

———

"Welcome to Phase II," T. Brown said loudly, and woke us up. She didn't seem to have any other voice except loud.

I was tired from being awakened all night. Giggles and I figured the only way T. Brown was able to keep up with our lack of sleep was to take naps when we were with other trainers, otherwise there was no way she could have maintained the perfect suit, hair, and makeup.

Somehow in the middle of the night, the girls from Team Blue had disappeared. How they managed to get them out without waking the rest of us was a mystery. It was unnerving to see them gone, and I believed the others felt the same as they glanced around the room with puzzled looks. With the three members from Team Blue gone, it left only seventeen of us remaining, with Green and Orange at four each, Brown at three, Yellow at three, and Pink with three.

Then they introduced an extreme hardship for me. I would say that none of us needed to lose weight; in fact, most of the girls could gain a few pounds, so I was surprised when we were deprived of our food choices.

"You must be able to operate with limited food," T. Brown said as she ate a sandwich in front of us. "There will be many days you will be hungry and you will need to work through it. The girls you will be looking for are often deprived of food as a form of punishment."

We continued our advanced weapons and self defense training, but no more did we have a smorgasbord to choose from at the cafeteria. Our breakfast consisted of a small bowl of sugarless hot cereal, lunch was limited to a grain roll and a portion of cheese, and the evening meal was some sort of watery soup. Seconds were not allowed. We were also given "supplement shots" weekly.

This wasn't the first time I'd gone to bed hungry. Back in Africa, after I'd been torn from my home in Uganda, I would count on my hand how many nights I'd slept with a full stomach. Hunger was nothing new. That was less than a year ago, but the torment of hunger still brought back painful memories of a time and place I wished I could forget.

"For the conclusion of this phase, your tolerance and ability to control narcotic substances and alcohol will be tested. It's non-habit forming, so there is nothing to fear for you former drug users. The last thing we want is for you to become addicted to anything. Group up!"

We clustered in our color team formations, as we'd been trained, and waited for direction. I bit my tongue, resisting the urge to ask what "narcotic substances" were. As the doctors entered our quarters, T. Brown assigned each group to a doctor.

"Team Brown will follow Dr. Earnest and Pink will follow Dr. Sethnoa," she concluded reading off a metal clipboard.

We followed Dr. Sethnoa to one of the study rooms, which was in the clinic where we had previously received our medical exams. Inside there was a bed with a metal frame attached to a solid concrete wall, three metal chairs bolted to the concrete floor, a television mounted in the corner, and a large mirror that took up most of the white wall. There was nothing else. I got nervous after I saw that the bathroom had only a toilet and a sink, but no door for privacy. I hoped that I didn't have to use it anytime soon. Aside from the television, the room was a prison cell without bars.

"Have a seat and take off your shoes and socks," Dr. Sethnoa said motioning to the chairs.

We each sat down on a chair without hesitation, and I chose the one closest to the door. He collected our shoes and socks, and placed them in a plastic bag that hung from his wrist.

He had to have been the strangest person I'd ever met. He had completely white, wild hair that matched his lab coat, and spectacles that rested on the tip of his nose, threatening to meet their demise on the cold concrete floor. This gave him the cartoon mad scientist look, instead of a prestigious medical doctor one. One of his hands shook, but pride glistened in his eyes as he moved around with the enthusiasm of a person completing his most valued life's work.

I was the first to receive a shot in my arm from an apparatus that looked like a futuristic needle pistol. The sudden jolt was like a blast of frozen air as it penetrated my shoulder.

# CHAPTER 22

Almost immediately, I felt the strange sensation move through my body. My mouth began to water, my vision became blurred. When I lifted my hands, they multiplied, creating an effect that was both surreal and unnerving. I struggled to think straight and looked around for the doctor, who had strangely disappeared.

Giggles laughed and crawled on all fours, going in circles as she chased her tail – I never noticed she had a tail before – while Pilly held fast to the chair, eerily swaying her multiple heads back and forth. I knew we were not supposed to speak but no one was around so maybe this was considered free time. I started to get antsy just sitting on the hard metal chair, so I tried to focus on the blank TV screen to keep from pole-vaulting through the ceiling.

Another shot to my arm was delivered by the invisible Dr. Sethnoa. He sure had a way of defying physics. Then there was that brief moment one feels before they pass out; however, I was unfortunate enough to linger in that state, forever teetering on its brink. Soon, I could no longer see my hands before me, and the antsy feeling was also gone, replaced by a heavy fog that seeped into my bones. The sounds in the room, the muffled movie, Giggles' laugh, and now Pilly's moans became white noise and indiscernible.

"Sit up straight," a man's voice broke through. He didn't shout, but his voice tore past the barrier like music, so soothing.

"Yes, sir," I wanted to say, but my mouth would not cooperate. I practically lay in the chair at this point. I attempted to shuffle my weight, but it felt like I wore a two-hundred-pound suit made of cement, and though I tried, I couldn't move.

Then I felt strong hands lift me by my waist. My vision became tunneled. I couldn't make out his blurred face, but I found my eyes trying to follow his movement. He was like an angel helping to bring me to heaven. I tried to reach out and touch him, but discovered my arms and legs were in fact, restrained. Even though I felt vulnerable yet subdued in this state, deep down inside I knew no harm would befall me.

Several moments passed, and I heard Pilly scream. Or was it me? I tried to look in that direction, but my neck wouldn't turn. Despite everything, I wanted to go to sleep. Wasn't there a bed somewhere? Yes, but only one, so I needed to get to it first. I tried to move again, but neither my arms nor legs would budge.

"You must learn how to work though the drugs and always listen. Do not lose yourself to it." That voice spoke in my ear, though the owner was not present. "You are no one, from nowhere. You are mine to own and shape however I choose. What's your name?"

"Matika," my voice said on command as my mind rose from the brink of unconsciousness.

"No, it's not."

I was struck across the face with what felt like leather straps. It didn't hurt but its sting irritated me. Again and again, the straps were rubbed against my face and neck, and I was slapped with it every time I tried to move my head away.

"You are no one. Who are you?" the voice repeated.

"I don't know." Again, I was struck multiple times, and each time stung more than the last. Again and again I was slapped across the face with the straps, each time I bit my tongue as I grew more agitated. What was I expected to say? I searched my mind for something I'd been told; anything...nothing.

"What's your name?" the voice said never breaking its calm rhythm.

"I have no name."

My hands pulled against restraints and I was struck again. My eyes stung from the tears that ran down my cheek. It was driving me crazy. There seemed to be no right way to respond. The feel of the leather straps nearly drove me insane. And my inability to move was awful.

"What is your name?" His voice was so soothing, it was a wonder that pain and annoyance could come from him. "Who are you?"

"Whoever you want me to be," I said as I finally discovered there was no other answer.

"Where are you from?" he asked coolly.

"From wherever you want me to be from," I said evenly. I began to understand and was rewarded when my hands were untied. Fighting the urge to rub my face that still stung, I waited for the voice to instruct me.

"Kneel on the floor."

I got to the floor as steadily as I could, my balance off, my eyes unfocused still. Kneeling on the cold cement floor, I sat on my ankles with my hands placed neatly in my lap, and my eyes cast down to the floor.

"Sit up straight."

"Yes, sir," I complied but was immediately slapped with the strap across the face.

"Don't speak without permission." The straps were once more rubbed against my face in a fashion that grated my nerves, and was akin to nails clawing on a chalk board. I would rather get slapped with it and be done because this was so much worse.

"Shoulders back, chin up, eyes down…" The orders were given in rapid succession. When I was finally in a position that pleased him, it stopped.

I never had bad posture as my Mama taught me to always stand up straight. "You must distinguish yourself from the common beggar on the street so you can attract a wealthy husband," she'd say. "Your father is a military general and a very successful banker. You should be proud."

Even so, my back ached from being kept ramrod straight and my head just so, all without moving a muscle. Try as I might to stay still, after some time, my body began to tremble from fatigue. Plus, my knees ached like an old lady and I could no longer feel my legs.

Giggles' yelp broke my concentration.

"Don't move," the voice said from far away. I wanted so badly to just lie on the floor but there was no reprieve. Soon, it took a massive effort to draw each breath as my chest tightened and every muscle in my body shook. I thought of everything, anything, to take my mind away, but when Chaz entered and seeped through, it scorched the giant hole that had been left in my heart.

I banished him back under lock and key, but then thoughts of my family surfaced. That was simply too painful, almost as much as the thought of Chaz who had betrayed me.

Finally, I realized I just couldn't think of the past at all. It only weakened me in my vulnerable state. Instead, I tried to remember what I needed to do for Suda.

"Lie down," came the command in a low but stern voice.

At his command, I let my body fall to the floor in the most unladylike manner. My legs were asleep, therefore gracefulness was not an option. Vaguely, I recalled being told to lie flat on my back before I drifted off to a dreamless sleep.

The toilet flushing brought me back to the present. I glanced over and saw Pilly as she dry heaved, the sound made me nauseous as well. My body was stiff as I turned on my side before sitting up, wondering how long I'd slept. Giggles was sound asleep at the far end of the room, also on her back.

Water bottles were left for us near the bed as well as nutrition bars. Groggily, I got up to retrieve a water bottle and a bar. After drinking several gulps of the water – which did nothing to sooth my cottonmouth – I took a large bite of the nutrition bar.

"I don't recommend that," Pilly said as she sat on the bed, "or you'll be hovering over the toilet like I was."

Though we were on the same team, it was the first time she had ever spoken to me.

"But, I'm so hungry," I complained like a child.

"Suit yourself," she said in her heavily accented English before stretching out on the bed with her hands behind her head. I didn't have to listen, but after I'd seen her sickness a few moments before and her pale face with nearly bloodshot eyes, I was wise enough to heed her advice. I set the bar and water aside and headed to the bathroom to get cleaned up as best as I could without a shower. When I exited the bathroom I felt much better. The cold water had lifted the final fog from my brain.

"That was crazy," Giggles said heading out of the bathroom, briskly rubbing her arms to get warm. "I can't stop shaking."

"Me, neither," I said and rubbed my sore jaws that I must have clenched in my dreams. "I wish we had blankets."

Giggles nodded in agreement as she sat down beside me. We huddled together trying to stay warm, while Pilly just ignored us, her expression unreadable. She then got off the bed and knelt on the floor where she sat and stared at the wall. Our trainer was no longer present so there was no reason for that. I really didn't understand her need to always be perfect, which irritated me because it made me and Giggles look less so. Compared to Pilly, we were an unruly and disobedient pair.

Over the next cycles the doctor kept us in a very docile state. I had very little memory of that time aside from the quick medical exams with a flashlight that shined brightly in my eyes, and the administration of medication. There were words and phrases that we were forced to repeat again and again, and every time I would try to remember them my head would ache to the point of total debilitation. I couldn't even recall when I ate or used the latrine, a total blur. One thing for sure was that my body and mind no longer felt the same. Everything was touched and explored from the inside out to the point of defilement. My thoughts felt different, like they were not my own. Incoherent phrases forever drummed in my ears. It was now hard for me to even think clearly, I no longer felt like myself. And I knew beyond a doubt that I could never leave the organization.

As the medication's effects wore off, I felt a profound sense of fatigue in mind, body, and spirit. Though I was nauseous, I didn't vomit when I hung my head over the toilet. Then, after showering, I stretched out on the floor and fell asleep for what seemed like days. I awoke to complete darkness and started to scream. I was blind.

# CHAPTER 23

"Help me! Help me!" I flailed my arms around for Giggles or Pilly. Though disoriented, I never forgot where I was and this wasn't right.

"I'm here," Giggles said heading to my voice. "They must have turned off the lights. It feels like this is never going to be over."

"I know and I feel the same way," I replied with a voice on the verge of tears. This had gone on far too long and I was ready to give up. "We can never leave our handler or this organization."

"Even if I wanted to, I have nowhere to go anyway," Giggles' voice was sad and she began to cry softly.

The tears rolled from my eyes and dropped onto Giggles' hair as I held her thin body. The regret I felt was so strong it threatened to destroy me. My decision to come here was so ill-thought-out and irrational that I wanted to kill myself a thousand times over. I missed Chaz so much it tore me apart, especially now that I knew I would never see him again. I felt so sorry for Suda....

There was nothing to do in the darkness but sleep or go crazy in the silence. Pilly was quiet the whole time. I was so bored and nothing could make the time pass any faster.

"Are you still awake?" I asked, as I tapped Giggles' shoulder where she lay beside me.

"Of course I am," she whispered back. "There is only so much sleeping I can do."

I sat up and basked in her body heat. I was taking a chance, but since we were in complete darkness, I figured that no one could see us. I couldn't imagine the trainer would walk in.

"What do you think it will be like – what do you think our handler will be like?" she asked as I settled in beside her.

"I wish I knew, but I hope he'll be nice. I'm really nervous about that. He could easily mistreat us, and there won't be anything we can do about it. No one will even know."

"You're right. And if we run away, the agency will make us disappear forever."

"Besides that, we don't exist anymore." I didn't know why but I knew it to be true, beyond a doubt. "What's your name, by the way? I think at this point I should call you something other than Giggles."

"You call me Giggles? Hmm…I guess I can see that. My name's Mei-Ling. And yes, it's Chinese. What's yours?"

"Matika. I'm from Uganda."

"Oh, that's much better than me calling you 'Big Mouth' like some of the girls do."

"What? Why would they call me that?"

"Because you talk too much," Pilly said to my utter surprise and horror. "And you always ask questions when we aren't supposed to be talking. Take now for instance." She had stealthily moved closer to us on the other side of Mei-Ling and I could feel her look directly at me in the darkness.

"She's right," Mei-Ling stifled a laugh, her body shaking with her poor efforts to control another outburst.

"I do not," I defended, challenging her. "I only seek clarification when I don't understand something. Like you can talk Mei-Ling, you're always getting in trouble with your laughing."

"I can't believe I'm stuck on a team with children. You two are going to get us killed in the field, you know," Pilly complained as she shifted. I could hear her turn her back to us as she loudly expelled the air from her lungs.

"You need to lighten up; you're always so serious," Mei-Ling said with a hint of sadness in her voice. "It's not good to always be so serious."

"What's your name?" I asked Pilly. "Since we're on the same team and have to live together indefinitely you might as well tell us."

"Why should I tell you? We'll all be dead soon."

"Fine! I guess we'll continue calling you Pilly. Yep, that name suits you well."

"Pilly! That's so immature. What does that mean anyway?" she asked.

"You know what? I don't even care what it means. I'm not here for your entertainment."

"OK, Pilly," Mei-Ling said in a singsong voice, pouring salt in her wounds.

"Oh, for goodness' sake! I can't have you imbeciles calling me that in front of our handler. If I tell you, I don't want to hear another word from you the rest of the time here."

"Agreed," we both said in unison.

"My name's Yana. And it's none of your business where I'm from."

"Now that wasn't so hard," I added, pleased at her admission.

"Not another word."

As promised, and despite my need to scream and bounce off the walls, I didn't speak for the rest of the time. It may have been few hours or a few days that we spent in utter darkness. I was famished, and when the light finally came back on it nearly blinded me. Soon after a quick beep sounded, the door was opened.

"All right, Pink Team, get up and group up," T. Brown's voice was a welcome homage. "Congratulations, you have made it out of Phase II. Now it's time to recover for your final segment."

I wanted to hug T. Brown in relief. I eagerly stood up, ready to go instead. If I never had to see that room again, it would be much too soon. We followed T. Brown back to our old living quarters. The squad bay was a five-star hotel in comparison to where I'd just been, and I would never complain about it – not that I ever did, anyway.

The Yellow Team of three was missing. With the Blue Team now gone, it meant that at least one more team would be eliminated before we were done. The teams were eradicated one at a time, and each looked far worse than the last. T. Brown had said that it was team cohesion that was important in our mission because we would always be with the team for our protection as well as the safety of our handler.

"Get cleaned up and prepare for lunch at the top of the hour," T. Brown said absently before turning to speak to T. Rayes. She hadn't yelled, so maybe she had a small amount of sympathy for us.

The idea of a shower was a luxury at this point. My body slumped, and standing under a hot water spray would take away some of the aches and pains in my joints and muscles. I quickly gathered my clothes and headed for the bathroom.

We were given the rest of the afternoon to square ourselves away, clean the layer of dust that had collected in the squad bay in our absence, and finally rest up for training the next day. I used my time to rebraid my hair because it had grown out several inches in the roots. For the first time in months I looked at myself in the mirror, and didn't recognize the haunted look in my eyes that was one of shame and fear. A seed had been planted deep in me that took root and spread like weeds.

"I just don't get it, Mei-Ling," I said in puzzlement. "This place is changing me into someone I don't like. We are supposed to be a gatherer of intelligence, the eyes and ears of our agent, a protector and, when necessary, a killer. I have no problem with any of that. In fact, I feel empowered. I could have used these skills in the past. But what gets me is that they also want me to be submissive to our agent – to be a sexual being that only lives to serve him in all things and nothing short of worshipping the ground he walks on."

"It's confusing," Mei-Ling said as she brushed her hair. "We are like creatures that only live to please and provide pleasure in forms of erotic dance, drugs, and – without being told directly, from what I recall – possibly sex, who is to do everything she told us and nothing less. The contradiction is dizzying and would be impossible to distinguish between a submissive and a killer."

I could die a thousand times inside doing everything that was required of me, but I could not let that girl inside me perish. At that moment I made a vow to always remember who I was and who I would always be…Matika. I was here for Suda.

That night, I slept soundly in my soft bed, under the warm covers that cocooned around me. Though I'd gone to bed very early, I could have slept for days if they'd let me. Unfortunately, at a quarter to five, T. Brown woke us. As usual, she was dressed impeccably, complete with runway makeup, heels, and not a hair out of place. The women in the magazines that Suda liked so much had nothing on T. Brown. T. Rayes stood beside her in all her splendor as well. It was unusual for her to be present at this hour.

After we ate breakfast, we were taken to what I would only term as beautification training. I supposed that being submissive and seductive was one thing, but being beautiful was an art in itself when it came to hair and makeup.

"If you don't look good, it doesn't matter how you act because your enemy will not take the bait," T. Rayes said with a flourish of her hand. "You can't have chipped nails, hairy legs, and a unibrow."

Giggles burst out laughing, which got me laughing, and ended up with us both on the floor doing pushups for the next fifteen minutes while the others began their hair and makeup details. It was fun once we got started; I had access to hundreds of hair and makeup products which truly over-whelmed me, and I didn't know where to start.

"You look like a drag queen," T. Brown said to Pilly, who managed not to change her expression.

I'd never heard the term before but knew it wasn't good when Giggles stiffened in an attempt to hold another outburst at bay, which would only lead us both to nothing but trouble…again. Pilly had the bangs of her long blonde hair stiff as a board, fanning around her head like a peacock. Although most girls sported the "wave" in one form or another; she'd managed to make hers higher than the rest and included the sides as well, and used a whole can of hairspray at the very least. Her makeup was heavy, the dark lipstick in a deep red hue, almost black, contrasted despairingly with her pale creamy skin. The blue glittery eye shadow and clumpy coat of mascara made her hazel eyes stand out. To her credit, she did a whole lot better than the girl with the shoulder-length black hair that painted in her eyebrows, which made her look like she was headed for a surprise party.

Not a single one of us completed our hair and makeup to T. Brown's satisfaction, and while Giggles had drawn an extra eye with the eyeliner, I was told that I didn't put enough on and looked the same as I did when I'd started, so my technique to keep it simple with natural colors simply wasn't enough.

"Makeup must complement you, not have you looking like a whore or a common prostitute that anyone could have off a street corner. You must present yourself as kept ladies, which will ensure that you are above the fray of just a common sex slave."

T. Rayes showed us the proper way of application, and then we were coached individually to assist with our unique needs. After our makeup was applied to perfection and our hair done, T. Brown took photos of each of us. I was disappointed because we didn't get to see them.

"Ladies, you have come a long way to get this far," T. Brown began after breakfast the next day, uncharacteristically positive, "but you are not done yet. This final phase will be the most difficult. You will need to rely on all the training you have gotten so far in order to succeed. From here on out, your agent will be with you. How well your team works with each other as well as your agent will determine if you make it to assignment. I would urge you to all do your best because there is no place for failures in this organization."

As surprised as any of the girls, I glanced over at Mei-Ling to my right. She shook from head to toe, and I found myself doing the same. Her large almond eyes grew rounded in her fright. Yana's eyes were trained ahead and never wavered.

"There are women and girls out there that are depending on you to succeed. You may have to do something you don't want to do, but remember it is only your role, not your life. And most importantly, remember your training. You are a team for a reason. Give strength to one another so you can succeed together. It was a pleasure working with all of you and I wish you the best of luck," T. Rayes said with a hint of sadness in her voice that belied her expression.

"Group up and assume position, now. The agents will be here at five sharp."

Fighting the urge to ask some of the hundreds of questions that floated through my head, I bit my tongue and got in position. Mei-Ling nestled as close to me as she could get, her warm thigh touching mine. Quickly I reached over and gave her leg a reassuring squeeze before I placed my hands stiffly in my lap as I knelt with my back straight, head down, eyes to the floor.

I wondered where we were going and for how long. Then I realized that it didn't matter. This was going to be our new life, one full of uncertainty, living day by day. And we wouldn't return to this room or see T. Brown or T. Rayes again. At five o'clock sharp the door was opened and a group of men strutted in.

# CHAPTER 24

I lifted my head quickly and stole a look at the men. Each wore tailored pants and shiny dress shoes that clicked like rain on a tin roof as they entered our dwelling. All wore buttoned-up shirts but were tieless. They were grouped two by two, one white shirt and the other in trainer blue. The men in trainer blues sported buzz cuts and were clean shaven, while the others had longer hair of various lengths from just below the ears to long hair pulled into ponytails, and facial hair from goatees to mustaches to long beards. These men looked menacing and deadly, unlike the clean-cut trainers.

One of the white shirts had a visible tattoo that ran from his left cheek down his neck to beneath the collar of his shirt. He was so big and dwarfed the others with wide shoulders and muscled arms that couldn't be hidden by any shirt. With a goatee around his square jaw, and a lip that was actually pierced, he looked much more than lethal. I prayed that he wasn't our handler.

Commandingly, they approached the groups. I dared not look up again, then two pairs of shoes were placed in front of me. One had feet the size of my forearm to hand, completely massive. Fighting the urge to rub my cold, trembling arms, I felt naked in my yoga pants and tight-fitted tank I'd slept in.

"Blindfold them." The order presumably came from the blue shirt. He was our trainer from the cell. I would recognize his voice, a gentle yet authoritarian tone, in my sleep.

A cloth was tied snugly over my eyes. After another few minutes my team was led away through a series of corridors that echoed with the men's shoes, unlike our tennis shoes that barely made a sound. Mei-Ling, who walked too close behind me, gave me a flat tire when she stepped on the back of my shoe, causing my heel to disengage, sending me colliding into the solid wall of the man in front of me. He was as still as a statue while I hit the ground with a solid thump.

"You clumsy fool!" A baritone voice boomed with a slight Southern accent.

Not our trainer. I recognized the accent from my teacher at the refugee camp in Kenya. He too had a similar accent, though much more pronounced.

"I-I'm sorry. It was an accident," I stammered and tried to get my feet, but I was hopelessly disoriented.

"Be mindful. They can't see," a trainer said to calm the other man. With his strong hands he held onto my shoulder for me to right my foot in the shoe.

With the tight confines of the small area coupled with our subsequent ascent, I assumed that we had taken an elevator ride. Soon, after a few more corridors, we exited the building as a blast of hot – albeit fresh – air stopped me in my tracks.

"Keep walking," the baritone said pushing me forward, his accent now undetectable.

We got in the back of a vehicle. After about thirty minutes, the van or truck slowed down just before I began to get really carsick. I was never one for bumpy roads, which was a curse in my home country if you ever wanted to travel anywhere and not walk. As it was, between the nerves and the roller coaster ride, my stomach bile was only moments away from greeting us all, which would enrage our handler. I certainly didn't need any help in that area as he'd already reprimanded me twice and we hadn't even made it to our destination.

The vehicle suddenly stopped, slamming us forward. The engine was killed, the silence deafening. I waited for the door to open. This was it. After this point, we were going to be with our handler from this day forward, assuming we made it through this experience. The door was unlocked and thrown open, letting the warm air and soft breeze inside.

"Boy, it sure is hot out here," said the man with the country twang.

Our trainer helped us out of the van, and we were led inside. My blindfold was unceremoniously pulled off. It took a moment for my eyes to adjust to the brightness. A house? We were in the main room of a small, sparsely furnished cabin. There was a dark-brown couch with red pillows against the far wall, a cherry-wood end table, and a matching bookcase full of encyclopedias that had identical book jackets of gray with red borders. Two doors were straight ahead, which I assumed must be the bedroom and bathroom, and a kitchen to the left that housed a small table and four chairs.

"Now listen to me," the trainer began promptly. "You have been prepared well. Listen to your agent's commands carefully. Now get into position."

I felt strange as I focused on him for the first time. I'd never seen him while fully alert. Though he had a kind and expressive face, there was no real emotion displayed that I could feel. However, like the other trainers, he took pride in his work and only wanted what was best for us. And, successful performance was a direct reflection on him and his tutelage.

Our agent was supposed to be the same. If we didn't work well together convincingly, we would all fail. Failure was not an option. Suda needed me. They would take no risk with a dysfunctional team. In the field, our lives would depend on how well we worked together. Our agent was a veteran in espionage so he didn't have as much to lose. He would undoubtedly be reassigned to another mission, or perhaps be recycled and receive another set of girls. It wasn't clear what would happen to us. They kept that part a mystery, another layer of secrecy that was the story of our lives.

In position, we faced the closed doors as our trainer exited the cabin. The agent was still outside as well. Our trainer spoke with him, but I failed make out their words. Then the van's engine roared to life before pulling away just as our handler pranced through the door, dropping three heavy green duffel bags near the entrance, vibrating the hickory floor boards.

"I'm about to tell you how this is going to go," he said. "Now all of you stand up."

Without hesitation I attempted to stand up but stumbled over my feet that had gone numb like the rest of my body. It was him.

# CHAPTER 25

Of all the bad luck I could have had, this was surely the worst. It could have been any of the others but nooo…it had to be the meanest and scariest of them all. His evilness leapt off his deeply tanned skin like invisible flames that heated my body with his mere presence. His lip wasn't the only thing pierced. Silver rings ran across his eyebrows and up his ears. And that tattoo…

"You are as clumsy as they come," he said with smirk that was more like a sneer. His facial tattoo, which resembled a part of a reptile, was creepy. Although there were no such things as black eyes, his were the exception. His long lashes did nothing to soften those obsidian pools that bore into my soul, and completely contrasted his handsome, yet rugged, facial features.

"I-I'm sorry," I said stumbling over my words. I stood up on shaky legs, lowered my eyes to the ground, slumped my shoulders in defeat, praying for a way to dissolve into the floor.

"Did I say you can speak?"

"No, sir," I croaked breathlessly.

"Then be quiet," he said in exasperation, throwing his hands up and shaking his head, which made his wavy locks sway. He barely contained his temper that was sure to explode before the day was out.

I winced at his words, but made a mental note that when he was angry he had a Southern accent. At this rate I wasn't going to make it the rest of the day, let alone the week.

"Now, your job is to do as I say without any hesitation. And, you only speak if I say you can speak." He directed his last comment to me. "Now you, clumsy girl, make me some food. You two unpack the bags and don't touch the black metal box."

Without hesitation Yana and Mei-Ling began to drag the duffel bags, which were too heavy to carry, to the room. I, on the other hand, was in a dilemma. I didn't cook very well. At all.

"Sir, may I speak?" I asked in apprehension at his brows that drew together. He was so much taller than I thought. I would have to crane my neck to look up at him. Not that I wanted to anyway.

"It seems you are already speaking but no, you may not. You can call me Reid, by the way."

"How am I supposed to ask permission to speak without talking?" I countered. He was impossible.

"I'll fix you," he said as he reached for me roughly and pulled me around so my back was against his massive build. Shuffling around in his pocket, he produced a blindfold that he tied it tightly around my mouth. "Make some food, woman," was all he said as he pushed me toward the kitchen before he sat on the couch and watched me intently, as if he dared me to disobey him.

I got to work but noticed that there were padlocks on all the cabinets and the refrigerator. Luckily, none were locked. The refrigerator was completely stocked with an assortment of fresh food. I took out one of the cartons of eggs, and some milk and cheese. With the loaf of sourdough bread in the small pantry, I would make some toast and eggs. That seemed easy enough.

There was no toaster, so I put the bread in the oven and set the temperature to broil. Although I managed to take out all the egg shells, unfortunately I forgot to add butter to the bottom of the pan so they clung to it, creating a burnt outer layer that looked unappetizing. It took me quite a while to scrape all the eggs off the pan and put them on the plate. I thought to make coffee but after I fumbled and spilled the coffee tin on the floor, I changed course. While I poured a tall glass of milk I noticed a faint burning smell. I realized I'd forgotten the toast. Once I had scraped the top two layers I added it to the plate as well, setting it and the milk on the table.

I waited by the table for long minutes and didn't say a word as he looked at me expectantly.

Finally, he rose from the couch and walked slowly over to me. "I suppose I have to get up myself, seeing as I don't like cold food. Let's see what we have here." He sat down at the table, the chair squeaking under his solid weight. "Looks good. Burnt toast and eggs are my favorite." Sarcasm dripped from his voice. He took a huge gulp of his milk before he tore into the food. To my surprise, he ate. He was a big man and required lots of food to maintain his build. When the agent got up, he headed for the pantry and handed me three cereals bars. "Take that to the others."

Before I was off, his large hand wrapped around my wrist, stopping me. And, without another word he took off my gag. I bit my tongue to keep from saying "thank you," and went to the room.

Yana and Mei-Ling had just finished the unpacking when I entered. The room was large, slightly bigger than the living room, and featured a king-size bed with a floral-print blanket and oversized pillows, two narrow dressers, and a large coffee table that was better suited for the living room. Like the rest of the house, the furniture was cherry wood, very solid. There were two floor lamps on each side of the bed and nothing more except for a small door that I assumed was a walk-in closet. With no bed for us, it was safe to assume that we would be sleeping on the hardwood floors.

"Are you okay?" Mei-Ling asked as she came over to me. "I think you make him angry."

"See what I mean," Yana added, "you talk too much."

"You're right about that," I said rolling my eyes to the ceiling in defeat. "Breakfast is served."

As we ate the cereal bars in silence, I couldn't help but wonder how I was ever going to make it through this phase. Instead of feeling bad about myself, I explored the room. Checking the closet door, I noticed it was locked. It could have been a water heater inside. Next, I looked through the dressers to see what was packed for us. Everything was ultra-short, tight, or see-through. At least it was warm and humid outside so we wouldn't freeze to death. There was no underwear in the drawer that

I could see. This was clearly a mistake. The other dresser had his clothes, toiletries, and a backpack that was locked. What caught my attention was heavy black metal box on the floor. I crouched down over it.

"He said not to touch it," Yana said in a hushed tone. "You shouldn't be nosy."

Mei-Ling came over as well, her almond eyes large with curiosity. She pushed back a lock of her hair that had gotten in her face and crouched down as well.

"I'm not," I said observing that it was locked and required a combination to open it anyway. "I just wonder what's inside." I attempted to lift it but it was much too heavy.

"Don't even bother. Yana and I had to drag it over here together." All of us were a little uncomfortable at the use of her name.

"It's probably weapons," I said to break the tension.

"What's going on?" the agent's voice came from behind, startling us all.

His voice sent chills down my spine, causing me to straighten my back.

"I was just helping them move the box out of the way," I lied smoothly and didn't miss a beat.

"I said not to touch it."

"That's what they told me, and I didn't. That's why I couldn't move it."

Wow! I was starting to even convince myself of this tale, though he didn't seem persuaded with his raised eyebrow.

"Get down," he commanded with his hand on his hips.

We knelt down before him in submission.

"I'm going to go over the rules of the house and any house we enter. Hold your questions to the end. Understood?"

"Yes, sir," we said in unison.

"This room, our private bedroom, will be the only place where you may speak freely to one another, but quietly. Any conversation or discussion will not leave this room, ever. Speaking freely doesn't mean acting freely. All intel will be shared here." I followed his gaze to the bed that now loomed before me.

"Why there?" The question shot from my mouth before I could stop it.

"How hard is it to hold your questions to the end? Do I need to gag you again?"

"No, sir, I was just afraid that I would forget my question."

"If you would let me finish then you would have the answers. In the bed is the only safe place that a submissive can share intelligence. No one would suspect anything there. We'll be close enough to not be overheard. Also, if you have an extremely urgent issue, you will bite your lower lip. These are subtle signs that will not be detected. I'll do what I can to get you in a secured location as soon as possible."

He smiled with his eyes letting me know that he enjoyed this way too much. We also learned that if we had information that couldn't wait until we were in the room or safe place, he would give us permission to kiss his hand in acknowledgement and at that point would make an effort to give us an opportunity to divulge it.

There was a major problem with all of this. First, the thought of being in the same bed with him frightened me. I didn't even feel comfortable with him in the same room, let alone share such an intimate setting – a bed no less. Second, kissing his hand was out of the question for me. Put my lips on his tawny skin…I lost my breath as I just imagined it.

"Are you listening?" he asked me sternly, deliberately enunciating his words.

"Yes, sir," Mei-Ling and I said together. We must have both lost focus for a moment.

"As you have already guessed, our weapons are in that black box there, which will be kept beside the bed. While we are in the field, you will all carry tactical poison pens, pepper spray, and other undetectable weapons. This is the only protection permitted by a submissive. However, during social events and extreme situations, I'll need backup. You'll carry guns then, which you'll strap to the inside of your thigh. We'll also be provided with special weapons when we are in the field."

"Why–"

"Before you ask," he interrupted, holding up his hand, "no one would ever give a weapon to a sex slave. In the field there will be plenty of men groping you and could easily discover it if you have a fully loaded gun. That would blow our cover and jeopardize the mission. I will be the only one with the combination code to the weapons box. In the event of a kill zone, we will all be armed and there will be no survivors, so we shoot to kill. We leave no one, armed or unarmed. Understood?"

"Yes, sir." It was much more quietly uttered than before. This would soon be very real for us.

"You don't have to call me 'sir' in this room. Now, moving on to the more domestic rules, which are equally as important for believability. You'll not be allowed in the kitchen unless I tell you. I'll be preparing all the meals from now on. All cabinets have been secured. I'm the only one with the key to the padlocks, so don't bother snooping around there, either. You'll do all the cleaning and clothes washing. There's a stackable washer and dryer in the bathroom, which will also remain locked at all times. I don't care if you're taking a shit, no doors will be closed in this house unless I've instructed you to do so. Lastly, cameras are everywhere, so don't think you can get around any of the rules we've gone over. I don't fail at anything, so do as I say for your sake, and we can get our assignments done, 'cause I'm itchin' to get back in the field."

There was that Southern drawl again. He went over to the black box, and punched in a code before it clicked open. "These aren't live bullets, but they hurt like hell." He loaded one of the three guns with the rubber-like bullets. In the box were a stun gun, flares, metal bars, and two small red boxes of hypodermic needles. I couldn't hide the *what the hell* look on my face, but luckily he hadn't noticed.

He put the loaded gun in a holster at the small of his back, shut the weapons box with a click, and looked satisfied. He ran a hand through his long dark waves before he turned back to us. "Let's see what you can do. Get dressed in something more decent and make it quick."

He didn't close the door but had the decency to leave so we could change in privacy. Yana was the first to head to the drawer without hesitation, and picked out similar outfits for each of us. The halter top and miniskirt were as narrow as the width of toilet paper, and didn't cover my ass. Though I was much thinner than I'd liked, my butt and breasts were still quite full.

"Take off your panties," Yana hissed at me. "You look silly with them on, and you're going to get us in trouble."

"Why do we have to wear this, anyway? Just because you picked it out doesn't mean we have to wear it."

"I assure you that it doesn't get better than this."

I pushed my way past her and rummaged through the drawer, only to discover that she was indeed right. There wasn't anything more decent. Baba would have a heart attack if he saw me now. The thought of Baba riggered a massive migraine, and I doubled over in pain.

"Are you all right?" Mei-Ling asked with concern. She bent to put her hand on my back, and rubbed it gently.

"I'll be fine," I said closing my eyes as I fought to stave off the painful assault. "You two go ahead. I'll be there in a minute."

"Ok, but hurry if you can." She followed Yana out the door, and left me alone.

With my pounding head, I made my way to the bed, and lay at the foot end. I couldn't remember the last time I had a headache, but this had to be the worst by a mile. It wasn't normal and I hoped nothing was wrong with me.

I felt his presence before I heard his voice. "You think this is a game?" the agent asked sarcastically with an underlying anger seething from his voice.

# CHAPTER 26

I tried to get up but couldn't move without causing excruciating pain in the uppermost region of my skull down to my forehead. The world became more disoriented as the room began to spin.

"No, sir," I managed. "My head…" I couldn't finish.

"You need to stop thinking about the past." He headed for the box, opened it, and rummaged through its contents.

A long syringe was at his eye level, glistening as a sample of its liquids slid down the metal tip. "Matika, I got something that will make you forget."

"No, please, I'll be fine. How did you know my name?"

"I know enough about all of you, rest assured. Now trust me, it will only get worse and I can't have you being our weak link."

With a small pinch, cold venom was dispatched into a vein in my forearm. It effects began quickly as the fluids raced through the gridline of my body's map. It numbed all over psychologically, yet I was in tune with my body. The pain in my head was completely gone. I couldn't remember why it had even started but it didn't matter now. It felt great; I felt great.

"We have a job to do, so you need to get it together."

"Yes, sir." I sat up on bed, stood up, and followed him out of the room. My world felt different and so good. I loved this feeling. Like I was present but not really here, an out-of-body experience, yet in the body at the same time.

I was on top of the world. I listened to my handler's commands and didn't make a single mistake. Even when I knelt for what seemed like hours,

I never wavered. When I thought to get embarrassed when ordered to dance, I let my mind go, my audience completely forgotten. My handler's crude language and insults fell on deaf ears. I moved my body, swayed my hips magically with more seduction than I even knew I had, using a combination of rhythm from my homeland of Africa coupled with what I learned in training to create a dance unique to me and me alone.

At nightfall we were given a reprieve to shower and get ready for bed. And, for our good performance, our handler made us food to eat at the table. It was a simple meal of frozen lasagna and salad. I was ravenous since I'd had nothing since this morning's breakfast bar. I felt drained, and was beyond exhausted.

"Go to bed," the agent said from the couch he was perched on as he watched us eat.

In the room, the blankets were set out to the right of the bed, closest to the door. We settled in, with Mei-Ling in the middle as always, a human barrier between Yana and me. My relationship with Yana was cool at best and not in the hip sense. She saw me as a weak link in our team because she perceived me as a challenger to all authority. She looked to be the oldest among us, she assumed the role of a leader, the more responsible and reliable member.

"Matika, you danced amazing tonight. I didn't think you could dance like that," Mei-Ling said turning toward me.

"Me, neither. I'm so tired," I said with a yawn. "Goodnight, Mei-Ling."

"If we can perform like we did today every day, then we will pass this for sure. It's only going to get easier for us."

"Quiet, you two," Yana interjected. "And sleep with one eye open."

That was one night I couldn't oblige. My sleep was dreamless and deep. The hardwood floor could have been spiked with nails, and I wouldn't have known. Nothing could arouse me from my sleep short of a kick to the ribs. When I felt a firm pinch on my shoulder though, my eyes shot open angrily.

"Aw, what was that for?" I asked noticing Yana was on an elbow and, from what I could only assume from the small amount of light that flowed from beneath the door, glaring at me.

"You were snoring and didn't respond to anything else."

"I'm sorry," I rose up to look over at the bed. It was empty.

"He hasn't been in here all night, I don't think. Go back to sleep." Yana turned over and adjusted her pillow.

"I can't now that you woke me up. Besides, I really need to use the bathroom." I had to go so badly, it was a wonder that it hadn't woken me up.

"You know we can't get up without permission so you'd better hold it until morning."

"I'll explode by morning." I grudgingly laid back down with a bladder the size of a soccer ball, so uncomfortable that I had to squeeze my legs shut to prevent an accident. My bladder felt like I'd drunk at least a gallon of water before bed. Water. Just the thought of any form of liquid was a big mistake.

The rhythm of Yana's breaths signaled that she was asleep. I made a decision to make a quick trip to the bathroom because I couldn't hold it a moment longer. I got up slowly and tip-toed to the half-open door. Peering out into the darkness, I assumed that the agent was asleep, and hurried to the bathroom, shutting the door softly behind me.

I didn't turn on the light, nor did I flush the toilet when I was done to make sure I didn't wake our handler. My eyes were adjusted to the darkness. I stood at the closed door and listened. All was still quiet. The coast was clear. I opened the door to head back to the room.

Faster than I could inhale, my body was thrust back into the bathroom and slammed against the inside wall. A solid forearm pressed against my neck, choking off my airflow. The unmistakable cold barrel of a pistol was flush again my temple.

"I could have killed you," his gravel-filled voice was low, but his anger was barely contained as he continued to cut off my much-needed air supply. His hot breath teased my cheeks as his scarred face was only inches away from mine. "You would have been dead in the field."

I wasn't afraid of being shot by him. He was so strong and could have broken my neck as easily as snapping a twig if he'd wanted to. Still, he wouldn't release me though I struggled beneath his weight. Under the threat of being suffocated, I reacted the only way I knew how, bringing my knee up to his *makende* out of desperation. He let go of me then, and doubled over in pain as I did the same. We both labored for each breath.

Working to gather my composure, I scurried back to the room before he could react. There was nowhere for me to run or hide. I lay back down hid under the covers, and waited. Within a few moments, he stormed into the room and snatched the blanket off of us and, like I was a sack of grain, he scooped me up over his high shoulder.

He carried me into the living room and flung me onto the floor. "I'll teach you to never do that to me again."

"Well, you were trying to choke me to death just because I had to use the bathroom," I shot back as I stood to my feet. "What was I supposed to do?" I knew I was wrong to challenge him, and jeopardize the hundreds of hours of training, especially in this room but I held fast, and watched his eyebrows arch.

"If I wanted to kill you then, I would have done it already. Get into position."

There was nothing to say to that. He could have killed me. I was considered untraceable, erased. No one knew where I was or cared, so a grand search party, like the ones done for the young, blonde and beautiful, was not going to happen. Fighting to hide my annoyance that clearly showed in my eyes, I got into position in front of him.

"You puzzle me, and I don't like it," he said his voice deep and slow. "As it is, you have pressed most of the rules I have given you. You are openly defiant and even tried to kill me with your cooking. It's a wonder you made it this far. The worst part of it is that I can't get an assignment unless we all pass the training. That means I'm stuck because I don't fail at anything I do, and I'm certainly not about to start now."

The agent went over to the side table and produced the leather strap that sat on top of the bookshelf. His hands flexed and relaxed before they caressed the end of the strap. Then he came very close to me. I smelled the woodsy cologne and the masculine soap, and wondered when he had taken a shower and graced his body with the wonderful scent.

At that moment I admitted to myself what I had denied from the moment I first spotted him in the squad bay. My subconscious had worked overtime to show me that I was attracted to him. But...I didn't have to like him. He was not the most handsome man by any means – he was quite scary with a scar on his face, and eyes as black as the night's sky that bore into your soul. His square jaw and angular face, coupled with a nose that was on the large side, was not the look of a supermodel for sure.

But I felt his massive presence more than anything. I thought it was fear that made me tingle all over just knowing that he was under the same roof as me. It wasn't. How I wanted him to kiss me with his large sensuous mouth.

I flushed when he caught me as I looked at him and moistened my lips. I shifted my eyes in embarrassment before I lowered my head to the floor.

"Damn it," he growled as if he could sense my hunger for him. "I didn't want to have to do this at two in the morning, but you left me no choice."

Before I could even react, he struck me hard on my bottom, as if to say to never look at him like that again. I yelped in response. He had struck me harder than the trainer ever had, and the pain shocked as it sliced through me. I had little time to feel the welt that was sure to rise before he struck me yet again. I heard myself cry out as the tears slid down my cheeks. My pride was wounded. This was only the first day and things couldn't get any worse.

Without warning he threw the leather strap across the floor. Cursing, he ran a strong hand through his thick waves that were loose about his shoulders, and paced back and forth. I collapsed on the floor.

"Get up," he bit off his words before grabbing me behind the neck. "They gave me a hooker, a former druggy, and you, a freakin' runaway kid," he said coldly, and gave me a long and very insulting look.

Was Yana the hooker or the druggy, or was she both? I couldn't imagine Mei-Ling doing any of those things.

He roughly led me back to the bedroom, but instead of sending me to the floor where my warm blankets awaited me, he opened up the locked door, and propelled me into the darkness.

# CHAPTER 27

I whirled, frightened and shocked to be in an area the size of the small closet, without any racks to hang clothing, designed specifically for this purpose. I was at my wits' end. The fear of being confined in small places like this was my worst nightmare. I tried not to remember back to the time I was locked in a box while I crossed the Kenyan border. I tried to think of happy places instead when all I wanted to do was pound on the door and demand to be released.

This was enough to make me want to quit. Truly, I would give up everything if only to get out of this room. Trembling, I sat on the floor – it was strangely, carpeted – covered my ears with my hands, squeezed my eyes shut, rocked back and forth, and willed the time to pass. He could have done anything to me and it wouldn't have been worse than this. I would rather be beaten a dozen times over instead of locked away forever in darkness.

My heart seized in my chest. Gasping for air that wasn't forthcoming, I pounded my sweaty hands on the door, unable to stand it another moment. Though I had not the breath to spare, I screamed at the top of my lungs like a demon-possessed nun.

For reasons beyond my brain's comprehension, no matter what I tried to convince my mind that is was unreasonable, I knew I was going to die in this closet of asphyxiation. Everyone would forget about me and I would die. ...

When the door was finally opened, I burst forth on my hands and knees, and scampered to the agent. My head was on his bare feet, bathing them with my salty tears.

"I'm so sorry. I beg you, please don't put me back in there. I will do anything you say and will never talk back. I swear this–"

"Whoa there, little lady. You don't swear in my presence," he advised in a thick Southern drawl. He looked down at me, his brows furrowed in puzzlement as he studied me carefully.

"Yes, sir," I faltered as I made yet another mistake. I bit my tongue in penitence, tasting the metallic blood that ensued.

My team was awake, but they hadn't made a sound or changed positions for that matter. They too, like the perfect subs, didn't want to be the subject of his wrath. It was almost comical that they would even pretend to sleep through the noise.

"Luckily for you, I'm beat so I'll be doing us both a favor by letting you out, seeing as how you woke the dead anyway." With that, he stepped out of my grasp and headed to the bed.

Without hesitation, I slid under my covers on the hard floor and hid until morning. Sometime, after everything was quiet, I felt Mei-Ling hold me in my sleep. It was the most comfort I'd had in a very long time as her warm body was pressed against my back.

Two months had gone by – uneventfully – as we trained at a pistol range, exercised, and learned our life in new roles. Still traumatized from the closet fiasco, I was the perfect recruit, and even gave Yana a run for her money. I kept all my thoughts on lockdown, only focusing on the orders or tasks at hand, earning my standing and then some, which gave Reid nothing to complain about.

"Congratulations, you've completed the training," John Lee said as he came out of nowhere one night as we prepared to eat dinner. He was dressed in one of his endless supply of dark suits as if headed to a board meeting. "Now follow me, I have a car waiting for you."

"Oh, thank goodness!" Mei-Ling chimed in clapping her hands together in glee, as she cast all rules aside.

"Sir, it's an honor to meet you," Reid said extending his hand to John enthusiastically.

"Now we can find Suda," I said as I looked him directly in the eyes. I was so relieved to finally be able to go into the field and find my sister.

"Not quite," John said as we followed him to the white, windowless utility van. Another agent peered at us from the driver's seat, both hands on the wheel ready to go. Then turning around and opening the back door he said, "We have a hot trail for an urgent target. But it will be in the same location where Suda was spotted last. I'll give you instructions on the way to the safe house."

While Yana and Mei-Ling held expressions of bewilderment, Reid went with it like nothing was out of the ordinary. The only indication that showed he, too, was put off was a barely noticeable lift of his perfect brow. As he hopped into the back of the van with ease, I nearly stumbled to get my foot off the ground and into it. I sat behind Reid, who was next to John in the front row that faced the partition that protected the driver and prevented the passenger from any visual, while Yana and Mei-Ling sat beside me.

One moment we were in the middle of training for this grand mission and the next we were not. It all happened too fast. It literally made me dizzy. If I'd had food in my stomach, I would have purged its contents on the van floor before the door was closed.

For some reason, I had expected a graduation or milestone ceremony that would mark the completion of the program. Granted, it would be a private one because of the nature of our mission, but one nonetheless where we would be provided a few humble words of encouragement. A small but simple transition would have at least made this moment more real to me.

"Sir, to what do we have the pleasure of your appearance today?"

"You can call me John. I'm serving as your D.O. throughout your fieldwork for this particular caseload. I also wanted to be sure that Miss Matika was taken care of."

"What's a D.O.?" I asked quietly, bending forward to get closer to Reid's ear.

"Short for desk officer," he began and then added, "don't worry about it. You'll never see him again, anyway."

"The subject you need to locate is the daughter of a Mr. Shueler, former Navy intelligence captain, now a U.S. diplomat to Lithuania," John said as he took a gray file from the locked briefcase that rested on his lap. "She is believed to have been taken approximately forty-eight hours ago while vacationing with three friends in Ensenada, Mexico, by a well-known affiliate of a Russian sex-trafficking network. This network has many ties and is said to operate in over sixty countries. This faction has no boundaries, and its resources are unlimited, especially with the drug and arms trade. We're going to get a run for our money with this assignment."

"Where does Suda fit into any of this, Mr. Lee?" I asked, and leaned forward as far as I could. If I was any closer, I'd be resting in Reid's lap. The knowledge that I invaded his personal space gave me great pleasure. He was unsure of the relationship between John and me and therefore he couldn't say anything at the moment.

"I'm getting there, Matika," John said looking over at me. "Mr. Shueler possesses many state secrets that cannot and will not reach the Russians. It is imperative that you not fail, or we will be forced to neutralize the situation and lose the valuable intelligence that we currently have in our possession."

At that stage, I knew what "neutralize the situation" meant. If we failed, Mr. Shueler could find himself on the wrong side of the grass. There were two lives at stake here, and both depended on us.

"According to our sources, the Russians are the ones who requested to acquire the subject via the Santiago Cartel. It was through sources in the Santiago Cartel that Suda's picture was taken and later confirmed. She and many other African women have gone through this route. It's a cold lead, but it's a start. I know you are up to it and that you are well-trained."

"ID," Reid's confidence came easily as his years of experience in the field came forth.

As if on cue, John handed each of us a photo of the subject. The matte-finished photo I clutched in my hands surprised me. I don't know if I expected to see a dead body – like in those cop movies – or something equally gruesome. The word "subject" seemed so broad and impersonal to refer to the living, but this image never crossed my mind.

I held a picture of a beautiful girl who looked much younger than the nineteen years typed under the photo. With a smile that radiated to the twinkle in her doe-like eyes, her happiness was evident. The unique coppery color mix of her hair looked like she made a trip to the salon for those highlights that consisted of too many hues to be natural, though the text read "red/blonde."

With the plain light background, this looked like a quick snapshot taken for a school ID, but better than the terrible ones at school that captured my image with the worst possible expression, and in which my eyes were all but closed by the bright white flash. There were no re-dos for us. No, this girl looked like a model at a photo shoot.

"Memorize the ID, ladies. This will be last time you'll see it." The agent then handed Reid a small black phone about the size of my four fingers.

"Is that the best we got?" Reid asked sarcastically, leaning to the side to place the phone in the front pocket of his cargo pants.

I'd never seen a cell phone up close before, and the ones I saw from afar were much larger than the sleek black flip phone that folded down to half the size, and much thinner. This phone must have state-of-the-art technology not available to the public.

"Very funny, Mr. Reid Carson." John's smile was tight as he read from a passport he'd flipped opened. "Your English passport will be your primary, and there are others in case of an emergency. The team's passports are in there as well." He handed it, along with a small satchel, to Reid before he dug out three files to give to each of us girls, along with a wad of hundred-dollar bills secured with a paper clip. "Yana Staveinski…Matika Dayenda…Mei-Ling Chio. Study your names and history. If you forget anything, you better not forget how to spell your last name. That's the most important part when all else can be forgotten with trauma. That money is what you've earned so far during training. Your seven-thousand-dollar payments will be given to you in cash once a month in a bank account that we've created for you. But, you may not have the opportunity to spend it until after each assignment is complete."

Monthly! Not even in my dreams did I imagine having so much money. What would I do with it all? With my seventeenth birthday all but forgotten, I was now two years older than my faux age. The new "me" was fifteen years old from a small village outside of Beira, Mozambique. Though I had no clue how to speak Portuguese, the official language there, I was somewhat familiar with an Africana dialect used in a nearby remote village because Baba's cousins, who came to visit for three harvest moons to help clear the fields, lived there.

The good news was the fact that with so many languages spoken in Mozambique I would be able to pull it off without knowing Portuguese. Besides, according to my new identity, I was uneducated, taken from my family around the age of nine during the civil war, and sold into various houses and countries in Africa for slave labor. It was a miserable life, for which I was thankful wasn't true, but because of it, I could have easily forgotten my native language and culture.

Yana was now from Poland and Mei-Ling from Thailand. Although Yana was the only one among us who could read or write in her new language, what we each had in common was the fact that none of us supposedly spoke fluent English.

"You girls have all been together with Mr. Carson for the past year. Yana was acquired first by Mr. Carson, six years ago," he said looking back at her. "Because you best play the SS, or sex slave role, it would be the most believable." Then he turned to Mei-Ling and said, "You were acquired four years ago. And you, Matika, are certainly a work in progress. Therefore, at fifteen, and as the youngest, you've had the least amount of time and training with only nine months under your belt, so to speak. Because you were bought as a working servant, this is your first time as an SS.

"You may call the agent 'sir' or 'Mr. Carson' when others are present, and you can call him 'mud' for all I care when you're alone. The most important thing is that you stay in character all the time, at all costs. You never know when you are being watched."

"Are we flying to Mexico?" I asked as soon as he finished because no one else came forth with any questions. I was anxious to be there to look for Suda.

"As a matter of fact, you are all taking a flight to San Diego's Lindbergh Field where a car will be waiting for you at Seaport Village on Pacific Coast Highway. Everything you'll need is in that vehicle. Reid, you'll drive it across the border with the girls and head down to Ensenada. There's a deep ally, or 'green,' that will pass on some sighting information to you. Again, that profile is top secret and will be in the car as well."

Sometime after that, I tuned out, the direction of the conversation completely lost on me with more acronyms than the alphabet. I was struck with a sudden case of nerves that tore into my empty stomach. What was I thinking? This was beyond my limited knowledge and no amount of training could make it any different. I was the weakness on the team and it was hard to swallow. Not in a physical sense, by no means, because I was far stronger than Mei-Ling in pretty much everything, but in an emotional state. Sure, it could have been attributed to many things, but my age and background should have made this role easier. Besides occasional laughter with Mei-Ling, and a few questions for clarification every now and then, I was a good recruit. At least until Reid was forced into the picture. It had to do with my feelings for him. As plain as day, I knew that he could be my downfall.

"Sounds good. What's our ETA?" Reid said.

"1400, 1630, and 2100 West Coast arrival. Take care of Matika, Reid."

Just then, the van pulled up short, and the engine killed. The door was thrown open by the driver, who escorted us up the walkway of the safe house and never made eye contact. It was as if he were there but not really, his eyes constantly darted around searching for the enemy that was nowhere to be seen. This was a very nice and quiet neighborhood. What could possibly lurk in the shadows here?

Inside the enclosed screened porch of the lovely eggshell-colored house – which I discovered was in Alexandria, Virginia after I scanned an advertisement that stuck out of an overstuffed mailbox – was an older woman in her mid-sixties with snow hair and cream-colored suede skin that sat in one of two wicker chairs on the deck. She stared back at me, not in a rude way, but in a way that showed much interest and caring. As soon as Reid opened the screen door, the van disappeared as quickly as it had arrived.

"Come," the old lady said as she got out of a chair covered in dusty floral cushions. "I've made you some supper. I hope you like beef stew." She smiled wide at us before turning and hobbling into the house like old people do.

She was shorter than I expected, very short as a matter of fact, and had thin little legs that poked out from her long oversize dress like sticks from a tent.

"Shall we?" Reid said when we stood there like statues as the door that was left opened let delicious aromas escape from the confines of the house.

Silently we followed him – or more like followed our nose – past one of two living rooms to the eat-in kitchen in the rear of the old-fashioned house. Though it looked somewhat modern on the outside, similar to the others on that block, the inside was anything but. With more print than a fabric store, the furniture was full of matching colorful floral patterns. The creepy old-fashioned porcelain dolls in the two china cabinets were a scene from a horror film. All unsmiling faces stared at me, waiting for night fall to come out and kill the innocent children.

My eyes were soon drawn to the thick beef porridge being ladled from a large pot into dark ceramic bowls by the old woman's shaking hands. I was the first to plop down on one of six chairs seated around the square cherry wood table.

"Don't be shy, now." Her smile was bright, eager for conversation and company. "It's been a while since I had any visitors. About ten years, I would say."

"This looks really good," I added shortly, digging into the stew without preamble.

"Child, we always say grace before we eat in my house."

"Sorry," I added embarrassed, the blood rushing to my face.

Only when everyone took their seats did she say grace – an overly long prayer that gave thanks for the food and safety of too many people – and were we finally able to dig in.

"Are you not hungry?" Mei-Ling asked as she looked up from her bowl.

"Oh, no, that's much too filling for me right now. You'll find that as you get older you don't require as much food. Besides with the amount of flour I've put in the roux, I'd have to have three servings of fiber to get that out of me. Oh, dear…did I just say that out loud?"

Mei-Ling and I chuckled while Reid and Yana didn't crack a smile. They were ever so serious. Effortlessly, Reid mopped up the last of his stew with the freshly baked bread. Happy to serve, our hostess spooned him another helping before she headed over to the stove. The meal got even better when she pulled out a freshly baked sweet treat.

"Save some room for peach cobbler. It's my specialty." She sat it on the table leaving the oven mitten underneath it.

"I've never had cobbler before. It looks good," I said as she produced a large helping for me.

"The key is the splash of cinnamon and not too much sugar, because folks nowadays put too much sugar in everything, and, of course, our family's secret ingredient. I must say that my family has a secret ingredient for everything. That's why my mom, God rest her soul, was the best cook this side of the Mississippi. And she learned from my grandma, who was my pa's mom…"

At that point, my eyes glazed over from overeating and fatigue. Listening to the lady's voice was so soothing I nearly fell asleep at the table. It had been a long, long day.

"Ma'am," Reid said interrupting her chronicle of family cooking, "if you'd be so kind to let us get cleaned up before our departure that would be great."

"Oh, but of course," she replied standing to her feet. "Sometimes I get carried away. It's quite easy to do when you only have the television to talk to and my cat that, for the life of me, I can't seem to find. Come on, I got all your things situated in the rooms."

She led Reid to a steep staircase. "Pardon me, but I'm not up for climbing the stairs today. Everything you need is up there and should be to your liking. Turn all the way to the left for hot water, but give it a minute to travel up those rusty pipes."

Then she headed down a dark hall flanked by old black-and-white photos, with a colored one every so often that seemed out of place, showing us to a room that smelled of fresh linen and dust. She was clearly too old to do the heavy dusting, but the room was neat just the same.

"The bathroom is one door over, ladies. There are fresh towels and a lovely soap that I got from the Avon lady a few years ago. The drawers are filled with clothes, so I'm sure you can find something suitable. If you need anything, don't hesitate to ask. I'll just be in the kitchen tidying up."

After the "thank you, madams" were said, Yana was the first in the shower, followed by me, and then Mei-Ling. True to her word, the soap's fragrance was nice but clearly not designed for everyday use, as it was as strong as bathing in straight perfume. People would smell us from a mile away.

When Mei-Ling was in the shower and Yana and I were already dressed, Reid knocked on the door one time, as a quick warning before he entered the room.

"Yana, pack a few things in these bags. I don't care what you pack. Just fill the backpacks. Matika, you go see if our hostess needs any help in the kitchen. We'll be leaving here within fifteen minutes."

"Where are we headed?" I asked since I'd thought that we were going to stay here for a while yet.

"To the airport, of course. Have you already forgotten?"

Right. This all happened too fast for my liking, but I wouldn't let him see how it affected me. With my head held high and shoulders thrust back,

I squeezed through the door and only made brief eye contact with Reid as I passed, though he nearly filled the doorway with his solid frame.

As I entered the kitchen, I asked, "Can I help you with something?"

"No, I've got it," she replied as she struggled to put the large ceramic bowl in the upper cabinet.

Why was it that when you offered someone help who clearly needed it they'd say "No, thank you."? I ignored her and helped anyway, and took the bowl from her grasp. A broken hip wasn't going to happen on my watch. Although her thick-soled, cream-colored nursing shoes made her an inch taller at most, she couldn't have been more than four feet, ten inches in height, and probably weighed seventy-five pounds soaking wet.

The dishes were already washed and only needed to be dried and put away.

"So, how long have you lived here?" I asked to distract her from my intrusion.

"Oh, nearly sixty years," she replied smiling up at me. She drained the dishwater then dried her hands on the towel that sat on the counter next to the wet dishes. "David and I bought this house soon after we were married. You wouldn't know it, but we added the second floor when the boys got older. He helped build it with his bare hands."

"You had sons? How many?" I knew I shouldn't get her started, but her conversation was a respite from what was to come. In my country, people became happy when they spoke about their sons, because sons can bring wealth and pass on the family name for generations to come.

"I had many sons, so to speak, but never any daughters."

Her tone was strained yet firm and final, which let me know that further explanation would not be forthcoming. Did she refer to taking in agents or did she mean her own children? Deep down, somehow I knew that she had no children of her own.

"You take care of yourself," she said gently putting a hand to stay my arm.

"Yes, I will, madam." The sincerity in her words startled me but I forced a smile, as best as I could anyway.

"They seem to get younger and younger," she said to herself as she turned away. "Looks like your ride is here."

Strange, I hadn't hear anything, but sure enough, after glancing out the front room window, the van had returned and was now parked at curb, in front of the mailbox.

"Let's go, Matika," Reid called out to me, a light backpack over his shoulders. Yana and Mei-Ling were only steps behind him.

"It was really nice meeting you," I said and gave the small lady a hug, careful not to squeeze too hard on her frail shoulders.

"Take care, child." She held me briefly before she turned away and busied herself with a more important task. The feather-light floral fragrance kindly graced my nose before it drifted away.

I hurried into the opened door of the van, and moments later it pulled away.

# CHAPTER 28

We had arrived at the airport together, but per our instructions, we were like perfect strangers through security, boarding, and the flight where we each sat in different parts of the plane. Before we left, I mailed a total of eighteen thousand dollars to Baba's house, and only kept a few hundred, in the hope that he would forgive me. I didn't leave a note or a forwarding address, but he would know it was from me as he would recognize my handwriting.

We flew non-stop from Reagan International to San Diego, a five-hour flight that I easily slept through, and didn't wake until the plane had landed and taxied to the terminal. After I took my backpack from the overhead bin, I followed the signs to ground transportation. I had never been to this airport and was very surprised at how small it was considering that San Diego was such a big city. I wasn't worried about getting lost when I decided to take quick detour to visit the ladies room; my bladder was about to burst after so many hours.

Once relieved, I splashed cold water on my face in the hope it would make me more alert. For some reason, after I fell asleep on the flight, I felt more exhausted than before. It was like there just wasn't enough oxygen on the plane. Turning off the tap, I dried my face with the sandpaper towels, and headed out.

"Matika," someone shouted from the security line that weaved around the corridor where at least a hundred people stood as they waited to go through.

My heart beat loudly in my chest, and I was momentarily frozen by a voice from the past. Afraid of what I would find, I hurried though the first automatic doors that led to the darkness outside.

"Matika, don't run from me!" Chaz grabbed my arm, and the automatic doors stayed open.

His eyes were wild and large, laced with fear. He looked exactly as I remembered but perhaps a bit thinner, which made him look even taller. He wore jeans and a button-up collared shirt with material as fine as silk, which made him look every bit the son of the wealthy family that he truly was from. His brown leather shoes were no less perfect and shined brightly under the florescent lights.

"What do you want?" I said breathily, at a loss for what to do. Around us people looked with open curiosity while others rushed by without notice to make their flights.

"Don't do this. I've been looking for you for so long. Where did you go?"

"Away. I have to leave right now, Chaz," I said, but my words came out in a mass of confusion. There was a reason why I didn't want to see him, but for the life of me, I couldn't remember anything. He always had such a profound effect on me. It unsettled me.

"You can't do this to me again. I love you and will never stop loving you. You are everything to me. Come back home and I will take care of you. Things will be even better than they were, I promise. I will do anything you want, give you anything, too. I just…I just need you with me."

This couldn't happen. I grew angry at his words as my past with him flooded back, and the familiar pain in my chest sprang up anew. "Are you forgetting that you're married?"

"No, Matika. I love you. Please listen to me–"

"So you are in love with me and her at the same time? I'm better than that, Chaz. I have my own career that is just as important, or more so than yours. I can take care of myself."

He blanched at my words, and I knew it had hurt him to the core. He opened his mouth then shut it again, momentarily at a loss for words. "Yes,

I married her, but only as a favor to my father. It was for an interim special clearance my father's Canadian business partner needed for a top secret contract. By me marrying his daughter, they were able to pull strings with immigration to get his U.S. citizenship as well. It also helped with their partnership for control of assets in the company. Listen, it was only business, nothing more. I don't love her. I love you, Matika."

That was usually the case in my country. Fathers would arrange marriages for their sons and daughters that were beneficial to the family business, wealth, or influence. Of anything that could have been said that was the least expected. I was completely confused. Just when I had everything figured out, or at least as close to it as I could get...

"Sir," a security officer said with one hand on his baton at the ready, flanked by another officer. "You left your bags unattended in the security line. You'll have to come with us for questioning."

"Matika, please call me. We have to talk. I will only be gone for a couple of weeks and then I will wait by my phone for your call."

"Sir, you can either come with us peacefully or we can do this the hard way – your choice," the other officer said and left no room for interpretation about his intentions.

Chaz squeezed his eyes shut, lowered his head briefly before conceding, and allowed himself to be escorted away.

Turing around, I ran right into Reid like I had an interview with a solid oak tree.

"Leave it to you to be late. Who were you talking to?" he accused with eyes that had narrowed to small slits. His menacing stare was intimidating but I had done nothing wrong.

"No one important, okay? I'm sorry I was late," I said exhaling in a huff as I began to walk to the cab.

Reid was upset with me, and more so for walking away during his questioning, but he wasn't about to make a scene at the airport. That gave me the space I needed to gather my thoughts.

The cab took us near the car location on Pacific Coast Highway. It was an older, indistinct, dark Chevy Bronco with a Baja California license plate, parked alone near the small brick bathroom and faced the water. A homeless man slept on a bench in front of it, surrounded by bags of dirty clothes, cans, and other sordid personnel items.

"Wait in the car. It should be open," Reid said shortly in his Southern accent after he paid the cab driver. "Not you, Matika."

Yana shook her head in disapproval while Mei-Ling shrugged a shoulder and rounded her eyes in apprehension.

"I said I was sorry about being late. What more do you want from me?" I said crossing my arms across my chest in irritation. I knew that I shouldn't have been irritable toward him because he had nothing to do with my seeing Chaz, but I wasn't able to think logically at that moment. I was so confused and needed time to think.

"I need to know if you have jeopardized our mission. Who is he? And what exactly did you tell him?"

"He's no one," I said shifting my weight to one foot, while the other tapped the asphalt impatiently.

"You're not fooling me, so don't waste my time. You don't speak to some random guy in an airport like that. Nor does 'no one' touch you or look at you the way he did." His eyes were dark but steady as they bore into me.

"I don't want to talk about it, okay?"

"Now, I'm going to ask you one more time, Matika, or so help me, you will find yourself in the dark side of the room tonight. Who is he? And what exactly did you tell him?"

My petulance left with the cool breeze that blew between us. With that threat, I had no other option. I told him about Chaz and relayed our conversation. His brows grew together, but he didn't interrupt. When I was done, he ran his fingers through his hair and rolled his eyes. "You better keep any notions of that loverboy out of your mind. You're mine now and your life belongs to the team and its mission so don't you forget it. Now, how do you know Mr. John Lee?"

"I met him over a year ago. So what?" I asked shrugging.

"So what? The founder of this entire operation doesn't just pop in and serve as a D.O. for no reason. That's like the President of the United States deciding to drive you home and clean your house. It's so far beneath him it's laughable."

"I resent that. I have more to lose in this than any of you."

"Just get yourself in the car." His hand tore through his thick locks.

I climbed into the back seat with Mei-Ling, while Yana sat upfront. I was in no mood to argue with him or anyone else. There were battles to be had between him and me but this wasn't going to be the one I chose.

"Is everything all right?" Mei-Ling asked with concern, her hands in knots on her lap. "You're not in trouble, are you?"

"Of course she is, and, I'm not the least bit surprised. Nor should you be, Mei-Ling," Yana snapped, looking back at me without a hint of compassion. "What did you do this time?"

"I did nothing wrong, Yana," I grumbled as I buckled my seat belt that annoyingly retracted too tightly. I had to do the unbuckle-rebuckle, to get some slack.

Reid walked over to the homeless guy who, without sitting up, handed him a small envelope in exchange for all of our poorly packed backpacks. I had to wonder what we were going to do for clothes and the thought sent chills through me.

He opened the small package as soon as he got behind the wheel. "Ladies, get some sleep. It's only a few hours' drive, and I doubt there'll be traffic at this hour on a Thursday. We'll all be working tonight. I'll give you the POA before arrival." He backed out of the parking lot and headed south on Pacific Highway.

"POA?" I asked when it was evident no one else would. What would they do without me?

"Plan of action. Do you have to question everything?"

I didn't have to see his eyes to know they rolled to the back of his skull. But the truth was he'd been in the business for years so this was part of the language to him, while we newbies were hearing it for the first time. As much as I wanted to, I didn't state the obvious to Reid. I was only a step away from the "dark side of the room" so there was no reason to push my luck. I swallowed my pride and sat back in silence.

Reid turned on the country music station, but kept the volume low so we could get some sleep. I didn't know much about country, but I still recognized Dolly Parton's beautiful, high-pitched tone that drowned out the hum of the engine. This was the first time I'd listened to any music since I'd left San Diego to train at the facility. Though not my music of choice, it was enjoyable just the same.

My body was sluggish, but I was much too nervous to fall asleep right away. And, no matter how "obedient" Yana claimed to be, she only pretended to sleep. She leaned against the window, used her arm as a pillow, and stayed perfectly still. The rhythm of her breaths gently moved her head up and down. Such a show-off.

Mei-Ling and I both had scooted down and faced one another, our eyes wide open, secretly communicating our fear. I wanted to talk to her so badly or maybe just whisper in her ear about my feelings, but instead, I reached over and squeezed her small hand in mine as we both attempted to draw courage from each other.

By the time we reached the border some thirty minutes later, Mei-Ling was dead to the world. I sat up to look at the bright sign that read "Mexico" over the bridge, and moved forward to see out the front window, my body wedged between Reid and Yana. The border was amazingly busy. If you were headed into Mexico it was only a small wait, but the side to get back into the U.S. was nearly at a standstill.

"Why is it so slow coming back?" I asked when I saw that there was even a long line of foot traffic, which didn't make sense.

"That's nothing. During peak times the wait's as long as three hours, easily," Reid said as he shifted in his seat. "You're supposed to be sleeping."

"I know, but I can't," I remarked biting my lower lip. Only inches away from him, the woodsy fragrance of his aftershave drifted to my nose. Inhaling deeply, I took in the bouquet of scents, which included those natural to his body, closing my eyes in wonder. I stayed there for long moments as my mind traveled to forbidden territory.

He shifted in his seat again as if he had a leg cramp. "Sit back right now. You are not to bite your lip like that ever again."

"Yes, sir." My response was automatic but my tone was deep, husky. Still, I lingered for as long as I dared before slowly moving back.

As we crossed the border, I saw the drastic difference from the U.S. side to the Mexico side. Like night and day, the clusters of buildings were busy with throngs of pedestrians as they walked in, out, and between the structures that littered the streets. Shoeless children with babies strapped to their backs begged for money or sold gum, and walked dangerously close to our car.

It reminded me of Nairobi, because its feel was just as lively and crowded with street vendors that sold everything from food to clothes, to small trinkets, knickknacks, hats, and blankets. This border town of Tijuana had an abundance of pharmacies – in fact, one block accounted for more than I'd seen in my entire life. The people must really get sick here.

I rolled down the window with the automatic button, and took in the polluted city air that was heavy from car exhaust, spicy food, and the un-mistakable deep fried cinnamon churros sold in a nearby vendor's cart. When my window was suddenly rolled up, I pulled my head out of it just in time to prevent its loss. Before I had time to think, I scowled at Reid, who smiled sadistically in the rear-view mirror.

I was tired. After all, it was 10 p.m., which means it was really 1 a.m. Eastern Standard Time. Leaning my head against the glass, I fought the heaviness of my eyelids. The radio station grew staticky as a Mexican sta-tion overpowered the frequency, and finally took away the country one completely. Then, the fastest, most animated announcers began to speak, and even if I spoke fluent Spanish, I would have had a difficult time keep-ing up with the pace. As it was, my limited Spanish was at a toddler's knowledge, and I couldn't make out a single word.

There was so much to see under the bright lights of the city, but soon it all merged together as we weaved through the streets before we found our way to the MEX-1D Carretera Ensenada-Tijuana expressway. Finally, I gave up the fight and fell into a fitful sleep where my meeting with Chaz was replayed again and again, and dominated my dream sequence.

"Wake up, girls. We're here and it's time to work." Reid's voice was surprisingly festive with only a hint of sarcasm, which was completely out of character.

Alert, I peered out the window and viewed the location of my first assignment at the start of my career that provided insight to my destiny.

# CHAPTER 29

The large nine-story Hotel de Playa was intimidating. The building, arranged in a semi-rectangular structure, allowed for every unit to have an ocean view that overlooked the dark waters of the beach. The clusters of trees and palms swayed in the salty cool breeze that flowed into the car when Reid opened the door.

"Wait here until I get back," he said before he walked away.

At 12:30 a.m., there was little foot traffic besides a few wayward young adults laughing merrily, making their way back to their rooms, or perhaps another bar. I shook so bad my knees were getting bruised from knocking together. Yana, though she appeared calm as always, rapidly blinked her eyes as if she had difficulty adjusting to the light.

"We're finally here," I said softly to no one in particular suddenly feeling very cold inside despite the windows being up.

"I'm kind of scared. Are you?" Mei-Ling asked me, hugging her middle as she leaned forward. "I think I may throw up."

"You need to suck it up and swallow it if you have to," Yana snapped, turning to look back at us with her hazel eyes narrowed sharply and her skin clustered into a frown between them. "We can't have you making a scene out here. This is crucial and we are now on duty."

"Yana, can you put down the window so Mei-Ling can get some fresh air? It should help calm her nerves a bit."

I put my hand against Mei-Ling's cool, clammy forehead, and felt for a temperature. Though hair stuck to her forehead, she was not overly warm.

The beads of sweat that pearled over her upper lip were only a reaction to her nerves.

"I will do no such thing. Our handler said not to move."

"He didn't mean literally, Yana. He just didn't want us to wander off. By the way, you can call him Reid you know."

"It'll only take one time to mess up the whole operation, and I won't be the cause of it," Yana shot back. "So it will be on you, Matika, if you make that mistake. And then where will it leave us? You need to get acclimated to our new life and live it."

Yana was going overboard again, and she was truly – though I hate to use this word – brainwashed. All was quiet after that exchange. Then, after we had waited in the car for about ten minutes, Reid returned from the hotel with a slip of paper in one hand and a set of keys in the other.

"Take the bags out of the trunk quickly," he said after pulling the driver's side door open and left his keys in the ignition. "We're on a tight schedule."

I almost spoke but thought better of it. Getting out of the car as instructed, I never thought to consider that there could be bags in the trunk, which would answer the question about what we were going to wear. And, sure enough, there were two designer duffel bags, one standard size suitcase, and a large metal briefcase that Reid quickly reached for. I imagined its contents were precious, as he rotated it to his left hand carefully.

With Reid in the lead, we entered through the side of the building that led to the row of rooms on the first floor. The hallway was exceptionally long, which made it seem narrower than it really was, and which, to my surprise, was completely empty of guests. At the end of the corridor was the elevator that we took to the very top level where the rooms were much more spaced apart.

Reid opened the door to our...penthouse, and allowed us to walk before him. In wonder, I dropped my bag on the floor while my eyes explored the suite. The first thing I noticed were the high ceilings that, no matter how tall a person, were impossible to reach without a ladder – not that anyone needed to reach the ceiling but to change a light bulb, I suppose.

Then, there was the shiny butter-cream marble floor and the small set of steps that led to the elevated kitchen that was fully equipped, complete with a well-stocked wet bar and several bar stools for seats. The kitchen's granite countertops, a sister color to the floors, contrasted perfectly to the stained-black wooden cabinets with glass windows that showed off its porcelain china. The island in the kitchen was far from lonely and an array of fresh pastries filled a wicker basket in its center.

Finally, my eyes roamed to the formal dining room, made for entertaining many, with a table already set for ten guests, complete with the finest dishes and silverware, crystal wine glasses and cloth napkins folded like exotic birds. The living room and office combo was grand and cozy within itself. With two large sectional Italian leather couches, two easy chairs strategically placed by the fireplace, and a coffee table adorned with fresh cut flowers, it had the lived-in feel of a magnificent home. It was all so exquisite, from the chandeliers to the paintings on the walls.

"First things first," Reid said once he'd closed the door and engaged the deadbolt. "We always do a security sweep of our surroundings whenever we enter our dwelling, wherever that may be. There could be someone hiding inside and we never want to get caught off guard. Yana, take left, Matika right, and Mei-Ling center."

The penthouse was like a luxury apartment, but better, because there was a maid to clean and bring you fresh linen, and more closets than you could use. With two bathrooms but only one large bedroom, which I thought was peculiar, we completed our sweep in no time.

"A message was left at the desk by our colleague that indicated three ladies, one of which a possible redhead, were taken to a known drug dealer by the street name of Juego. HT – human trafficking – is only a side business for him, but his connections are vast and his movements quick. We'll be paying him a visit shortly, so keep your eyes and ears open. Find out what you can from other girls if the opportunity presents itself. We have to obtain a definitive ID before we can move forward. Now go ahead and take the bags to the room, get cleaned up, and dress in your street clothes. Meet out here in twenty. Got it?"

"Yes, sir," we said in unison before heading to the room.

After we filed in, Mei-Ling closed the double doors behind us.

"No closed doors, ever," Reid called from the living area.

"Sorry," she said softly, and reopened them. She was nearly in tears by that small reprimand. Mei-Ling was so sensitive.

Yana gave her the "I told you so" look. I felt bad for Mei-Ling because I had already forgotten the rule of no closed doors, so it could have been me. This was simply not the time to forget anything. I needed to stay focused because, despite Yana's belief, I refused to be the one to jeopardize the mission.

"We don't have much time," Yana said taking control immediately. "Mei-Ling, hit the shower and leave the water running when you're done. Matika, find the makeup and get it set up. I'll pick out the clothes for us."

Digging through the bags looking for the makeup, I was in awe at our new garments. It was nothing like we had before. With dozens of name-brand clothing that I had only read about in fashion magazines, thousands of dollars were spent on them. From the lacy thong, to designer jackets and platform heels, every piece of clothing was worth far more than anything I'd ever owned. Top-notch brands that I'd only read about, like Armani, Gucci, Chanel, and Yves Saint Laurent, reeked of the upmost quality. Suda would love this! A familiar pain shot in my heart at the thought of my sister. I wondered where she was or if I'd ever see her again.

"Matika, we're down to fifteen minutes, and you haven't taken a shower yet," Yana said, as she toweled her wet hair.

I must have zoned out. I couldn't even remember what I was thinking about. Hurrying into the bathroom and taking the fastest wash off of my life, I felt about the size of a flea in the oversized shower that was built next to the Roman oval tub big enough for three adults. I should have showered first to give me the extra time I needed to do my hair but it was too late for that.

Though it had bothered me in the beginning back at the cabin, I learned to appreciate and was now grateful that Yana picked out our clothes. She had a sense of style that was above and beyond anything I could've even imagined. What she lacked in makeup application, which she tended to overdo, she made up for in superb clothing selections.

For me, Yana selected a black fitted high-waist miniskirt and a neon-pink oversize sweater that came off my shoulders but was cut short to show every detail of the skirt. The black thigh-high stockings were a perfect fit and were not only warm but added a little modesty to the ensemble. The underwear was more uncomfortable than it looked with the string between my butt cheeks, giving me the urge to pick it out in the most unladylike manner. Finally, I shoved my feet in the high-heeled patent leather pumps knowing that I would surely be limping by night's end.

After I put on makeup and fixed my hair into a quick, high ponytail, I barely made it out of the room on time where I was greeted by stoic faces. Dressed to impress, Yana and Mei-Ling waited with Reid, who stood clenching his jaws, near the front door. Yana, donned in an all-black trench-coat-style dress with jeweled buttons and back opaque tights, was on the catwalk. Her hair was sleek and combed back with an obscene amount of gel that gave her the "wet look."

Mei-Ling looked adorable, in a childlike manner, wearing a dark-blue print baby-doll dress, flat-knit slouch socks, and quaint strapped baby-doll shoes. A large yellow bow in her thick hair – behind her high bangs – completed the outfit. She was a midget standing between the others, fidgeting with her hands as the blood drained from her face. The ruby-red lipstick and matching blush was a splash of red paint on a sheet of white paper.

Reid's dark tweed suit was impeccable, which made me wonder how he was able to get anything pressed in the small amount of time we had. Though he didn't wear a tie, his black shirt had three buttons undone, revealing a small portion of his muscled chest adorned with a heavy gold chain. The silver watch that cuffed his thick wrist was both elegant yet masculine. Reid had trimmed his goatee and cleaned up the stubble on his checks, which brought his tattoo to the forefront.

Reid was…angry. His eyebrows rose briefly then narrowed upon my approach, and his scar grew enraged as well as it wrinkled in fury. I was late, yet I looked down at the marble floor as I joined them, self-conscious of his gaze that burned into me. "Glad you could join us," Reid announced sarcastically.

I couldn't meet his dark eyes, at least not yet, anyway. I was still working my way up from his massive feet covered in alligator-skin dress shoes.

"These are your weapons to only be used in an extreme situation," he said handing us each a small cylinder of lipstick, "and by extreme, I mean life threatening. I mean a 'you-are-about-to-die' scenario."

"Like if someone is trying to kill us?" I asked perplexed, rotating the small tube with my fingers.

"Yes, then and only then," he responded checking the chamber of a handgun before he placed it in the waistband at the small of his back. "You may be hit or beaten and neither one would warrant using the weapon."

"So, how close to death do we need to be? Like guts hanging out on the floor?"

"Yes, that about sums it up," he said checking the chamber of a smaller gun that he strapped to his ankle.

"How does it work?" Mei-Ling asked as she opened the cap.

"Push this up right here," he pointed at its raised bottom that prevented the lipstick from being able to stand right-side up.

I pushed on it, which required a significant amount of pressure, and a sharp knife's edge sprang to life, its blade gleamed in the recessed lighting overhead. Wanting to test its sharpness, I was about to rub my index finder along the point.

"Matika, no!" His large hand firmly grabbed my wrist and his thumb sank into the base, forcing my hand open, releasing the weapon into his waiting palm. His breathing changed, and became erratic when he looked down at me, yet his face was emotionless. "It's poisoned. One prick will kill you instantly. I would hate to have to replace you before we even begin."

"I'm sorry."

Reid's grip was painful, and the amount of pressure he exerted was close to snapping the narrow bone like a twig. I attempted to pull away but he made it a point not to let go as his eyes bore down into mine. Only when my eyes began to water, and threatened to smear my fresh mascara and thick eyeliner, did he release me.

He retracted the blade before he handed it back to me. "Put it away. It should be concealed on your body in a place that's easily accessible."

There were no pockets or any hiding places in this ensemble, except for in my lacy bra, which I refused to consider in Reid's presence. With no other alternative, I secured the deadly lipstick at the skirt waist under my panty string at my right hip. My skirt was as tight as the fabric on an office cubicle wall shown on television, but I feared that it would still fall out if I wasn't too careful.

"Remember our cues. If you have some Intel that must be shared your sign to me will be biting your lower lip. Don't forget it and do it by mistake. Any questions?"

Silence. Reid raised an eyebrow at me. I was already shaking so badly that my brain was a jumbled mess, and as blank as a sheet of construction paper in a cooking class.

"If it's ever too much for you, I have something to help you relax. We use a lot of anxiety medicine out in the field. Mei-Ling, stop that with your hands."

"Yes, sir," she said, her eyes the size of saucers. She promptly ceased the knotting of her hands before staring down at them in longing.

"Let's go. The car should be here now. We'll be accompanied by hired guards of the black market kind. They have no idea who we are, so don't trust them. Don't trust anyone for that matter, especially the working girls." He opened the door, and allowed us passage before him.

From training, I knew that "working girls" was the demure name for girls in the sex trade or adult market. Still, I appreciated its use compared to the others I'd heard and was sometimes called in preparation for this very moment.

"We're on." It was the last thing Reid said before he led us to the elevator. His whole demeanor changed instantly, from one of cool aloofness to stone cold with menacing eyes that could frighten away a bulldog.

Who was this man who froze every molecule in the elevator making it impossible for me to draw a breath? He was the stranger among us and I was as insignificant as the insect under his shoe. I was humbled with the sudden realization that I was in the presence of a highly trained assassin. I was terrified.

# CHAPTER 30

Downstairs, Yana, Mei-Ling, and I were ushered into the dark Chevy Suburban with limo-tint windows by a middle-aged Latino male who wore a dark suit, and also lacked a tie. The tieless look was clearly in style in this country. Instead, he wore a thin cord with silver weighed down with decorative metal tips. The cords were clasped together by an elaborate metal clip engraved with a series of patterns and symbols. Though I burned with curiosity, I didn't dare ask him about it.

He wasn't much taller than Yana, minus her five-inch heels, but was twice as wide. His beefy hand rested on the door as he stood viewing Yana's backside while she climbed inside. All of our womanly goods were thoroughly exposed as we each climbed over the seats, thus receiving an appreciative "ahhh" from our escort. But it was our duty to be the eyes and ears of the agent, in addition to providing protection when needed, so sitting in the rear was a must. I imagined that it didn't please Reid in the least to have us cover his back. And that thought made me smile inside, as we sat like bowling pens in the last row of the vehicle, unmoving, waiting for the strike.

When I received a sharp elbow to the ribs by Yana, I realized I sported a silly grin from ear to ear. It instantly disappeared after I saw the escort's counterpart, who sat in the driver's seat, leering at me through the rear-view mirror in the most provocative manner, his mustache curled upward as the corners of his mouth lifted, exposing his teeth.

I was appalled that I had led him to believe I was interested in him. Biting my lip to prevent a grimace, I looked down at my nails like they were the most interesting things in the world; anything to keep my eyes out of the mirror, where I knew he would be waiting to make eye contact again.

Yana pinched me this time. It was a warning not to bite my lip, as it was our sign. I expelled a breath, and my shoulders slumped in defeat when I saw the anger in her bright hazel eyes. Her thoughts were plainly written on her face. She didn't have to frown or utter a single syllable. Within minutes, I'd made two mistakes, and the car hadn't yet moved. This was going to be a long, long night.

A few moments later, after a hushed conversation between Reid and the escort, and another look from the driver, we were on our way to the meeting point. Reid and his companion sat in the row directly behind the driver.

To my surprise, Reid spoke fluent Spanish with an undetectable accent – at least none that I was aware of. To me, Spanish was a rapid dialect. I had a better chance of understanding the South African *Xhosa* language, which is a dialect made of clicking sounds and used the same sequence of consonants and vowels that have different meanings with the high or low intonation in the voice.

So, for Reid's conversation with our hired help, following the crescendo of syllables, even if I couldn't understand more than every few words, I wasn't interested. I would rather not know the topic that caused the men to laugh, the driver to peer at me, or the "ohs" of understanding, as we were driven further and further away from the hotel. The more Reid spoke the more uneasy both men became.

"*Es muy peligroso,*" the driver said as he sat straighter in his seat, catching my wayward attention.

"*Si,*" the other man responded shifting as well, swiping a quick hand across his nose, and finally followed up with a sniff.

Whatever Reid asked, both men agreed it to be "very dangerous." Then, a large wad of American currency, wrapped loosely in a rubber band, slipped from Reid's hand to the gentleman with the now wary eyes, sitting beside him. He frowned as he snapped off the thin band, thumbed through the bills, stopping periodically to look at Reid, as if he was afraid he'd disappear.

The tension in the vehicle grew immeasurably with the transaction. It was odd because one would surmise that cash would be cause for celebration, but the amount of money offered seemed to further indebt our escorts to be more committed to Reid than they were clearly comfortable with.

Coming from a culture of bribes and side deals, it was completely natural for me to see commerce of this nature in action. It was a fact that back home in Uganda and Kenya, most business was done with bribes and bartering, to acquire everything from food, precious resources and jobs, to livestock, housing, land, education, and wives.

Everything has a price, and that price varied for each person. I was taught that it was fair for a rich man to be expected to pay three times as much, or more, for the same item than a poorer person would pay. Though I didn't know the economic health of our escorts, I knew that the large sum of money Reid had offered was more than I'd ever seen growing up. So it was safe to say that it gave them reservations as well.

"We'll wait on the outside only. If we don't, we will risk not be able to show our faces again by choosing a side if things go wrong," the escort who accepted the money said as he switched to heavily accented English. He had a way of rolling the "r's" and pronounced the "ch" like "sh."

"With that much money, you don't have to return unless it suits you," Reid said coolly. He, too, spoke with an accent, albeit British. "You wait inside, have a drink, and take a load off."

"How do you know we don't have family here? Or girls of our own inside?" the driver asked before slowing to make a right at an intersection.

We drove in circles at that point, right turn after right turn.

"I'm sure that can all be arranged quickly. You are free to use mine if it suits you."

Both men looked back at us, as if inspecting us for future use.

"This is only half," Reid continued, bringing their attention back to him. "The other half will come in due time. Besides, this job may last a little longer than I originally thought. And I can assure that you will be well compensated for your time."

The driver and Reid's companion exchanged a look in the rear-view mirror. Though it was indiscernible to me, they seemed to know what each was thinking.

"*Sí, pero*...if things do go wrong, we don't guarantee your safety."

I knew that "your" did not include us girls sitting pretty in the back, but I would have liked to think that if things did go downhill, we would have some level of protection. Reid had better clarify the terms of that agreement. We were a team, after all.

"Gentlemen, you have yourself a deal," Reid announced and ran his thumb and forefinger across his goatee before shaking the hand of his not so eager new friend.

I nearly narrowed my eyes at his words and fought hard to keep them rounded. I was seething in anger. How dare he make such a deal that completely disregarded our lives?

Moments later, we pulled up to the rear of La Chica, a rundown building with a large neon-lit picture of a naked girl lounging in a martini glass. The attendant, who had the appearance of a person causally waiting for cab, opened the chain-link gate and allowed us entrance into the dirt lot that belied the expensive cars parked within. He immediately secured the gate behind us.

The men exited the vehicle first after a quick, visual sweep around the area, and left us to follow. My anger fled and was replaced by fear. By the time my high heels made contact with the dusty ground, my knees shook so badly I was afraid that I would fall. With my heart rattling in my chest, drawing in a breath was difficult. I was getting lightheaded. Reid casually walked over to me, and I just knew I was in trouble and immediately downcast my eyes.

"Look at me. You need something?" he asked Mei-Ling, who, with doe-like eyes and the ashen face of a Geisha, resembled a ghost.

She nodded intensely, the yellow bow bobbing briskly, and threatened to come undone.

As usual, Reid was prepared. Grabbing her jaw with one strong hand, he forced her mouth open and slipped a dissolvable pill under her tongue. "Let's go!" he called sternly, then snapped his fingers and pointed toward the back entrance.

We milled forward to the back door, scaling with peeling paint that screamed "stay away" louder than the music within. After we descended a dry-rot lumber staircase more suitable for firewood, and which threatened to crack under our weight, we were greeted by the thick smoke and enclosed by the brown stained walls of the club.

The room seemed smaller than I expected, considering the exterior. It had two small dance floors that showcased three naked women, who undulated their bodies in time with the tune. One of the women performed a dangerous acrobatic stunt at the top of the pole near the ceiling, using only her see-through heeled shoes to suspend her body upside down, while her hands groped at her breasts. These dancers would make T. Rayes proud and maybe even teach her a skill or two.

Surprised that the customers' attention could be pulled away from such an impressive show, I was taken aback by the looks in my direction. Completely in a trance, I had walked in front of the stage and watched the dancers.

"Keep moving," Reid said sharply, nudging me forward by the small of my back.

"I'm sorry," I said and scurried forward to the door on the side of the bar.

Another hallway, another door, led us to a much nicer room where a man, who stood watch, let us in with no problem. It was like a club within a club, but much flashier than the other had been, with speckled white lights that reflected off the walls and ceiling, and much softer and quieter music that ensured a relaxed atmosphere both comfortable and serene. This room had marble-like floors, or more like shiny black tile.

A handful of scantily dressed women sat on the laps of men as they did lines of cocaine, each involved in their own satisfaction, totally disregarding the dancing platform straight ahead. With only one stage, it was an intimate setting, up close and personal.

My eyes traveled to the stage where I waited to see the most experienced dancers who would have the privilege of performing in the nicest section of the club. At first I couldn't see them or my mind disregarded the images all together. But then I could not believe my eyes.

# CHAPTER 31

Of all things to expect, this was not even in my mind for consideration. The trio onstage did not dance at all. Instead, they were engaged in sex acts with one another that were beyond explicit and shocking. I had no idea that women could even do such things to one another.

"Move it!" Reid snapped, urging me forward, forcing my eyes away from the scene that would forever be engrained in my head. "Get it together, Matika," he said for my ears alone.

Our escorts headed to the small bar to order a *cerveza*, or beer, while Reid led us to the far side of the room where a group of men sat with two young ladies as they did lines of cocaine on a glass table littered with half-filled tumblers and liquor bottles. While one was completely relaxed with a girl on each arm, the others became instantly alert, and acknowledged our presence as they stared us down.

"You are right on time, quite early by European standards, wouldn't you say, Carson?" the relaxed man spoke with an authority and control that befit the leader of the group. He was dressed in a printed black shirt unbuttoned to the middle of his chest, which showed off a set of thick gold chains that was worth more than year's salary for the average worker. His shirt was tucked in his coal-gray slacks cinched with a black leather belt. His attire was quite cool and casual compared to the others, who wore sports coats that probably concealed weapons. Like the other men in his company, he, too, had a mustache, but it was much thinner, like a young man entering puberty.

"Indeed. I've recently adjusted to the American standard, which has served me well, Juego. I see you don't take your pleasures lightly." Reid motioned around the club with a wave of his right hand while the other encircled Yana's small waist.

"Have a seat and partake of the purest snow you'll ever have," Juego said slowly. All seats were occupied. Then, without taking his eyes off Reid, "Don't be a statue, *quitate*," he commanded his girls.

Juego cruelly flung the two girls to the ground where they stayed at his feet like lap dogs. Three of the men across from him also rose and moved to stand a few feet away. They seemed to enjoy the provocative show but kept an eye on the lot of us at the same time. Two were of average build, while the third was quiet large, yet still lacked in height and stature when compared to Reid's imposing physique.

"Don't mind if I do," Reid smiled, and took a seat across from the leader where the men had recently vacated. Without the slightest hesitation, Reid snorted a line of the white powder from end to end.

Both men nodded their approval. When Reid motioned for us to assume the position, we too, knelt at his feet, poised like the servants of kings.

I felt so comfortable in this position I'd learned so well. It surprised me. It was the only thing that was familiar, constant, and unchanging. In this basic pose, everything else around me ceased but for the voices and the commands I waited to receive. I was receptive to all and nothing would get past my ears. I was well-trained to listen and feel for the slightest change in atmosphere and inflection of voice.

"They are well-taught," Juego remarked, impressed by our stillness.

I didn't need to look up to know his gaze lingered on us, although for far too long in my opinion.

"My clients are diplomats, presidents, kings, and distinguished guests. They are worthy of only the best in breeding, training, and rare beauty. Anything less would be insulting and could cost me my life."

"I see," Juego said as he expelled cigarette smoke that I caught from the corner of my eye. "Well, it's a good thing you come here to acquire.

My products are always clean and free from disease, which, by the way can be a real pain the ass."

"So they say."

It was Reid's turn to take a puff of a cigarette that, now that I thought of it, didn't smell like a cigarette at all. It was an earthier, herbal odor, both sweet and soft.

"You have a book?" Reid asked resting a strong hand on his knee.

"Fuego! *Dame el libro!*" One of the men moved quickly with his words. He shuffled around before he handed a thick black binder to Reid. "That's how my main man got the name Fuego, by the way. Years ago he had fire from one of the girls every time he took a piss. The name stuck with him ever since. He hasn't touched any of the girls since." He chuckled but Fuego remained silent. "I have a video for most of them, so if you see something you like, we'll let you get a closer look and see them in action."

"Thank you, chap." Reid opened the book and began to thumb through the plastic pages of Polaroid pictures. It seemed to take forever.

I couldn't see the pages but heard them as they were turned, which made me feel uneasy. Reid looked at women that were lost to the world, forever missed by someone but never forgotten.

It's human nature to nest and crave a small amount of something or someplace for one's own. Whether a person was homeless or lived in a mansion, it didn't matter. Since everything that had happened in my life, I found my special place at that moment. I found comfort sitting in the position that I'd been taught to do so well with my team at my side. It took me to a place that was mine alone.

Then, there were Reid's hands. He had strong hands with beautiful long fingers, two of which pinched the small hand-rolled cigarette that emitted the earthy order. So many days and cold nights I had spent watching them, unnoticed, as they worked or simply rested on his knees like they were now. Together with the songs that played in my head, I was at peace.

"What's the turnaround time?" Reid asked after a while.

"All are on site and available unless they are onstage or occupied with a client. Still, I can have them cleaned and handed over in thirty minutes or less."

"Mmm, maybe this one. What is her background and breeding?"

"You like redheads? This one is a natural, if you know what I mean. The natural redheads are hard to come by, and they go quickly. As a matter of fact, we had one go through here a couple of days ago that sold within the hour."

"What I want is of no consequence because it's my clients who dictate what I like. Wouldn't you agree?"

"Now we are talking business. Fuego, take these girls to the room and get them prepared."

"Come," the one called Fuego, who was the biggest of the three, said as he pulled Mei-Ling to her feet.

He seemed angry, disgusted, and downright mean. Where did they plan to take us? Prepared for what? I guess this would be a good opportunity to speak to the other girls if they came with us.

"My girls stay with me," Reid said casually, his deep voice as cool as always. "I have just lost a girl that I was supposed to deliver in three days' time. Extenuating circumstances, you see, have put me in a precarious position. Not to mention that a very large sum of money has already been exchanged and thus my capital has depleted significantly. I also lost two men because of this, forcing me to deliver my own product. There is no more room for delays or errors."

"I'd like to help you ... really. But, here, we show good faith when doing business to prove worth and trust. It is the cardinal law; I sample your merchandise and you sample mine. My girls are very experienced. This one can suck the paint off a car, and both have the ass of an eight-year-old boy." Juego laughed at his own joke and Reid joined him. "After we've had our fill then we talk business."

"Sounds like a jolly good time, indeed. Unfortunately, I'm on a real time constraint, and my customers have a particular appetite that I cannot disclose. Don't ask. It's my trade secret."

"OK. I'll just use one of them for an hour. My balls are blue just look-ing at them, which says a lot because in this business it's nearly impossible to have my interest piqued. I will say it's been a while since I've had a *ne-grita*. She has tits as hard melons." His hands reached to his privates, shift-ing his package that had grown considerably on the left side of his pants.

My blood ran cold. Was he proposing to have sex with me? I had to chew the inside of my cheek to keep from reacting.

Reid had better fix this scenario and fix it quick. "She's not bad to look at, either. Don't you hate it when you get the 'butter faces' – when every-thing looks good 'but her face.'" He laughed at his joke before taking a pull from his cigarette. "That one is still in training and is practically useless at this point. I've only had her for a short while." His voice fluctuated as if he were bored with the topic.

The temperature in the room dropped below freezing level. It was clear that Juego didn't like to be denied his pleasure.

"Carson, I have been breaking in the product for over twenty years. I've had it all, from the experienced street walker to the young virgin. You are here today because of my skills, success as a businessman, and the superior products that I offer. Don't insult me or my intelligence. You are outnumbered and outgunned."

As he said this, his men drew closer to us, preventing any escape if needed. Though I was terrified, there was no indication that Reid was at all affected by the threat.

"That is true, and I don't disagree with that in the least. As a matter of fact, it is because of those reasons you should not be offended. I don't wish to insult you or my business with this one." He waved a strong arm to me. "I'll tell you what. You take this one. Her long legs can wrap around you twice. She's experienced and knows how to please."

"No. That's not what I asked for. Those two *putas* at the bar won't do you any good. They pack light, and their loyalty is even lighter. So my friend, you are alone here. Play well or you will lose the game."

"I see." Reid took a long draw from his cigarette with no apparent urgency. Though there was an ashtray on the table he let his ashes fall to the floor like fallen snow. "Mr. Juego, I need to do business with you, but it is as I've said. I cannot jeopardize my own skin. Likewise, I'm in a predicament because I need to acquire product stat, and I know you have the undisputable best quality and rates in these parts. How about she dances for you instead, and next time I'll have something worthy of your time. As it is now, I've got less than an hour to spare here."

The silence that stretched between them was enormous and wasn't ignored. The air of tension between them belied their casual demeanor. Juego's girls shifted nervously, and another man held a gun that was now visible. This was about to get very bad and we were in the middle.

"You strike a hard bargain," Juego paused, and then took another puff from his cigarette. "I always love a good dance, as you can see. Yes, a private dance will do this time."

"Excellent. You two, up!" Reid barked and snapped his finger at Yana and Mei-Ling. "Go over to the bar and wait until I collect you."

"Fuego, take the little *chocolate* to the *quadro*."

Though the order was given, Fuego made no move to collect me nor did I move to follow him. I was trained, or more like it was drilled into me, to only respond to our agents' orders.

"Matika," Reid said leaning over to me. His deep voice was raised but gentle to my ears. He lifted my chin with his thumb, and I was nearly lost in his dark bottomless eyes that were unreadable. Even through this heavy cologne, I could smell him. Then, slowly, as if he spoke to a simpleton, "You are going to perform a dance for Mr. Juego. Do you understand?"

"Yes, sir," I responded, my voice brittle through an ever-drying throat.

"Do well. Up, up."

For a moment, I simply stared at him. Then, he snapped his fingers, and I fell into zombie mode. I got up on shaky legs and followed Fuego.

# CHAPTER 32

The months and months of training could never have adequately prepared me for this moment. I was being tested in a real-life situation that was crucial for all our sakes. This was only a start, and God only knew what else I'd be forced to perform. At that moment, it all became very clear to me. It was something I'd never even considered. Reid may have gotten me out of having sex with Juego this night, but he may not always have that option in the future. There would be times that no matter what he proposed, things may turn out much differently. What if he didn't even try? I would have no choice but to do as I'm told or risk our mission.

I pushed those thoughts out of my head and concentrated on my surroundings as I was led through a door that opened up to yet another narrow hall with rows of closed doors, which took fire hazard to a whole new level. The faded, hanging lights coupled with the disturbing moans of men and women that echoed off the concrete floor were a scene from a horror film.

Fuego opened the last door at the cul-de-sac, and stepped aside to allow me to walk in before him. He didn't touch me, and I found his politeness both creepy and peculiar. Inside, the décor was striking; though there wasn't a raised stage, the clear path in front of the overwhelming king-size bed with dark-blue silk comforter complete with a pole obviously used for dancing or other entertainment.

Much like the rest of the building the walls were white, but the glow from several black lights illuminated them with an ambiance of colors and patterns that danced off the marble floors over the stage. The only furnishings, besides the massive bed, were a dark-stained mini-bar about waist high that held an assortment of liquors within its glass confines and a decanter of dark liquid next to four crystal glasses on top; a TV and VCR; a small side table with two drawers next to the bed; and a large stereo near the silver dancing pole.

Fuego turned on the stereo to play Mexican music, drowning out the loud noises from outside, for which I was thankful.

"Juego will join you shortly," he said in a heavy accent.

For some reason, he didn't seem as mean as he looked before. Though his expression was cryptic, his dark eyes were kind and framed with long, sweeping lashes.

With the first and only words from Fuego, the door was closed and locked, which left me alone in the windowless room. The walls seemed to get smaller and so I did the only prudent thing I could think of to control its shrinkage. I headed over to the mini bar, picked up the entire decanter, didn't bother with a glass, and swallowed as much of the fiery substance as my empty stomach would allow. It burned all the way down, warming up my insides in the way that only hard liquor could.

Within ten minutes it took effect, dulling my senses, as I had hoped. Still, I needed more just to be sure because my nerves were still on edge. I attempted to down more of the fire water, choked, and sprayed it out of my mouth and all over the wood floors. With hands on my knees I doubled over, coughing and hiccupping at the same time until my eyes watered in protest. I held my breath to rid the spasms in my diaphragm. Then, in effort not to smear my heavy mascara, I dabbed at the corners of my eyes with a black cocktail napkin as soft as a folded sheet of construction paper.

A quarter of the bottle was now MIA, and at that point I had overdone it when I swayed slightly in time with the music on the stereo. At that point, I began to chuckle out loud, now finding the whole situation amusing. The floor was soaking wet from the alcohol that I was not given permission to have, and now I felt more intoxicated than I'd intended.

"Why don't you make yourself comfortable?" said a voice that dripped with sarcasm.

Immediately, I got down on my knees and assumed the submissive position. My heart made a foul attempt to pick up the pace, but had to settle for a light skip. Juego had entered the room so quietly he'd caught me making a total fool of myself, dancing to his music, drunk on his booze that was all over the floor. Why didn't I think to dry it up?

"Don't waste my time. Get up and entertain me," he said and went over to select another CD and then pressed play. The music was changed to a more erotic beat with no lyrics.

He was a lot shorter than I thought now that he stood before me. Still, he was taller than me, but shorter than Yana with much broader shoulders. He walked over to the bed and began to disrobe. I was in total shock. In that twenty or so minutes that I'd waited was there another deal made that I wasn't aware of? I felt a huge sense of dread, even amid the buzz, and it must have shown clearly on my face.

"You act as if you never seen a naked man before," he said smoothly, smiling like a leopard, exposing all his yellow-stained teeth. A life of over-indulgence had given Juego a small round belly and soft muscles that were veiled beneath his clothing. He poured himself a drink, filling up the tumbler to nearly overflowing. "Very interesting…"

What was I expected to do for this naked man who enjoyed my discomfort way too much?

"No, sir. I mean yes, sir," I said stumbling over my words.

He downed the drink in one gulp, like it was Kool-Aid. Then he lay on the bed with his legs slightly open and both hands behind his head, and waited impatiently. I forced my eyes away from his growing part that I didn't care to see, and slowly got up from the cold floor on unsteady legs, uncertain how to begin.

Though my judgment was a bit cloudy and grew more so by the minute, I knew the job I had to do, and I was determined to do it well. I refused to be a failure and face Yana, or worse…Reid. I loathed the sight of disappointment in his eyes. Reid. With the thought of him, I settled my resolve and began to move.

When I danced for Juego, I pretended as though I danced for Reid. In my imagination, it was his eyes that looked at me longingly, his seductive lips that smiled at me, and his deep voice that sent currents down my body and urged me on. I danced an African dance of seduction, love, and fertility with movements that I'd seen the girls do at the village festivals and tribal ceremonies. I mimicked the women and girls, as they called out to the gods to grant them favor.

I removed my clothing with reckless abandon, and tore them in the process – the complete opposite of how we were taught. When I heard something fall to the floor my heart nearly stopped. The deadly lipstick came to the forefront of my mind. My weapon! Dancing had caused it to fall out and roll to the side of the stage, leaving me unprotected. It was supposed to be on my person at all times.

I knew I needed to secure it promptly, and inched along on all fours like a sexy kitten, stopping every so often to move my hips and butt until I reached my target. Surreptitiously, I placed it in my thigh-high stocking, praying he hadn't noticed. As if nothing were out of the ordinary, I continued my dance with a surge of fury and emotion.

I danced with a boldness I never had before, and touched where I'd never touched before, undulating my hips with total disregard for gravity, giving a silent yet forceful invitation for Reid to take me else I be consumed with wantonness. I pulled the fastener off the ponytail, letting my hair fall in a dense mass to my shoulders.

I took pleasure in every movement, and lost my mind to my inner woman's burning needs as the music soared to new heights. I flaunted my wares like honey before a hungry bear, and teased him as I came up close to the bed before I retreated to the stage again. Shamelessly, I ignored my vision that swam before me, and chose instead to feel my way to the rhythm of music where I synchronized the dance of seduction.

"*Muy bien, chica*," he said as he sat up in the bed, a touch of admiration in his voice. "I've never seen anyone dance like that before. And I've watched many dancers come through my club. Where did you learn to dance like that?"

I looked down at my stocking covered feet, and remained silent as I curled my toes.

"Do you speak English?"

"Little," I replied mimicking Suda's heavy accent. I almost smiled as I thought about her lack of desire to refine her English. No matter how hard Baba pushed us, her refusal to embrace the language was tenacious.

"You would be good money at my club. I bet you would like that. Come here," he ordered, his eyes hooded with unfeigned desire.

I hesitated.

"Come, I won't bite. At least, not today."

Knowing I couldn't refuse, I paused only a moment before moving toward the massive bed. An eerie feeling began to envelope me as I walked. The black lights seemed dimmer, and made it impossible to see the far corners of the room, which added to my unease. I chewed nervously on my lip as I scanned the chamber.

"Sit down," he cooed and patted the silky comforter beside him. Though he had sat up, he hadn't moved to make more room for me. Instead, he drew even closer, leaving less than a foot of bed space. "Your body is tight and curvy at the same time."

Immediately I complied, and felt the cold satin against my bare bottom. Biting my lip harder, I felt the blood flood my face when I realized that I was still topless. It was one thing to dance without clothes, because I still wore underwear that covered only the most intimate part, but another thing entirely to sit vulnerable before him...exposed.

Only a year ago, I would have died from humiliation a thousand times over. I was never bold enough to be scantily dressed in front of anyone, let alone a stranger of the opposite sex. But I knew that my body was only a vessel and though it was uncovered, it didn't reveal the inner spirit within me that was most sacred. So at that moment I was only shy because of how seductively I had performed for him while I'd pretended he was Reid, which gave him the impression that I wanted him.

Though this was all an act, thinking of him in that way was a dangerous combination.

Without preamble, Juego's sweaty hands were roughly stroking my breast, hardening my nipples against their will. Shivers raked through my body as chill overtook me, weakening my knees. I trembled as I worked to tune out his roaming hands, unable to ignore the sinking feeling that this situation was heading downhill fast.

Where was Reid when I needed him? Probably off with those beautiful brunettes doing...

A stab of jealously tore through me. I couldn't let my mind traverse that dangerous path that would only lead to pain and self-destruction.

Soon, Juego's hands and mouth were everywhere they didn't belong as he kissed all over my shoulders and neck. Thankfully, he avoided my mouth, which was far to intimate a place. When Juego pulled me under him, I was in trouble. And, within moments, he suddenly had the poisonous lipstick in hand.

"What is this?" he asked curiously opening the tube as he pulled up slightly from me. Its purplish hue glowed against the black lights.

"It's my makeup," I said reaching for it a little too swiftly.

"Really?" he asked suspiciously, moving it out of my reach as he rotated it slowly before he brought it closer to eye level. His eyes briefly shot down to mine. Concentrating once again on the deadly object, his expression was angry and sinister, like the killer he truly was.

Juego was about to release the spring. In moments it would all be over for us. My heart pounded in my throat at the thought of risking our mission. I did the only thing I could think of. I pushed up and began to kiss him with an urgency that no man could deny. His lips were soft, but not full, and tasted of alcohol as I imagine mine did as well. Soon, the deadly cosmetic was lost on him and dropped between the formerly neat bedding. He began to move against me. I felt every inch of his body, and coupled with the smell of intoxicants, my stomach churned violently. I forced the bile to subside, and swallowed hard as I choked on his tongue.

He spread my legs and ripped the thin barrier of my so-called underwear. We were only moments away from the inevitable, and yet it was the only thing I could do to distract.

"Juego!" Fuego called from the other side of the door. Then a momentary double-tap on the wood just before the hall lights flooded the room. "We're being raided!"

"Damn!" The frustration in his voice was palatable as he reluctantly tore himself from me. "How much time?"

Juego was off the bed and pulled on his slacks in seconds. While he dressed, I took the opportunity to rummage through the bedcovers for my lipstick. I found it, and hid it once again in my stocking.

"Seven minutes at most. As usual, our friends at the department couldn't give us more notice than that." Fuego was in the room and loaded a gun that he had taken from the mini bar.

"Secure the product," Juego barked as he bent to put on his shoes.

"It's being taken care of as we speak," he replied, handing the pistol to Juego's ready grip before he took out another.

"This is the second one in as many months," Juego said as he checked the chamber of the semi atomatctic weapon before he placed it in his belt.

"You know how they can be sometimes, always looking for more money. They should be thankful for the services we provide."

"Perhaps we should pay our friends another visit to their homes to remind them of our kindness. A friendly reminder on the front end usually does us well, for a while at least."

"This surge is just another pony show for the new governor's party," Fuego said. "I hate politics. There is nothing to worry about. Things will die down as they usually do in time."

"*Bueno.* Business as usual in two nights. The new shipment should arrive by then, anyway. It'll be a good time to break it in and get it ready for market."

What ensued was a fire drill that they'd practiced numerous times. Their movements were in sync, as they prepared for their speedy departure from the club, completely forgetting I was even in the room. Equipment was shuffled around, bags rearranged, air freshener was sprayed, and strangely enough, the bed was even remade.

Gathering up my torn clothing and shoes, I watched the two of them speedily move around the room, unsure what to do next. Was Reid going to come for me? Or was I supposed to go with Juego and reunite with my team later? Though it was risky to leave without Reid, I knew that I couldn't risk getting picked up by the police. That would be an even worse option. I was a foreigner in the country with no form of ID on me, and now so drunk I saw double. Not to mention the fact that I was below the legal drinking age.

"Put this on," Juego said throwing an article of clothing on the floor in front of me.

Only then did Fuego notice me as I stood there like a statue. His dark eyes swept over my nakedness, his expression though muted, was a mask of concern. When our eyes locked, he turned away and continued to shuffle around the room.

Blushing, I stumbled forward and picked up the white long-sleeve button up shirt. I dropped my useless clothing and extremely high heels, which were an ankle break waiting to happen. I threw the garment over my head where it thankfully reached two inches above the knees.

"Let's go," Juego called as they exited to the hall that burst like hive with activity.

I gathered up my belongings and quickly followed the men.

# CHAPTER 33

The chaos became deafening. Men, who seemingly were only patrons, stood and barked orders, while they led the throng of more than a dozen terrified women in their wake as they rushed for the stairs. They, too, were in all manner of undress, completely off guard, with some completely nude. With no sign of Reid or my team anywhere, I had to assume they were topside or perhaps already in the vehicle.

Instead of following the herd, we took a private route through a room beside the one we exited that had a narrow trapdoor in its ceiling that led outside. Fuego pulled down an emergency fire ladder and stepped aside to allow Juego to go up first. I was helped up next while Fuego trailed closely behind me.

I emerged from the escape door in utter shock. We were now in the adjacent parking lot of the building next door where a sleek car awaited us, engine running. The other two gentlemen from the club were inside in the driver's and passenger's seat.

"Get in," Juego said, pushing me toward the open door. Fuego was already in the back seat. The apprehension in his eyes was unmistakable. The authorities were moments away.

"But…but," I stammered at loss for words. I didn't want to get in the car, and I knew that I would be lost if I did. But I didn't see the team anywhere as my eyes struggled to adjust to the darkness.

"But nothing," the driver snapped. "The cops will be here any minute."

"Get the fuck in the car," Juego commanded through clenched teeth.

He shoved me through the opening, and I hit the top of my head in the process. Thankfully, my thick hair, that was down and about my shoulders, provided some cushion.

"Mr. Carson will be angry with me," I cried in desperation when I was sandwiched between Juego and Fuego, who took up the lion's share of the space.

"Or maybe not," he chuckled as the car peeled out of the lot and weaved through the streets. "You can make me a lot of money with your moves. I think I'll keep you for myself." He brought his head down to mine, grabbed the back of my neck, and licked my face with his slimly tongue.

Only then did I realize the seriousness of the situation, which sapped the effects of the alcohol right out of me. I needed to get out of the vehicle. With my left hand, I carefully extracted my weapon. Reid's voice rang out in my head reminding me to only to use it in a life or death situation. Could this be considered one? No telling what would happen to me. If I were forced to stay with Juego, I could very well die. I had no way to get out of this country nor did I know of anyone who I could call to help me. Not a single emergency number was provided to any of us that I was aware of.

"It's bad business, *señor*," Fuego said cautiously, his gaze focused out the window as *la policía* raced by, their lights and sirens disturbing the tranquil night.

"He's probably a nobody. I've never heard of him before yesterday," he countered as he pulled me even closer to him.

"You may be right but he came highly recommend by Deats. And Deats is never wrong, you know."

"What does he know anyway? *El puto* is a kiss-ass and thinks he knows about everything. Besides, I don't think we should trust him. I've been thinking about breaking off from those ties, anyway." He pulled me closer to him until I was perched on his lap.

"I don't recommend it and you know that I've never steered you wrong. But if that's a risk you're willing to take you know I'm behind you one hundred percent."

"It's only a girl! There are many more like her." Juego was angry with him but he held fast to me.

"*¡Exactamente!*" was Fuego's only response.

They exchanged rapid words in Spanish. I felt Juego stiffen in anger. He let out a grunt of disapproval, but pushed me over to Fuego. I still carried my weapon in my hand, ready to strike as we stopped at a light. "This better be worth it! Pull over. Get Carson on the phone, Fuego." He cursed under his breath in Spanish again, but it didn't take a rocket scientist to figure that out.

Used to getting his way in all things, he was like a spoiled child denied his favorite toy. I was already his, and he had to give me away. I wanted to stab him in the eye for the audacity to think I belonged to him. The only person who owned me was me – not Juego, not Reid, not even the agency.

When we pulled over, Fuego used the car phone to call Reid while Juego sat back and sulked. Thankfully, the SUV pulled up within minutes, and I fought hard not to climb over Juego and burst through the door. Fuego stepped out of the vehicle quickly, and I followed even quicker, still clutching my belongings.

Fuego escorted me to the car. Never in my life was I so thankful to see Reid. I nearly leaped in his arms as he stood waiting for me. His expression was stoic; his eyes bore in to mine briefly.

"Get in the car," he said before turning his attention to Juego. "Until we meet again." That was all he'd uttered, for he remained silent the entire trip. Our escorts spoke among themselves quietly about the raid.

After we arrived at the hotel, we did a thorough sweep of the suite. It was secured. It was such a welcome feeling to be back here. It was our home even if it was only temporary. I was suddenly so thirsty. If I could drink a gallon of water it still wouldn't be enough to soothe my parched throat.

"Get ready for bed," Reid snapped. "Not you, Matika."

Reid stormed to the far bathroom, and clearly expected me to follow. With apprehension, I slowly made my way to the open door, which was promptly slammed after I'd entered the powder room.

The décor of the room was quaint and elegant and twice the size of the one we all shared back in San Diego. Beautiful tan embroidered towels that matched the decorative rugs hung on the racks. A lonely shower with a glass window was in the far corner.

"I ordered you to dance for him. What the hell were you doing?" His English accent was now gone and that country twang up front and center.

He voice was menacing as he came up over me and crowded my space. I tried to back away but the far wall greeted my back. "I did nothing wrong, sir."

"Don't you dare call me 'sir' right now!" he fumed. "This isn't a joke, Matika."

"I never said it was, Reid," I added clutching my clothes tighter to me. As much as I wanted to, I just couldn't bring myself to look away from him. For one, it was a sign of weakness in my eyes, and I just couldn't let him intimidate me.

"How could you get in the car with them? If you were lost, there would be nothing I could do about it."

"I had no choice. You were nowhere to be found. What would you have me do? Go off running to the police?"

"You should have stayed. I would have come for you," he said running his hands through his thick hair. "If it wasn't for our friend deep under, you would have been done. Finished."

"Fuego?"

"Don't ever say the name again. You can never say a name without risking a life."

"Sorry," I said lowering my head. Deep down inside, I had known there was something different about Fuego. His eyes gave him away. Just then I realized how much in the dark I was about this mission. And it really upset me. I swallowed heavily as I glanced back up at him. "Why is it that I don't have anyone to call if trouble arises? That doesn't make sense to me."

"Because we can't risk it," he said flatly.

"What do you mean 'we can't risk it'? I risk my life out there the same as you. How can you tell me that I'm to be all alone out there if something happens? This is crazy and unreasonable." It was my turn to be angry. It was my turn to glare up at him.

"We've all been embedded with a tracking devise. Though it doesn't show our exact location, it comes pretty close, like a cell phone signal. But, by the looks of it, you'll be just fine with or without a tracking device," he quipped raking my body with his piercing eyes.

"The hell I will!"

"Don't give me that shit. You put out far more than you were supposed to."

"I did no such thing–"

"Then you come here smelling like booze and cheap cologne and wearing his shirt, no less."

"For your information, my clothes were torn!" I cried in frustration.

"Oh, really?" he said sarcastically.

Reid's gaze traveled to my clothes on the floor. I flushed, biting my bottom lip as memories of the dance flowed over me.

"I have no reason to lie to you." I pushed the clothes to him but he let them the fall to the floor. Then I grew even angrier. "Like you can talk. What were you doing with those girls? Reciting a poem? Or were you singing them a lullaby?" I threw back at him and jabbed my finger into his hard chest.

"That's none of your business. I do my job and you do yours."

"Oh, really? Well then it's none of your concern what I do," I said smoothly as attempting to walk past him to leave. I'd had enough for one night, and this conversation was headed downhill fast.

He roughly grabbed both my shoulders, and pinned me to the wall. "I didn't say you could go."

"Let go of me," I said breathing heavily. I just couldn't seem catch my breath with him so close to me.

"You play a dangerous game, Matika."

"You would know," I hissed, as my eyes blazed into him. I wanted to slap the silly grin off his face. He infuriated me, yet my body responded to him like liquid fire. He was so close to me.

Then to my astonishment, Reid's lips pressed firmly against mine with a fiery passion on the verge of explosion. His mouth was savage and fierce as it seized upon mine. His pierced lip was tantalizing but surprisingly smooth. Instantly I melted against him. He picked me up as if I was a feather, and I wrapped my arms and legs around him. I felt every inch of his hard body though my thin shirt. I was ready for him and burned to my inner core for him to take me. I whimpered with pent-up need, demanding all of him.

Then he pushed me away from him, my weight dropping to the floor with only the wall to break my fall. I blinked in surprise.

His back was tense and his jaw clenched tightly. "Stop! This is enough," he said through clenched teeth. His eyes blazed dark with a feral hunger but his blistering words greeted me like a slap in the face. "Get out of here, Matika."

"Why?" It was all I could ask as the hurt and rejection in my voice nearly choked me, which made my voice high and shaky.

"So help me," he said looking up at the ceiling, "leave now or you'll be sleeping in the nearest closet."

I fled in a blur of tears, heading straight to the master suite bathroom, bypassing Yana and Mei-Ling's startled expressions. Needing to be alone, I closed and locked the door behind me, damming the rules.

# CHAPTER 34

The chaos and adrenaline from the night coupled with the alcohol turned me into a hot mess emotionally. Looking at my reflection in the oversized mirror made me feel that much worse. The smeared eyeliner and mascara, swollen lips, and the man's shirt I sported made me look like a cheap date doing the walk of shame out of the men's college dorm. I made up my mind to never let that happen again. I wasn't sure at this point who kissed whom, but one thing was for sure, I knew it would only lead to pain and rejection as my feelings for him had steadily grown.

I turned the shower on and got in before the temperature adjusted and cried until my eyes refused to let out another tear. I stayed in the shower until the water ran cold. Then after I brushed my teeth and put my hair in a French braid, I left the bathroom to the darkness of the room.

That night we all slept in the extra-large king-size bed. All except for Reid. Despite my confusion and the many thoughts that ran a marathon in my head, I feel asleep as soon as my head landed on the feather pillow.

The next morning, I was awoken by voices in the front room. Glancing over at Yana, who sat up on the bed, I gave her a questioning look as our bedroom door had been closed.

"They've been talking for over an hour now," she whispered. "Maybe he's gotten smart enough to finally get rid of you."

I chose to ignore her remark though it bothered me more than it should have. Mei-Ling, who slept between us, stirred as she let out a cat-like yawn before she rubbed the sleep out of her eyes.

"Is everything okay?" she asked placing a gentle hand on my arm. Her genuine concern for me warmed my heart. She was a welcome distraction from the others.

"It's fine," I assured her, "There's no need to worry about me."

"I'm glad. So, guess what?" she said happily, smiling brightly. "We were able to get a positive ID on the subject," she finished in a low tone.

"Really?" I asked sitting up on the bed and pulling the blankets up to my chin.

"Yeah. One of the girls actually spoke to me. She said that Yana was stuck up like the redhead."

Yana stiffened at that comment but didn't refute the claim. Instead, she got off the bed and headed to the bathroom. I couldn't help the smile that crossed my face. Yana's demeanor could easily be interpreted as "stuck up." And that comment didn't come from my mouth.

"Through casual conversation, I learned that the subject was never meant to stay in the club as a working girl. And that they got her for the foreigners. At least that's what she had overhead the men say. They said that she was taken with some of the other girls to be routed through the Santiago Cartel. Apparently he is a bigger deal than Juego. Much bigger. Any girl of worth will get sold at a high price to an elite market. He does the high-priced negotiations."

"Does Reid know?"

"Yeah, I told him last night when he came in the room."

"He slept in here?" I asked in a high voice that was a little too interested.

"Of course not," Yana retorted as she came back from the bathroom. "Not after how angry he was at you last night." She began to rummage through the clothing bag.

"He was acting strange. He just stood over the bed for a while like he was unsure of what to do." Mei-Ling sat up, her brows wrinkled in puzzlement. "It was almost as if–"

At that moment, Reid swung the door open and stepped inside. "Pack up, we leave in fifteen minutes."

"How should we dress?" Yana inquired.

"Comfortably. The hired men will be taking us down to first drop-off point in the city of Leon to try and meet up with them before they head to Guatemala. Hopefully, we will be able to intercept the package in time."

"Why didn't we leave last night?" I asked the simple question that I wished to take back as Reid turned his attention to me.

"They're watching us for some reason. It would have been too suspicious. The men are waiting in the car, and we still have to go over the POA, so get moving."

Once again we were in another mad dash to get dressed, packed, and go over the Plan of Action, or POA. There was nothing about this job that was slow. I longed for a short breather and to sleep for more than six hours at time.

"Okay let's get this straight," Reid began when we were ready to go. "For now until whenever, those hired men will be with us at all times. Don't be fooled by them. They know the business, the people, and dabble in the trade occasionally. But, no matter what, don't trust them. They are mercenaries and will betray anyone for the love of money. Understood?"

"Yes, sir," we replied.

"At all times we have to play by the rules. *No* deviations."

His dark eyes snapped to mine, and showed that the last comment was directed at me. It took every ounce of control for me not to respond to his words or the rules that seemed to increase exponentially. Time seemed to drag at an excruciating pace though it was only minutes. The walls in the room seemed to move closer, and I itched to break free. I needed to exercise in the worst way as my anxiety was getting the best of me. I shifted from one leg to the next, unable to stand still. A good long run to sweat it all out would have been the perfect remedy.

"Are you listening?"

"Yes, sir," I responded but had tuned him out and lost some of his instructions. His eyes were locked on mine but thankfully he didn't grill me.

We left shortly thereafter and loaded up in the SUV parked at the side of the hotel. My stomach growled loudly when I got a whiff of what looked like a breakfast burrito that one of the men ate with gusto. The salt of the pork made my mouth water. I couldn't remember when my last hot meal was.

Constantly being in the role exhausted me. Most of the time was spent on the road; the inability to talk freely or ask questions drove me crazy. Mei-Ling had bought a pen and pad at the gas station and taught me how to play tic-tac-toe, hangman, and MASH – a pointless game that was supposed to determine if you'd live in a mansion, apartment, shack, or house, to pass the time. Yana, too, was bored and joined in on a few of our games.

Reid was adamant about getting to Leon quickly, so he refused to stop for anything more than a bathroom break. Also, he wanted to keep a low profile, so when we finally stopped for the night we all stayed in a shabby motel that smelled of urine, where the rooms were adjoined by a door that was left open. The men didn't trust Reid as much as he didn't trust them.

Reid and Yana slept in one bed and Mei-Ling and I slept in the other in shifts. Reid took the first watch shift followed by Yana, me, Mei-Ling, and then once again Reid. To play it off, we had to stay awake while we lay down, which was very difficult.

The next morning we were given *pan dulces*, or sweet breads, and tea that reminded me of home.

"It will take us another two days with this traffic, but we are making good progress," the driver spoke in an even tone. "I'm ready for a good lunch."

"Yeah, me too. It will be a week before I can take a good dump after eating plastic shit out of a bag. I know a good place that serves the best *chilaquiles* off the road. Just a small detour."

"All right," Reid conceded reluctantly, before he inhaled deeply and closed his eyes briefly. "It wouldn't hurt to have a good meal. However, I'd like to try another place down the road. Something a little more English – no offense," he quickly added.

I understood his line of thought; he didn't fool anyone. He didn't want to be on their domain at their known restaurants. It could be a trap.

"Let's just compromise and stop at the next exit. I'm sure there's food that'll suit both our tastes," the driver said.

"Sounds like a jolly plan," Reid drawled with his fake British accent.

We stopped at a dingy hole-in-the-wall diner that was quaint and homey. The soiled, thin carpet on the floor reminded me of home, and the walls didn't look much better but were decorated with pictures and relics. The staff, which consisted of an entire family, was friendly and helpful. I asked Reid if I could use the latrine, which was surprisingly not in the restaurant but at the adjacent store that was also owned by the family.

"Make it quick and take Mei-Ling with you," Reid said sternly before he sat down at the large table.

"You're very trusting of your girls," said the driver, who I learned was named Javier. "To let them out of your sight is pretty bold."

"They've been well-trained and will never run," Reid smiled wistfully as the server came over to pour ice water in porcelain cups. "I'll take a bottled water, if you will."

"That's what they all say. I'm sure they're worth quite a bit," Lorenzo quipped, taking out a cigarette.

Reid waved us away as he picked up the laminated menu. "Don't tarry or you'll both miss lunch."

"Yes, sir," we answered and quickly headed out the door.

Outside, the temperature was perfect – not too hot or cold, in the mid-80s. Having the sun glow on my face without the fear of being watched as we walked across the dirt lot to the adjacent store relaxed me.

"It's so nice out; I need a tan in the worst way," Mei-Ling said looking up at the clear blue sky. "To lay out by the pool and relax." She spoke in a dreamy, singsong voice.

"I think Yana needs that more than you do." We both giggled at that. It felt wonderful to laugh, even if it was at Yana's expense.

The bathroom required a key that was attached to a large wooden spoon, and was the size of a closet.

"After you," Mei-Ling said with a sarcastic smirk on her face as she mimicked the queen of hospitality.

"Great!" I cried with mock enthusiasm.

Inside was a major violation of the health code – at least it should have been by any standards. The mirror was a rectangle sheet of metal; the deep sink was also metal, and the toilet required a water hose to flush because the water in the back did not fill up on its own. It was also filthy, with a white bucket of used toilet paper beside the toilet. More used paper stuck like papier-mache to the wet concrete floors, and smelled of the foul waste.

After I used it without touching anything – if only that were possible – I headed outside the store and waited for Mei-Ling. That's when I saw the pay phone that beckoned me. I couldn't remember the last time I was alone for more than a few minutes to relieve myself. Even then, someone was always just outside the door, assuming it was even closed.

No one was around, and this was the best opportunity to call Baba. I wanted to talk to him so badly, though I knew in my heart that may not be possible. Since Baba believed that answering the phone was a woman's job, akin to a secretary, I knew that there was a good chance Namazzi would answer. With only a slight hesitation, I briskly walked over to the phone booth, stepped inside, and made a collect call to my family's home.

# CHAPTER 35

The call system was automated and a bit confusing, but soon the phone rang on the other end and my heart beat quickened. I held the receiver in a death grip in my sweaty palms as a thousand thoughts raced through my head. What if the call wasn't accepted? What would I do then? The feeling of rejection already overwhelmed me.

"Hello?" Namazzi's heavily accented voice made an attempt at English. She had been in the States for months and must have begun to pick up the language.

"Oh, thank God!" I cried in relief, my hand flying to my throat.

"I'm sorry, but there is no God here. You have the wrong number," she said sweetly. "Goodbye–"

"No wait!" I pleaded in Swahili. "Namazzi, it's Matika. Your little sister."

"Oh…" After a short but uncomfortable silence. "Are you well?"

"I am now. Is Baba home? Can I speak to him?" I rushed out in a single breath, scanning the area to make sure the coast was clear.

"He is home, yes, but he is working in the garage with Walyam. Our brothers are coming home soon, so we will need the extra space to convert to additional rooms. Now that Baba has come up with lots of money, it will be ready in no time. He also bought a van yesterday that we can all fit in."

I was filled with a sense of pride that Baba had received and used the money I'd sent. Namazzi's voice was excited, as if she hadn't spoken to anyone in a very long time. I imagined that life for her in Baba's home was lonely at best. She no longer had me to confide in so it broke my heart to interrupt her but time ran short. "Listen, I don't have much time. Can you please get Baba for me?"

"I cannot because he won't talk to you. Mama would also be angry if I even spoke to you or Suda on the phone, but she is out shopping now."

Getting Namazzi to break the rules was like persuading a cop to let a murderer go free, so I didn't waste my time. "Have you heard from Suda?"

"She called twice to ask about baby Walyam. He is getting big and very handsome you know. He's walking very well, too. Perhaps he will be a runner someday." She spoke with pride in her voice. "She says that I can keep him forever. But I'm worried about her. Her spirit is filled with anger and bitterness. I fear that she is in trouble. She said that she will find a way to get back to Uganda for unfinished business. I asked her what she meant by that but she wouldn't elaborate. But, I heard men yelling at her in the background...and then the phone went dead. She hasn't called since and that was many months ago. I think that she's in danger."

I knew what she meant. Suda was being held as a sex slave against her will. She risked much to make the call home. I also knew there was only one reason for her to return to Uganda. It was to seek revenge on our half-brother, Lutalo. Baba nearly died because of Lutalo. And what happened to Suda in that prison left her scarred for life.

"Next time she calls, please get her location for me. I will find her. You are right; she is in danger. How are you doing, Namazzi?"

"Very well. I do miss you but things are a little more peaceful without Suda."

"Is Walyam...treating you good?"

"He is still the same, insatiable, very hard to please, though I have tried and tried. I cannot conceive, and I fear that I never will."

"Don't blame yourself, Namazzi. It's not your fault. It can be the man who cannot conceive, you know."

"That's impossible, Matika. Walyam said that it's me who can't have children," she said dismissively.

I knew that it was Walyam that couldn't have children, but that was not my secret to tell. She was so dense and unreasonable sometimes. Namazzi would never believe me over her husband. I had already spent too much time on the phone with her though there was still so much to catch up on. "Please give Baba a message for me. Tell him that Suda is in trouble but that I will find her. Tell him that I love him very much. And that I will do anything to prove that I am worthy to be his daughter again." I pressed my forehead against the cool glass.

"The money came from you, didn't it?" she asked shrewdly.

The coincidence that I'd called within days of its receipt was obvious. I had to admit that she impressed me. Perhaps she wasn't as unaware as I'd thought. "Please just tell him that," I said choosing to ignore her question and apparent answer. "I don't know when I can call again, but I will try soon."

"Matika, Baba still loves you deep down in his heart. He is filled with pride."

"Please, just tell him what I've said..." I swallowed my emotions and my voice broke.

"I will try...if I can..."

"Goodbye, my beloved sister." I cradled the phone. Turning around, I ran right into Reid's hard chest. My skin heated at the contact.

"Please, chat away. Don't stop on my account."

I backed back into the phone booth against the glass and he followed, filling the space with his large body. The door was closed behind us. He crossed his arms across his chest as if he worked hard not to touch me as he continued to bore down on me.

"Reid, I didn't plan this. I just needed to check up on Suda. I needed to see if they'd heard from her. I was only going to be a minute."

"You mean your lover boy, Chaz. You know something? I don't know... but something deep down inside told me not to trust you." Reid got closer, stared down with blazing eyes. "And if it wasn't for Mei-Ling who got my attention, you could have blown it for all of us."

"Oh, I'm so sorry," I began, "it won't happen–"

"Damn right it won't. Matika, you are a loose cannon, and no matter what I say, you refuse to listen or submit to me. We are risking our lives out here, and I'm stuck with you like some sort of sick joke."

"And, aside from kicking your ass, which I'm this close to doing," he said too calmly, holding his thumb and first finger together, "there isn't much more I could do without resorting to desperate measures, for which you have given me no choice."

"Reid, what are you going do?" I asked nervously biting my lip.

"Whatever the hell I want, just like you. Fuck the rules. You don't give a shit about them, so why should I?"

That was the first time I was truly afraid of Reid, and my mind rebelled against the possibilities. Even his tattoo that ran along his cheek and small scar were angry. I drew in a deep breath and straightened my shoulders before I tore my eyes away from his nearly black ones.

Before I knew it, Reid roughly grabbed my arm, pulled me out of the phone booth, across the dirt lot, and into the restaurant where the men had begun to eat. Yana and Mei-Ling waited for Reid to give the word to dine.

"Eat up, you two. We are going to hit the road soon," Reid said as he sat down in his chair, a large plate of enchiladas smothered in red sauce topped with goat cheese sat before him.

Reid had ordered a carne asada burrito for us girls that was filled with meat, beans, and rice and smelled heavenly. My mouth watered in anticipation.

"Not you," he said with a mouth full of food. "It seems you've lost your appetite. You might be coming down with something, and I wouldn't want you to throw up in the car."

He made me sit in front of my food unable to take a single bite. In the past, there had been many days I had gone without food where I was weak from hunger, and didn't when my next meal would be. Even in training, we had lived on protein bars or nothing at all. But today was different. A meal was placed before me that I couldn't touch though my stomach growled loudly to the point of pain.

My pride was wounded, and I fought back the tears that stung my eyes. I wanted to cry, yet the thought of being looked down upon by them would have made me feel much worse. I hated the world and everyone in it because they hated me.

"Let's do this," Reid said, and he threw down a hundred dollar note. Far more than the bill I'm sure, even with the four beers the men had consumed. "Keep the change."

"*Gracias, senor*," the waitress wearing a traditional Spanish-style long floral skirt and blouse said as she picked up the bill off the table. She smiled brightly as she grabbed the lion's share of the cups.

"*De nada*," Reid responded and took a final swig from his sweet tea.

We left the table soon after with my cold burrito left behind to be cleared with the rest of the dishes; a total waste of good food in my eyes when there were people starving.

With a good meal in their bellies, everyone seemed to be in better moods, except for me, of course. Reid made me sit in the very back, and insisted that I lie down...alone. I was nearly bored out of my mind. I took the opportunity to sleep most of the time and before I knew it we pulled into another shady motel. With only one room available – which was a mystery to me because who would want to stay here – we all had to share a room. Though they gave us extra blankets and a pullout bed, it was tight. We didn't even have a good or safe place for our luggage aside from the space in front of the bathroom.

"You two can take one of the beds," Reid said once inside the room.

"No way," Javier responded, shaking his head. "I don't swing that way. Only a dead man gets in the bed with me." He turned on the TV and began to flip through the channels, then stopped on a *novella*, or Mexican soap opera.

A small smile crept across Lorenzo's face. "I'll be happy to sleep with one of the girls. One of them can keep me warm tonight. There are three of us and three of them. Just enough to go around without getting into a cockfight."

"No can do, my friend," Reid interjected. "This is my money you're talking about, and I don't share my money unless I have to."

"That's an unusual way to do business," Javier said as he lay on one of the queen beds. He looked up at Reid with suspicion in his eyes.

"Yes, my friend. You are being possessive over these girls," Lorenzo added stretching out on the pullout bed. "It's like you don't trust us or something."

An uncomfortable moment drifted between us. How was Reid going to get out of this one? Reid's face was unreadable but the tension around him was thick and his jaw ticked rapidly. He stood as if preparing for a fight with his feet shoulder-width apart. His eyes narrowed as his hands clenched into fists, and he looked slowly from one man to the next.

"Come on, man, we are not going to fuck them. Honestly, I'm too tired to even think about that right now. Besides, I don't like an audience." Lorenzo was clearly the negotiator out of the two. He had the ability to smooth things over rather quickly with his lighter side.

"I suppose that can work considering the circumstances. Matika, you sleep with me. You two pick a bed," he ordered Mei-Ling and Yana.

"They better be worth the same tomorrow as they are today," he said to the men.

"My word is gold," Lorenzo said in mock indignation.

# CHAPTER 36

My heart did a somersault. I was shocked that Reid wanted me sleep with him. I had never been that close to him before, and I knew that night he would have no choice but to lie beside me. Though I knew nothing would happen, the thought of being so close to him in a bed unnerved me. I was secretly thrilled in my heart, yet fearful in my head. This could be another part of getting back me somehow for the phone call that I had made. He didn't seem to believe that I had spoken to my family, anyway.

After a quick shower, and I mean quick – Reid gave a two-minute time limit – I brushed my teeth. Although I didn't want to stay in the shower too long with the door wide open, I at least would have liked to have given the water a chance to heat up. Yana hustled in right after I came out in my spaghetti strap tank top and cutoff shorts.

Reid already lounged in sweatpants and his bare chest on the bed closest to the bathroom, reading a magazine by the time I came out. His gaze traveled to mine briefly before he focused his attention back on his reading. I eyed him warily for a moment as I gingerly slipped under the covers beside him. It was strange being so close to him. I desperately wanted to ease closer, or have him touch me.

"Close your eyes," he said gently but didn't look at me as he turned the page.

My cheeks colored at being caught looking at him. I closed my eyes, but there was no way I would fall asleep anytime soon. Even if I hadn't slept the day away in the car, or the fact that the television blared for the whole complex to hear, it would still be impossible to relax my stiff body. I hated my reaction to him. It was just another weakness I had to overcome, for my desire for him wasn't dimming, but grew stronger by the day.

Once everyone had done their business and settled down in bed, Reid got under the covers and pulled me closer to him. I was so nervous that I shook like a leaf in his embrace. He drew me even closer until the backside of me was flush against his front and his chin rested lightly on the top of my head.

"We are being followed," he whispered in my ear, the noise in the background dispelling any notion of being overhead.

"Really?" I asked turning my body around to speak into his neck. He smelled so good it was unfair. I nuzzled into him inhaling his scent of sandalwood aftershave that was wonderfully masculine. The comforting aroma relaxed my body against his.

This time it was Reid's turn to stiffen. I felt his body heat up and the gentle pounding of his heart as my hands were now against his chest.

"Three men in a green pickup truck were watching you on the phone."

"They could have been anyone. What makes you think they were following us?"

"It was the same truck at the gas station with the same three men shortly after. I also noticed that same truck last night at the motel. There is no coincidence in this business."

So that was why he didn't overreact when I was caught red-handed in the phone booth. Reid had a short temper, and I had seen more than a few times at my expense. I had expected him to yell, or at least react a little more animated than he did. To onlookers, I was merely doing as I was told and simply relayed the information to him.

"I heard something when I was in the car with Juego the other night." I bit my lips in concentration as I worked to recall the conversation. "Juego had mentioned to Fuego that he didn't trust Deats and was thinking about breaking off ties with him."

"What was Fuego's reaction when he said that?" Reid said, his body going rigid.

"Fuego told him that he didn't recommend it but would support him. I really got the feeling that he was uncomfortable with idea of 'breaking off ties' with whoever this 'Deats' is. Is there something we should know?"

"Deats works up high and is someone we will never speak directly to or have any contact with whatsoever. Honestly, I don't know what side he's on. Fuego, on the other hand, has been in deep for many years. He's a good man, so I've heard, but will do what he must to stay under."

"Hopefully, everything will be OK."

"Something is going down, and we've got to be prepared." His sweet breath fanned my check. "I'm going to put some weapons in your clothing bag. Tell the others when the time is right to be on the lookout and to be armed from this day forward."

"So it wasn't such a bad thing that I took a quick detour to use the phone?" I said smiling up at him.

"Don't push me, Matika. What you did was unacceptable and you know it. I'll find a way to make it up to you and that is a promise," he said with a trace of a smile pulling at the corners of his lips. His lips ghosted over my temple.

"That's the closest to a joke I've ever heard you make," I said teasingly, feeling bold, grinning like a fool.

"Oh, I'm far from joking. Now get some sleep. Who knows what tomorrow will bring?" He snorted before he placed his chin on the top of my head again.

"I've been resting all day. You sleep. I'll keep watch tonight."

"Fair enough."

I turned my head to face the others. Reid made no move to scoot away and I made no move pull away. It felt so good to be held by him though I knew it was part of the role. I found myself wiggle even closer to him until my backside was flush against him. Just the feel of his bare chest against my back aroused me. I could tell that it had affected him as well by the heat of his skin, the unmistakable hardness of his manhood, and the rumble in his chest.

"That's enough, Matika," he voice was deep and filled with need as he placed a hot hand on my hip to stay me. "You're teasing my instincts as a man."

"Yes, sir," I murmured and closed my eyes briefly, shivering at the additional contact of his strong hand. Despite the added sensation, I was content.

After several hours of deep thoughts, my eyes grew heavy. When I woke up, Reid dozed off. Sometime later there were mumbles. Then we were all told to get up and move out. The small clock displayed 2:30 a.m.

"What's the meaning of this? The sun is not even out yet," Javier complained, glaring at Reid who was busy gathering up is possessions.

"We leave now and complain later," Reid said giving him a sharp eye.

"Can I at least take a piss?" Lorenzo said pulling on his boots. "Everyone needs to take a piss in the morning." Both men had slept in their clothes.

"We'll make a stop early. Don't touch that light," Reid barked at Javier who was just about to flip the switch. "Let's go."

With no time to dress, we gathered up our belongings and were headed to the car within minutes. The green truck was nowhere to be found. The night was chilly, and we girls changed out of our night clothes while we drove down the road.

"What was that all about?" Lorenzo asked, looking back at Reid who sat in the first row of seats.

"I couldn't sleep, so there was no use of wasting my time in that room. Besides, we are behind schedule."

"We were making pretty good time," Javier stated as he made a right turn onto the expressway. "Just because you have insomnia doesn't mean we should all have to get up at this ungodly hour. Sleep is precious, you know."

"Well, we will get there sooner. That just means you will get your money that much faster. We can sleep when we're dead."

After we drove for eleven hours, we arrived in the city of Leon and looked tired and worn out. This time, Reid secured a nice two-bedroom, two-bath suite in an upscale section of the city. Though it wasn't nearly as nice as the first hotel, it was akin to a small apartment, complete with a kitchenette.

"You three get cleaned up and be ready to go in an hour," Reid said turning to us. Strangely enough, he closed the door once we were in the bedroom.

"What's up with him?" Mei-Ling asked puzzled when Yana turned on the shower.

"Come, there is something I need to tell you both." In the bathroom I relayed all of what Reid and I had talked about in regards to the green pickup. They were both quiet for a while when I'd finished.

"We have to dress a little more comfortably just in case," Yana said picking up our clothing bag. "And we will have to have a place to hide our weapons."

Reid had ordered a full breakfast for all of us that was delivered to our suite, of which he and I ate the lion's share. Before the hour was up, we headed out the door. I had on the first pair of boots I'd ever worn. Made out of the finest Italian leather, they were dark drown and somewhat form-fitting with a zipper that ran down the inside calf. That went perfectly with my short, tan high-waist skirt and fitted blouse that showed an ample supply of cleavage assisted by a padded pushup bra. I hogged up the blow dryer and flatiron, and wore my hair straight that night, with it falling past my shoulder blades.

Armed with the fatal lipstick in my purse, a tactical pin, a full-length blade in one boot and pistol in the other, I did feel safe. I would've felt even safer with a more powerful long-range gun but obviously there was no good place to hide it.

I felt all the men's appreciative looks on me and knew I had dressed well. Yana and Mei-Ling were both dressed lovely as well. Yana looked chic in classy shorts and heels. Her hair was out and feathered with hair-spray. Mei-Ling wore a short baby-doll dress and high heeled boots as well. They, too, had weapons on them and Mei-Ling and I felt safe around Yana, who was an expert shooter.

We drove through rows and rows of farmland before we turned down a dirt path followed by another and another. The drive was made slowly, as if to avoid the dust that was sure to gather on our car.

"I'm here to make a quick deal at this house. I want to get in and out with no trouble," Reid said to no one in particular as we pulled up to the gated manor. "You two stay as my side at all times."

"*Tienen un appointment?*" the scratchy voice asked from the box at gate.

"*Si, Senor* Carson *esta aqui!*" the driver shouted in the intercom. Soon the gate was opened and he cautiously drove up the paved road flanked by trees.

"I don't want any trouble either with Santiago. This is one group you don't want to mess with," Lorenzo said. "At least we are on the same page."

"After this job, I pay you and we will part ways if all goes well."

"Sounds good to me," Lorenzo said as he pulled to a stop in front of the villa where several other cars were parked.

Four armed men waited outside the door and three others stood on the various second-story patios that carried automatic rifles. At that moment, I understood the seriousness of our situation and the danger we were all in. I felt like I should demand a gun for myself. We were sorely unprepared, outnumbered, and outgunned.

"Get out of the car!" they shouted at us.

If I were the driver that would have been the perfect time to slam on the gas and take off. Money was not worth my life. Instead he got out quickly, as did the rest of us. There were others who appeared from behind, thus surrounding our vehicle as they pointed death barrels at our heads.

# CHAPTER 37

The men had their hands up and were quickly searched by the guards, while we girls huddled together and whimpered like scared lambs waiting for slaughter. We were taught to do this in order to not be perceived as a threat. It worked. The guards shoved us through the front door like lost luggage.

"What's the meaning of this?" Reid said indignantly once we were in the courtyard. His briefcase was taken from him hastily. "Is this how you treat your fellow businessman?"

We stood in a cold white foyer, larger than Baba's entire home, with marble floors and white plastered walls, and two-story-high ceilings. To the left, a curved white staircase with metal railings led to a balcony and a seemingly hallway with rows of white doors. A long side table with two small tan shaded lamps, a candle set, and a pair of leather white bucket chairs were also on the left. To the right, a large window covered the entire side wall, which showed off the beautiful hillside view of an indigenous forest. Straight ahead, a red door sat like a splash of blood on a white canvas. The combination was striking, but with a modern feel to it.

The odor in the air was odd. Though I couldn't place it, the smell was strangely familiar. It wasn't a type of consumable food or drink that I could remember, nor was it a cleaning solution, though the interior was impeccable. The scent was acidic, almost sulfurish – if that were a word it would be the only way to describe the tang.

"Oh, Mr. Carson," a man in a tweed suit said with a slight Spanish accent. He looked down at us from the balcony before beginning his descent. "One cannot be too cautious nowadays. What with the war on drugs, you never know who is out there lurking behind the bush."

All the men laughed at that. I didn't see the humor. I instantly hated this man, especially the way his heels clicked on the marble stairs like a woman's pumps, and the way this thin mustache curled at its ends, making him look like an evil villain in a cartoon. But what I really hated about him were his eyes – cold, hard, and devoid of humanity. There was so much I could tell about a person's eyes and his reminded me of the colonel who had tracked me from Uganda to Kenya to enact his torturous revenge on me and my family.

"Point taken, Mr. Santiago," Reid remarked, but didn't take his eyes off the new arrival. "If you would be so kind as to have your men return my case. I fear I'm incredibly naked without it."

"But of course. How rude of them." He nodded to one of his men who did as he was bid. "Come and partake of the refreshments in the *sala*."

We were led through the large red door into a living room furnished in red leather.

"I see what your favorite color is. Remarkable, nonetheless," Reid said lightly to Santiago.

"It has its purpose, that's for sure. And, is far easier for the maids to clean when things go astray, if you know what I mean." Santiago swept his hands to the couch motioning for Reid to sit across from him.

"Indeed." Reid glanced at us and we assumed the position at his feet.

With two claps of his hands, Santiago summoned the maids who brought out an endless supply of alcohol and lines of cocaine on silver platters. They also brought out enough corn chips and limes to give everyone swollen ankles from the amount of sodium. "What well-trained ones you have. They are almost as good as my personal ones." He took a line of cocaine and Reid followed suit.

"One still needs work but the other two are ready to get me a high return on my investment. I already have the buyers for them all."

"The trick is to get them trained from infancy. Their minds are like sponges at that age. They become perfect in no time at all. Unless they turn into trolls, but at least they will be good for something, anyhow."

The very idea of such a repulsive practice was mortifying. I bit my tongue hard to not react to his words. It was a horrific reminder, but I knew why I was here. Regardless of Reid and I not getting along or having to put up with Yana, there were young girls and even boys who needed me, who needed us, our team, and our mission. With no one to help them they became lost in hopelessness in a life not worth living, my resolve was strengthened with renewed purpose.

"It's rare that I do business in my home, but I hear you are seeking one of my more special items." He took a sip from a dark liquor, the ice clinking against the side of tumbler.

"Yes. I've lost one en route. Very unfortunate, if I might add. You see, good ones are so hard to come by these days."

"That is true," he nodded slowly before he snapped his fingers. "Put them with the good ones while I chat with Mr. Carson and his men."

"Very well," Reid complied but the men moved with Santiago's words, not his.

We were herded away while they conducted business. Two men led us to the east wing that was built more like a maze that was unfinished, boarded up and sealed, and led to hallways, a few stairs, and more rooms within. The architecture was deceiving. As each door closed it was meticulously locked before another one was opened. Then there were security cameras that I noted in two corners of each space; one that captured the exits and entrance; though stationary, the range was ninety degrees for each with straight intersections.

As we traveled further within the narrow catacombs, I got the sense that the men were purposely trying to confuse us. I noted that through the labyrinth of entrances and passageways, we were still in the east wing of the building. The only turn we made was in a large rectangle with all left turns. Without a word, we were thrust into a small opening that smelled like a latrine, the door bolted behind us.

Inside was complete darkness without a single window or source of light. I was tempted to pull out my small flashlight at the tip of my tactical pin but decided against it. I heard soft whimpers and knew that there was no threat within. Still, I remained vigilant as my eyes fought to adjust.

"Move away from the door, or they'll take you first when they return," a small voice said with an American accent from the far end of the room. The way her voice projected showed that the area was roughly twelve by twelve, give or take a few inches from additional bodies – from which I could sense the hot breath throughout – clothing, and perhaps bedding. I was thankful it wasn't a small closet.

"It's hard for me to see in here, so please excuse me if I bump into anyone," I said as politely as I could in a heavy accent, and slowly worked my way toward the voice while I held on to Mei-Ling's sweaty hand. The ground was a type of rubber that reminded me of the all-weather track and field at my high school, cushy but firm.

"You'll get used to it in time," the voice said as I drew closer. "It's not as dark as you think. You can sit over here."

A rustle of movement sounded as a body shifted to make room. I felt for the wall, discovering that it, too, was rubber, before I sat down. Yana and Mei-Ling followed my movements and sat beside me.

Despite my full belly my stomach growled in happy digestion.

"You'll get used to that, too," the girl said thinking that I was hungry. "They only feed us once a day if we're lucky, and you missed that meal. God help us if we gain any weight."

"Will you stop talking? You'll get us all in trouble if they hear you," another girl snapped. "This is a palace compared to where they can take us, and you know it."

"It's not like they can hear us right now, Lupita. It's we who need to hear them and get ready when that door opens. And when that door opens there is no place to hide, anyway," she said slowly. "I'm Camryn by the way. What's your name?"

"I'm Matika. It's nice to meet you, but I'm sorry you're here."

"You're here, too. And, I'm sorry, too." Camryn grew quiet, her sadness hung in the air between us.

"I hate the dark," Mei-Ling snapped a small glow stick for additional light. "I'm Mei-Ling. And this is Yana. Her English is not every good. She doesn't speak very much, anyway."

"Well, it's not like anyone here is a chatterbox. There's not really much to talk about. All you need to know is that if you perform well and do as your told you get to stay here."

"How long..." I couldn't finish, the words nearly choked in me.

"I'm not sure, really. I tried to keep track of night and day as best as I could, to keep sane, you know? About six months I think...yeah maybe. They make it really hard and keep us disoriented. And then there are the drugs...But sometimes they send girls to work the streets for money. I hear it's hard work, but at least you get to be outside and not waiting in darkness. And also it might be a chance—"

"Don't you dare speak it," Lupita snapped angrily. "You are trying to get us killed. I could tell on you, you know."

"I was just going to say that it might be a chance to smell the fresh air." Camryn stopped speaking after that threat.

As my eyes adjusted, I noticed that it wasn't as dark as it seemed with some light coming from around the door in addition to Mei-Ling's glow stick. There was a small vent on the ceiling with very little air coming from it. With roughly a dozen girls dressed only in men's long cotton shirts, it wasn't as crowded as it could be. No furniture was present, only mats and blankets. Two buckets were in the far corner, one looked to be full of paper, and the other was waste. That explained the foul odor.

"They keep us like animals," Camryn whispered as she saw my head turn toward the makeshift toilet. "The only time we get to shower or wear clean clothes is when they take us."

Camryn was a beautiful girl with sharp regal features as if she were a queen in the fifteenth century. Her straight hair was light brown, from what I could see, and hung just past her shoulders. Her lips were full and pinched together. But, it was her eyes that struck me. Not their color or large size; it was what was nested deep inside hidden beneath the sweeping lashes. Where the others looked defeated as they waited for the inevitable, Camryn's eyes shone with determination. A strong spirit rested within that wouldn't die. I'd seen that spirit in Suda's eyes. It was what got her through the prison in Kenya.

"Are you American?" I asked turning back to her.

"Yeah, like it means anything now. I'm from L.A., and not the nice part."

"How did you get here?"

"Typical story, really. Nothing special. Mom was a drunk who cared more about her booze than her kid. Never met my dad, but she made it a point to tell me how bad he was. Anyhow, she'd bring home random men who were more interested in me than her. I ran away, or got kicked out. Met some guy – who turned out to be a total ass, by the way – and ended up sold like a car. Guess it could be worse. No…not really."

"What's your story?"

"We're not staying," Yana said sternly in that voice that brooked no argument.

"Whatever. That's what they all say." Camryn sighed and pulled her knees to her chest to rest her chin. "It's not like anyone is going to come for you. Anyhow, take me with you when you go." She chuckled at that but it was no laughing matter. "No really, take me with you."

"Is everyone American here?" I asked casually to change the subject, as the wheels turned in my head. "How many girls are here?"

"There are, like, five of us Americans, I think. No, make that six because there was a new girl they brought last night when I was topside. A little fiery redhead."

"Where is she now?" Mei-Ling asked joining the conversation. "She's not in here, is she?" Mei-Ling did a show to look around the room, though she knew our subject wasn't present.

"She's probably in the hole. That's where they keep you at first. Until you learn–" "That's also where they put you if you don't stop talking,"

Lupita interrupted. She had to be the leader of the group or the closest thing to it.

That was the last time Camryn spoke for the next hour. During that time, I went crazy as I thought about what was going on with Reid. How long were we supposed to sit here like mice in a snake hole? We weren't at his back and our escorts couldn't be trusted. Just then, a shot rang out, and echoed through the house.

# CHAPTER 38

"Oh my God," Mei-Ling gasped the words we thought but couldn't utter. Her panic-filled face froze in shock.

My heart pounded in my chest, my breathing grew rapid and shallow. Please don't let that be Reid, I thought. He was our only hope to get out of here, and without him... I couldn't finish the thought that was unspeakable. Was it all over for us?

"You'll never get used to that," Camryn sighed before she got to her feet and paced the floor. "Bastards." Her words were only a whisper, barely audible.

Then there were multiple footsteps. Everyone began to panic, and all tried to hide behind one another in the furthest corners of the room, an impossible task.

"What should we do?" I asked Yana as the three of us huddled together. Despite everything, Yana was our team leader and we looked up to her, especially in these uncertain times.

"We do nothing for now," she said calmly, her voice never wavering.

"And if they take one of us? What about the weapons?" I hissed back angered at an answer that was far too vague. I needed answers now. "Reid could be dead for all we know."

"Our cover will be blown, and we'll get killed," Mei-Ling began to pant in hyperventilation, as did I.

"Listen to me," Yana said grasping Mei-Ling's shoulders, "if they try and take one of us, then we'll fight to the death. If they take all of us together then we wait until we know what's going on. Wait for my signal to strike and not a moment sooner."

Mei-Ling and I nodded our heads in agreement. Satisfied at having a POA we huddled closer together, and looked as fearful as the others who cried and moaned softly. Having something as simple as a plan of action calmed me. The footsteps grew louder until they paused before the door. Clinking. The locks were disengaged. Pause. The door opened slowly and let in a flood of white light. Hands. The hands were everywhere as they roughly turned our faces to identify whom they wanted.

We held on tightly to each other in order to know if one of us was taken, because it was difficult to see through the blinding light. Two girls were grabbed, and though they didn't put up a fight, their whimpers could be heard long after the door was closed and bolted.

"We can't wait here like sitting ducks. We have to investigate before they return," I hissed to Yana.

"Let me think," she said taking in a deep breath.

The girls were still distraught and many of them cried hysterically with a sense of doom while others cried in morbid relief that they were not chosen.

"There isn't time for that," I insisted and grabbed her by the shoulders. "I have a plan. Lift me up to the vent."

Yana and Mei-Ling helped me up until my knees were planted on Yana's shoulders. I used my full blade and made quick work of the screws, prying the vent open. It was a tight fit but I managed to push through to the large area above. Mei-Ling came up next.

"Please take me with you," Camryn cried out to us as Mei-Ling and I pulled up Yana.

"It's too dangerous. We're just going to have a look around. Don't worry, we'll come back for you if it's safe."

"But I can't stay here!"

"Camryn, you can be our lookout. Hit on the vent as hard as you can if you hear them coming back. Got it?"

"Yeah. But what if you don't come back?" she asked, her doe eyes looking up at me.

"Then consider this a very, very bad idea," I said before navigating through the vents with Yana and Mei-Ling close behind. It was easy to work my way around the large house. The walls were solid, and so was the ceiling, thankfully. The vents made little noise with our weighted disturbance. I knew we needed to be on the first floor and headed down between the walls where the rodents and cockroaches lived.

I saw the two men as they herded the same two girls like cattle, one in front and the other behind as they marched. They took the same trail back and made multiple right turns this time. We hustled to follow as they emerged from the same unfinished set of rooms. Glancing at Yana, I could see the uncertainty in her eyes as she took a visual survey.

The group approached the sitting room where we had left Reid, and the men's animated conversation echoed off the walls in rapid Spanish. I listened carefully and strained to hear Reid's deep signature baritone but picked up nothing. The men continued to speak unaware of our presence.

The room smelled of death and was clearly a murder scene. A trail of fresh blood was smeared from a large puddle by the chairs, and disappeared beyond the far corridor. With the body gone, we had no way to know if it was Reid who had been shot. My heart began to race double-time and my ears succumbed to its beat as I spotted one of our escorts who casually held a drink in his hand. It was Lorenzo, and he looked more serious than I'd ever seen him while he listened to the men speak out of turn.

"Sit them down right here, they'll be done in a minute. Man, they stink!" Another man said waving a negligent hand toward the girls. He was almost irritated that his conversation was interrupted with their arrival.

After what seemed like hours, a glorious sight appeared before my eyes. The leader emerged from the hall, and Reid followed close behind, taking stock of his surroundings. At that moment, I knew that I was not only attracted to him, but felt something even more. I nearly fell out of the vent and wept with relief, but our job was not yet over.

"Since we made our deal, why don't you stay the night?" the leader said eying Reid smartly as he took a seat on the small couch. "We could share our women and perhaps discuss other business. These girls can keep you company tonight in the long hours."

"Though it sounds tempting," Reid drawled before he took his seat across from him, "I'm on a tight schedule. Not to mention I'm one man short, no thanks to you. But, do not fear, we will be doing business again. The rest of the money will arrive within the hour, once I return to the meeting point safely."

"Are you sure you don't want to sample any more of my products?"

"I'm sure, but thank you anyway. Until next time, my friend."

Another man came through the door and pushed our target before him. She was bound by the wrists and gagged with a white cloth that had seen better days. Her eyes were watery, swollen from the many tears she'd shed. Her hair was a cloud of red around her shoulders in a tangled bird's nest. Her clothes were skimpy but present all the same. With a skirt that covered half of her butt, her long white legs were in bad shape. Though she sported many bruises on her legs, face, and neck, she was alive and well and able to carry herself forward on her own accord.

"What do you think?"

"Her marks will heal, but I believe she'll be perfect for my client." Reid rubbed the scruff under his chin.

"Ahhhh," her muffled cries were ignored, as she fought against the man who pushed her forward.

"She's a feisty one. You must know that I'm doing you a great favor. The foreigner who requested her was offering to pay top dollar, but not nearly as much as you, Mr. Carson. Still, they are a treacherous group, so I'll need to find a replacement soon enough. I'm sure I can squeeze out another redhead. They won't even know the difference. They all look the same."

All the men laughed at that joke. The leader clearly had no idea that the target couldn't be replaced. He was smug as the final transaction had taken place. He clasped his hands together, and the corners of his mouth lifted slightly as if pleased with the outcome.

"The remaining funds will be left at the alternate location as discussed. Well, gentleman, without further delay, I must be off. Lorenzo, get the package. Santiago, I'll need to collect my merchandise and be on my way."

"Not so fast," Santiago said as he held up a finger for a pause. "Your belongings will only be released to you when the transaction is complete."

"You're joking," Reid said and worked to hide his alarm that was evident only to us from months of living with him.

"You may take my products as collateral. Now you may go. My men will escort you to the gate."

They had planned this all along, and we fell into the trap. It was evident to me that they had no intention of honoring their end of the deal. Those girls were clearly expendable and were plain, scared, and filthy. With all due respect, they didn't come close to measuring up to us.

"Oh my God," Mei-Ling whispered to no one in particular.

"We've got to get out of here," Yana said urgently. "Matika, lead us out now, before it's too late."

"Yes, okay," I responded but I needed to think. I bit my lip in concentration. Even if we all had a tracking device, that wouldn't stop anyone else from finding us before someone came for us. *If* they came for us...

I headed left and scurried to the rear, or south end, of the house. My mind focused on where the potential escape routes were located. This kind of business ensured a certain type of occupational hazard that Santiago had to be prepared for. I was positive that more than one escape route existed, and I was going to find it.

Just when I came across another dead end, I noticed an edge of a wall was out of alignment. I quickly headed over.

"Come, help me get this open quickly," I said as I took out my knife once again. Within twenty seconds we'd pried open the vent and I was being lowered to the ground.

"Hurry," Yana said to Mei-Ling who was the shortest among us and was nervous to jump down into our waiting arms from the high ceilings.

"God, help me," she prayed just before she let herself go.

Mei-Ling had a habit of praying before each major challenge and it seemed to give her strength. She told me once that she grew up in a Christian household, as well as attended a Catholic school.

We were more than ready to catch her slight weight as she dropped into our safety net of arms. Footsteps. Someone was approaching. I ran over to the wall and felt along the seams with my hands until a small latch grazed my fingers. Pulling the wall open, we quickly stepped inside the space and sealed it just as the room was invaded.

"Take the new girls to the hole. Let's have some fun with them before Santiago does."

"Sounds like a plan."

There were a least two men in the room and by their voices, it was the ones that brought us to the hidden room and the same ones that had retrieved the two girls.

I started to run, and followed the logical drop in elevation. It led to a narrow tunnel that was supported by beams to prevent cave-ins. There was no time to delay, for they were about to discover us gone within moments. The very thought made me run even faster, which was a bold move considering the tunnel was dark save for Yana's flashlight.

"Hurry, Mei-Ling," Yana said between pants.

"I'm trying," Mei-Ling huffed, fighting to catch up.

She was falling behind. Though she was in great shape, her legs were too short to keep up. Just then, she let out a high-pitched squeal as she took a tumble.

"Are you okay?" Yana's concern for Mei-Ling surprised me. Her concern for anyone, for that matter, was out of character.

"Oh! My ankle. I-I think it's broken," Mei-Ling said between clenched teeth.

"I can see light," I said speeding up at the prospect, since I trusted Yana to see about Mei-Ling. I had to get out of this dark tunnel.

"Wait!" Yana called stopping me dead in my tracks. "Listen."

Silence. Then a grinding noise, or maybe it was scratching. It was hard to say. Or maybe it was my ragged breaths…or the gnashing of my teeth in impending doom.

"We have to be careful. Something doesn't seem right." Yana promptly turned off her flashlight before she helped Mei-Ling to her feet. Complete darkness, save for a few slivers of light, came from above.

I felt it, too. Something wasn't right.

# CHAPTER 39

"Yana, we have to get out. I'm not going to be stuck down here." The tunnels were closing in on me, and a tightness took root in my chest, threatening to cut off the precious air.

Despite Yana's warnings, I continued consciously on until I reached a narrow rope ladder.

"It's not safe." Yana said pulling at my leg.

"It's a lot safer up there than it is in here. It will be like shooting fish in a pool. You can stay if you want, but I'm leaving," I said and kicked my leg out in desperation to disengage it from Yana's grip.

"Me, too," Mei-Ling said as she climbed up right behind me, not using her injured ankle.

At the top, I had to push up hard before the heavy wooden plank slid away. Cautiously, I surveyed the area. Surrounded by indigenous growth next to an outlying field, we were in the middle of nowhere. Other than a lonely parked car that was covered with dirt and shrubs, we were alone.

"I think we're clear," I said emerging from the ground. I helped Mei-Ling out of the tunnel, and swiveled my head again for good measure.

"Should we take the car?" Mei-Ling asked as Yana pulled herself out. Mei-Ling was unable to put any weight on her ankle. "I can't walk, let alone run anywhere."

Pulling Mei-Ling's arm over my shoulder, I assisted her forward toward the vehicle.

"I don't know. It might be a trap." Yana said as she ran up to it. "Look, the keys are still inside. That doesn't make sense."

"Yes, it does. Come on Yana, let's go!" I cried opening the door which was, thankfully, unlocked. "You have to drive because you are the only one who can right now."

"Fine. But if something bad happens it's not my fault," Yana said and opened the door with resolution.

Mei-Ling and I both crammed in the front seat. Yana started the car, exhaling in relief when the engine turned over. She drove down a dirt path that went straight through the field. While Yana concentrated on the road ahead, I kept a watchful eye out for Santiago's men. We weren't out of danger yet. And even if we did manage to get away there was the dilemma of finding Reid.

"How are we supposed to find Reid?" Mei-Ling asked, stealing my thought. Her eyes were watery; a single tear rolled a clean spot on her dusty face. She clutched her left leg just below the knee to elevate her ankle that hung at an odd angle.

"There's only one road out of here," I brought my attention back inside the car. "He can't be too far ahead of us. He may be headed back to the hotel."

"Probably. Do you remember where it is, Matika?" Yana asked glancing over at me.

"No, but I do remember how to get there."

"I don't get it," she said as she barreled down the road.

"And neither do I." I rolled down the window and marveled at the dust cloud in our wake that Yana created from her car-wreck speed, as we passed farm after farm. It was just as well because they could be on us at any moment. Finally, we made it to the main road, and broke through it like a loose bullet down a greased barrel.

"I see the car!" I cried gripping the door handle to keep from clapping my hands in glee. "Right there, it's him! Hurry!"

"Calm down, Matika. I see the car," Yana assured as she began to come up on the car, and flashed her lights at him in warning. We were in an unidentifiable car and therefore needed to let Reid know that we were "friend" not "foe."

The van pulled off the main road, and we tailgated it until it stopped. I got out of the car first and helped Mei-Ling.

Reid was out of the car in a flash, scooping up Mei-Ling. The look on his face was incomparable to anything I'd seen on him. His expression was filled with relief and something akin to fear marred his brows. But, within a few seconds…it was gone.

We peeled away as soon as Yana was in the car, before the door was even closed. Our subject was tied on the floor near the passenger's seat and the other two girls were in the very back and cried softly.

"I would say all went very well considering I had help from the inside to get my property back," Reid said to Lorenzo, as if this was nothing out of the ordinary. "They just don't know who they are dealing with."

"You had me fooled," Lorenzo said "I didn't know that you had some-one on the inside."

"I'm always prepared. And this little redhead has an endless supply of energy that I'll need to get rid of. She fought the whole way to the car." Though Reid would never admit it, there was no doubt that he felt bad for tying her like rump roast. Though I felt bad for her as she struggled endlessly, it was for the best. Soon we were far from the compound and continued down the main road back toward the city. After a half-hour of driving, Reid told Lorenzo to pull over.

"Si, *senor*," Lorenzo replied as he slowed the vehicle to a vacant spot in a dirt lot where small shops were peppered in organized disarray. It was crowded with merchants as they sold an assortment of wares from blankets to hats, fruit to dried meat, and string jewelry to dresses.

"We part ways here for now," Reid said then added. "I'm sorry about your friend."

"It's the nature of the business. I had no idea that he was a turncoat for Juego. I've always told him to never play sides. It's no wonder he was try-ing to get this job so badly. He could have gotten us all killed. Shows how little you know about a person. On the bright side, I don't have to share the money with him." Despite Lorenzo's words to lighten up the mood he was clearly bothered by losing his co-worker and friend.

"Here is the rest of the money," Reid said handing Lorenzo a small packet. "It may not be safe for you with us right now so this is best for us all. Take the product out the back. I have no need for them. As I've said before, Santiago's money will be at the drop-off point and I have no hard feelings. You may send him my regards, as I'm sure his men are scoping it out right now." He ran his hands through his hair deep in thought. "I'll be in touch."

"A word of advice, my friend," Lorenzo said as he opened the door and stepped out of the vehicle. "Watch your back because they say Santiago doesn't like to be disrespected." With those final words, Lorenzo took the girls and headed inside the nearest shop, disappearing quickly among the people.

"Drug her," Reid ordered handing Yana a retractable syringe. "We need to debrief stat." He slipped into the driver's seat and pulled out of the lot, then rolled into the street, and narrowly avoided a cluster of women as they crossed.

The girl thrashed wildly at this point, which forced me to put my knees on her arms to hold her in place. She banged her head against the floor and arched her back. She fought as if her life depended on it. Yana plunged the needle into her arm none too gently. Her struggles became feeble attempts and then muscles spasms before her heavy eyelids gave in to their new newfound weight.

"Tell me everything from start to finish," Reid said. "How did you all get away?"

I let Yana fill him in on our escape, and she recounted most of the details. Though she downplayed my role, Reid looked at me in the rearview mirror with pride-filled eyes. It was most rewarding for me to have his dark eyes look at me in a new light. I was simply content at being in his presence, safe.

"Reid, we have to go back," I said turning to him. I'd forgotten about Camryn. She was still there and I felt like I'd betrayed her in my haste to leave that horrid place. "Stop the car!"

He slammed on the brakes. "What the hell!"

"Reid, Camryn is still at that house! We can't just leave her!"

"Who the hell is she?" Reid asked looking at Yana.

"She's an American girl Matika was talking to. She was a nice person," Mei-Ling added meekly. "We shouldn't leave her."

"All those girls in there will be lost if we don't do something," I cried as panic filled my voice. "We have to go back and get Camryn. And how can you leave those two girls with Lorenzo?"

"Are you serious? I was nearly killed today. As it was, I was forced to shoot our driver–"

"You killed him?" Mei-Ling asked, covering her jaw with her hand. She looked at Yana with questioning eyes. Then they clouded with tears moments before they closed.

"As the leader of them, it was my responsibility to seek justice by someone who betrayed me. Now, I don't like being put in that position as much as the next person, but I had no choice. Just as I now have no choice but to let those women go and never think of them again. I suggest you do the same."

"Reid, I can't live with myself knowing that Camryn is there. We can save her. We have to." I crawled between the seats beside him and looked him in the eyes. Though his were stern, I refused to back down.

"I've been an agent for over ten years. I was eighteen when I joined the company. I've seen and done a lot in my career, but this type of assignment is new to me, too. When you were in training, I, too, was in training for this. But there is one thing that I know for sure and will never forget. Matika, we have to make this work or it jeopardizes the whole team. That is our job. Our mission is to get our target and get out with as little waves as possible. Nothing more, nothing less."

"No, no, no!" I shook my head feverishly. "Reid, I swear to you that I won't leave this spot without at least trying to save them."

"Matika, my hands are tied," he said looking down at me, his eyes softening just a bit. "There is nothing I can do. There is nothing you can do."

I turned to head out the passenger door, but he grabbed the waist of my short shirt and pulled me back. Unfortunately, he pulled my thong as well, forcing it even further between my checks uncomfortably.

"Just listen for a minute," he said in his country accent, and pulled me close to him. "You know as well as I do that we did all we could at the moment. I'll tell you what. I can organize for a purchase of Camryn. Just give me her ID and I will see what I can do."

"You promise me?" I thrust my chin in the air, ready to bolt at any moment, challenging him eye to eye.

"Matika, I will do everything in my power to save her. You have my word." Reid placed his hand over his heart before he lifted my chin up further with this thumb and forefinger.

"All right," I said calming down just a bit though my heart still raced. Just the way he looked at me had an unnerving effect. I truly felt like I could trust him, only a little. Realistically, I had no choice. I couldn't go back to the house and save Camryn. Going in alone, I'd be as lost as the rest of those girls. "Thank you so much."

A tear slid down my check only moments before I let my lips slant over his, surprising the both of us. Though the kiss was brief and spontaneous, the effect was enough to send chills down my spine and leave me breathless. His mouth was so sweet and masculine that I loathed breaking contact.

Reid's eyes widened for a moment before they closed. "Matika, what am I going to do with you? You are too young and naïve, headstrong and unpredictable, but an invaluable asset to our team. I can't figure you out. You certainly keep me perplexed. I'll say that this job is never boring with you." He cracked a crooked smile that melted my heart. He ran his hand down to my arms then to my waist. At that moment we both became aware of the firmness in his lap. He lifted me up and sat me down in the front seat beside him. "Now sit right here and let's get moving. We need to finish the debrief on the day's events. There is something important that you all must know. We've definitely made another enemy, though I don't believe that we've blown our cover. Santiago is more likely to believe that

I had help on the inside to get you guys out. He's going to have a hell of a time rutting out a spy that doesn't exist."

I enjoyed the passenger's seat for the first time. It was the most comfortable seat in the car and I had a full view of the city that crackled with pedestrians. I listened half-heartedly to Reid's debrief, mourning over the lost girls. Mei-Ling cried silently as she, too, was affected by today's events and her possible broken ankle. This was much different from the club. It was much harder to ignore these women that we had met firsthand. We experienced their fears in the lonely windowless prison. That was life now, with an uncertain future.

Yana, on the other hand, seemed angry like the first time I'd seen her in the van. It had been a very long time ago but it wasn't lost on me. Her lips were tight and her eyes were haunted and vacant. After I briefed Reid on everything I knew about where the girls were within the compound, Reid told us that we had made adversaries.

"Now Juego's a for-sure enemy since I killed his mole. There is Santiago because I've seemingly outsmarted him. And finally, the Russians, who will know that I've purposely taken their collateral and will not be able to manipulate Mr. Shueler. Our cover is still intact, but we will always need to be mindful of our surroundings. We were not only in imminent danger of losing our lives, but more importantly we, like everyone else in this trade, have enemies. Therefore, our first mission was a complete success."

Reid paid a woman to drop off the car before we acquired another at a used lot. It was nearly seamless and thankfully the redheaded vixen was too doped on the tranquilizer to put up a fight, thus we were able to convince onlookers that she was simply drunk, another college girl under the influence.

# EPILOGUE

Six hours later Reid, Mei-Ling, Yana, and I waited with our subject at a private airfield about five hours north of Leon. It was a small space in the middle of an open field designed for nothing larger than a small private jet. Sheep, along with a few rogue cows, grazed the outlying fields dangerously close to the runway. It was humid and hot and the air conditioner didn't work in our recently acquired car, so all of the windows were down out of necessity, which let in the hungry insects.

We couldn't tell our subject who we were, but it soon became clear, based on our treatment of her, that something was happening. While she was sedated, we had cleaned and dressed her in suitable clothing that was much more modest than ours. Reid also bought her a coffee and a snack at the gas station en route, which she gladly took, to help her get past the grogginess of the drug.

"Please, if you let me go, I will have my father pay you anything you want," she said for what must have been the hundredth time. She was a feisty girl who refused to give up, but she didn't try to fight anymore.

"No more talking," Reid replied with the same response. He scanned the area again, and tapped a hand lightly on the steering wheel. The car was left running and ready to put in drive at a moment's notice. Reid didn't like being out here anymore than I. Out in the open we were an easy target, but had little choice but to wait. Our instructions were quite clear and they were thirty minutes late.

The plane engine sounded long before it came into view. After it landed on the airstrip, and subsequently scared the sheep, the engines remained idle even after it stopped moving. When the door was thrown open, two large men in black suits came out first and surveyed the area before a small man emerged. The man wore a dark gray suit with an unbuttoned jacket. His snowy white hair matched his collared shirt. He was tieless and alert, and he carried his body listlessly as if from extreme fatigue.

"Papa...Papa!" the girl cried in recognition. She climbed over me and tore out the door and headed for Mr. Shueler.

"Rachelle!" Her father nearly leaped down the small steps to meet her halfway. "Baby, it's you. Are you all right?"

"Papa!" She embraced him and buried her face in his chest. "You found me. I knew you would come for me. I never lost hope."

They cried together, and the older man shook so much so that I feared he would have a heart attack at the height of the emotional reunion. He pulled her back from him, just a little, before he planted several kisses on the top of her bright red head.

"I would never give up on you, Rachelle. Not until the day I died. Are you okay, baby?" He asked remorsefully with a voice of a broken man.

"I'm okay now, Papa." She said confidently, wiping the tears from her eyes before she looked up at him, brave and defiant as ever.

"Sir, we have to get going." One of the men said interrupting the moment, as he pressed two fingers to his earpiece. He was beside them now and moved closer to usher them into the plane.

Just then, Rachelle turned back to our car with a look of sheer happiness. There were no words to express the gratitude that filled her eyes, a welcome sight that I would never forget. "Thank you! Thank you so much. I-I..." She couldn't finish her words as she choked on her tears.

She didn't need to. I fought hard to control my emotions while Mei-Ling openly wept. I found myself holding her soft hand tightly. Yana's eyes were clear as glass but her mannerisms spoke volumes. She cleared her throat for the fifth time before she tore her eyes away from the window as Reid shifted the car in drive.

"The fun's not over yet, ladies," Reid said and looked over his shoulders before he turned back to the desolate path littered with grazing animals.

"This case was a walk in the park compared to our next assignment. I got a wire from our D.O., Mr. Lee. We have a cold case on our hands that we'll be pursuing, which could take us months to even get a lead on. It'll take much longer than that to complete. This one will require us to be deep under, which is much more dangerous for us all. Matika, Mr. Lee said that you'd be particularly interested in this case because it involves locating the lead trafficker of the African girls taken from Southern California. Next week, we'll get the intel. Until then, it's time for a short vacation to Cozumel. But first, we need to see about Mei-Ling's ankle."

Whether it was long or short, our new assignment didn't matter. I knew that this was the mission I was destined to do. My life had a profound meaning that filled me with a sense of gratification unparalleled to anything I'd experienced, a choice that I'd gladly make again. The lost girls depended on me and I would not give up on them. But for now, my sister was in my sights.

"I will find you, Suda."

# TRAFFICKING IN PERSONS

Trafficking in persons involves manipulating a person into some form of labor using abuse or other force, deception, or intimidation. Among the most egregious forms is sex trafficking, in particular that of minors. It is a world-wide problem, and while the magnitude is difficult to estimate, one can be certain that the victims number in the millions. The western hemisphere, including the United States, is not immune. In fact since 2003, the FBI working with partner agencies has rescued 3,400 children who were victims of sex trafficking. It is the responsibility of every person to report suspected trafficking so that someday there will be an end to this modern day form of slavery.

Sources:

FBI Innocence lost project: http://www.fbi.gov/about-us/investigate/vc_majorthefts/cac/innocencelost
US Department of State. Trafficking in Persons Report. June 2014. http://www.state.gov/documents/organization/226844.pdf Retrieved October 20, 2013.

# ABOUT THE AUTHOR

*Photo by Michael Fuller*

Latrice Simpkins has been passionately writing for over sixteen years. She holds a Bachelor's in Business from California State University, San Marcos, and a Master's degree in Management from Florida Institute of Technology. After serving in the U.S. Marine Corps for four years she began a career in civil service for the Department of the Navy as a Contracts and Grants Officer. Latrice is most noted for providing grant assistance throughout Africa, supporting the President's Emergency Plan for AIDS Relief (PEPFAR) program. She received a Letter of Commendation from the Commanding officer of Naval Health Research Center in 2012 for her outstanding work. Simpkins currently lives in San Diego with her two beautiful young daughters.

# AUTHOR NOTE

I hope you enjoyed the story as much as I've enjoyed writing it. Word of mouth is very important. If you enjoyed the book, please leave a review at the site where you found it, even if it's only a sentence. This will help others find the book and bring awareness to these issues.

Made in the USA
San Bernardino, CA
02 July 2015